To all you lovely people who have supported the series from Book 1 and stuck by us through the difficult last couple of years.
Thanks to Sandra Beer for allowing us to use her wonderful photograph of the Porthcawl lighthouse of the cover of this edition.
To both Caroline's (our wives) for supporting us in our writing endeavours and our families for forgiving us for the times when we were otherwise engaged.

CONTENTS

FOREWORD

This is the ninth book in the Terry McGuire series of crime thrillers and, whilst all previous books in the series were published by Wordcatcher Publishing, this one has reverted to the Artcymru label we used in the early days.

McGuire has reached a turning point in his career and, as the writers, so have we. We can promise a little more from Terry - certainly in some format - and hope you'll stick with us for the new series of novels featuring Abraham Quince (coming soon).

Thank you from the bottom of our hearts for supporting us.

PROLOGUE

 And the Raven, never flitting, still is sitting, still is sitting
On the pallid bust of Pallas just above my chamber door;
    And his eyes have all the seeming of a demon's that is dreaming,
    And the lamp-light o'er him streaming throws his shadow on the floor;
And my soul from out that shadow that lies floating on the floor
        Shall be lifted—nevermore!

Edgar Allan Poe

RAVEN

By

Arthur Cole

and

Nigel C. Williams

1.

"Everybody dies."

Titch ignored the comment. "Friends forever, right," he reminded the others. It was a statement not a question.

Lanky smiled but shook his head. "Can't be forever, nothing lasts forever, we'll die, everybody dies," he said again.

"No," Titch spat the word, refusing to accept that anything could separate them, even something as inevitable as death. "We made a deal. We spat in our hands. Friends forever," he spat into the palm of his hand again to reinforce the pledge they had made months before and held it out for Lanky to shake. Lanky grinned, spat into his own palm and accepted the soggy, slippery mitt.

Titch spat once more into his hand to top up the slimy contents and held it out to Tiny. Tiny grimaced as he too took Titch's hand. "Ew, ucky."

The three boys, dressed only in grubby shorts, laughed as they took off and ran along a coal-strewn path. The silky-smooth sound of Elvis Presley blasted out through the speakers of the portable music player that Lanky carried as they wound their way through verdant ferns and grasping thorn bushes that clawed and snatched at their exposed skin.

The entrance to the pit yard was four hundred metres from the winding gear tower. They took a sharp left at the chain-link fence and scrambled down the grass bank, slipping, tumbling and laughing as they raced towards the small man-made lake at the bottom of a natural valley basin.

The basin had been modified by the National Coal Board many years before to contain thousands of gallons of frigid water pumped from waterlogged mine shafts and to be recycled to blast the steam coal from rich seams deep beneath the ground.

The tall wire-mesh fence, barbed wire and warning signs that surrounded the man-made lake posed no problem for the trio. They had been there many times before and had already cut a hole in the fence with a 'borrowed' tin snips from the tool shed at the pit yard to access the cold but inviting water that only they seemed to enjoy. Perhaps it was the scary tales the miners told of kids drowning in the dark waters that kept the others away? It was all rubbish. Lanky had heard stories of an old house that was haunted too but knew it was only to keep people away.

A bush they had dug up from amongst the thick line of trees that surrounded one side of the lake was propped against the fence to hide their handiwork.

The sun began to burn the tops of their heads. It was another beautiful, cloudless summer day - one of the hottest on record - and a dip in the feeder would be a welcome relief from the heat. They stripped off their shorts down to their underpants and stuffed them behind the bush, out of sight, along with their tatty plimsolls they all called 'daps.'

More than just friends, Titch and Tiny were born brothers, two years apart and Lanky thought of himself as their older sibling. They had lived together for three years, since they had all found themselves in the childcare system. They knew that their care orders had nothing to do with them, they were good boys, but the same could not be said of their parents.

Bryn Bach Children's home was an eighteenth-century mansion, built for the local mine owner when Bryn Colliery near Treorchy was first opened in 1786. The Bryn was still a working mine but since the Miners' Strike in 1985 it had passed through several takeovers by private companies hoping to exploit the huge reserves of steam coal. Many locals believed the pit was destined to close – another inevitable victim of politically motivated interference.

The house was a grand but grimy limestone block building set in several acres of land just a mile away from the mine. Eight bedrooms and four reception rooms had made it a perfect place for conversion to a children's home now the original owner had long since died and no one else in the area was able to afford such an impressive property. Sixteen children were resident, but the three boys had found a common bond. They were inseparable and, as far as Titch was concerned, they always would be.

Tiny didn't seem to care about anything, he had never really known his parents, the drunken arguments, the beatings and verbal abuse, but Titch remembered them only too well and had never regretted the day they had come to the home.

The forestry, which was a short walk from the home, covered a hundred acres of mountain and valley and had become their playground and, unlike the experience of many children in care homes, their time there was as good as could be expected. They built dens from windbroken branches and dams in the shallow river and swam for hours in the deeper water pools they had created from their labour. This year, the river was more mud than water, so the feeder lake seemed more of an attractive proposition for a cooling dip.

Now stripped to their essentials, the boys dipped their toes into the cold water, squealed at the shock and then dived in. With the air temperature touching 30 degrees, the cold water took their breath away, but they were well used to it.

They splashed and ducked each other and swam around the lake close to the shore for just ten minutes when they heard something and froze. The boys were twenty metres from the bank as they trod water for a moment, trying to figure out where the sound was coming from. The rumbling noise seemed to emanate from deep below them. They had heard another scare story of a pump being used to draw water from the lake to feed the mine works, but they had always believed it to be a lie too, another fib to scare them from going anywhere near the place, but the terrified expressions on their faces made it clear that they were now all wondering if the stories were true. The water started swirling and seemed to pulsate, bubble, broil, and then the boys felt themselves being pulled towards the far side of the lake.

"Something's dragging me," Lanky yelled.

The other two also began to thrash, as the water became a churning morass.

As much as they splashed and struggled to stay above the water, the force was too great. The three boys frantically fought the inevitable but Tiny sank first, followed by Lanky and then Titch was also sucked beneath the surface.

**

A young nurse stood above Titch. He thought she looked like an angel, framed in the bright ceiling light behind her. She smiled warmly and bent over him to check something above his head. He smelt her perfume, nothing too strong, just a hint of something clean and fresh, like flowers he had smelt in the forest.

"I thought I was dead," he said as he looked around and realised he was lying in a hospital bed.

"You're a very lucky young man," she said as she stood upright and scribbled something onto a clipboard she held in her hand.

"Something dragged us under," Titch croaked, his voice weak and apologetic.

"Those were the suckers. What possessed you to swim in the feeder, didn't you realise that it was dangerous?"

"We saw the sign, but thought it was just to keep us out.'"

The nurse folded her arms and sighed. "Of course. That's the point of them," she shook her head bemused by the reckless stupidity.

Titch heard a cough from the corridor. Then he saw a man step into the open doorway, his eyes scanned the room and then settled on Titch's bed. He looked unsure of himself. Titch thought he looked worried.

DS Ralph Crane, a man who reminded Titch of Columbo, smiled awkwardly. He wore a suit that was ill fitting and stained at the lapels. He coughed again as he entered the ward, a means to draw attention to himself without having to say anything as he stepped towards Titch's bed.

Only three beds were in the small ward. The other two beds had curtains drawn and Titch guessed his brother and friend were recovering there.

The nurse turned and smiled at the detective. "He's still very weak. Five minutes, OK?"

The detective nodded and smiled back but the boy watched him closely and thought his smile seemed forced, perhaps false even.

The officer's brown shoes seemed at odds with his grey suit and they squeaked as he walked across the ward and sat on the chair next to the bed. "You alright?" he asked.

"Think so," Titch said. "Who are you?"

"Detective Sergeant Crane."

Titch could feel the blood drain from his face. They were in trouble, for sure. "We was only messing. We found the hole in the fence. We didn't cut it, honest," he lied.

DS Crane smiled again. "I'm not here to nick you, lad," he sighed and stared at the ceiling for a moment, searching for the words he knew would change the lad's life forever. "I've some bad news for you, lad," he said. There was no point in delaying it any longer. The boy had to know. "I'm afraid your brother wasn't so lucky as you. He drowned in the feeder. You and your mate were lucky to survive. If it hadn't been for the quick thinking of some of the miners all three of you would have died."

2.

Double twenty to finish. Not bad. Raven's aim was getting better. A *fifteen-dart-out* was the best he'd managed to date – a nine dart out being the Holy Grail of 501 darts.

He glanced at his desk and a flyer for the Elvis Festival in Porthcawl. Raven liked some of Elvis' music and he'd promised himself he'd go one year. The festival had gained a reputation for being a major event in the entertainment calendar in the town and it had to be worth a visit. It might take his mind off his money troubles.

He stared at the pile of unpaid bills that had been left on his desk and picked up the photo of a Birchwood TS31 motor cruiser offered for sale at Swansea Marina for a little over twenty-grand. The boat needed work – lots of work. The paintwork was rough, and the interior needed refitting after a small fire had destroyed the two-ring hob and the cabinet that had once housed it. The seller swore the thirty-one-foot boat was seaworthy and Raven was tempted to make an offer. He had promised his sister, Sue, that they would one day sail off into the sunset. Sue had loved boats ever since Raven had joined the Marines many years ago. She had taken an interest in all things to do with the sea and he knew it was her way of staying close to him whilst he had served overseas. Raven had also been drawn to the sea from a young age.

Having been born in Swansea, he had spent his summer holidays on the golden beaches of the Gower, surfing and sailing with a friend. Sailing was too much like hard work for him. He preferred the powered vessels that could take them down to France and along the coast to Spain without the extra work of dealing with sails and tacking. The boat was a pipe dream but one that had been close to fruition prior to the recent financial downturn in his business. He had squirreled away nearly all of the money for the boat but that would have to be used for the business if things didn't improve soon. The boat and the bills would have to wait. He had begun to think that he'd have to quit the investigations business and get a job somewhere else, somewhere with regular income.

He stepped to the dart board hanging on his door and retrieved his new set of tungsten darts, walked back to the worn patch of carpet that was more or less at the correct distance for a competition oche for another game as his phone began playing Layla. Raven pushed the darts into a piece of dark green floral oasis on his desk and answered. "Raven Investigations, how can I help you?"

The voice was strained and quiet. Raven's mid-range hearing was not as good as it used to be, too many years of gun shots had taken their toll. "It's my daughter, she's gone missing," the man said. Raven could tell the voice was that of an Asian, probably Indian or Pakistani. "It's not the first time she's done this, but the police aren't interested, they said that she'll come home, like before."

"Your name, please?"

"My name is Mister Patel, Rafiq Patel. I need your help, Mr Raven, I think my daughter is in trouble."

Raven believed he could pick up a lot from a disembodied voice on a phone - sometimes even more than speaking face-to-face, no distractions, just a voice and no misleading body language. Even though Mr Patel was forcing his voice to be clear and calm Raven knew he was worried – understandable where kids were concerned. "Call into the office, bring a photo of your daughter and we'll take it from there. I need a few details. What's her name, and how old is she?"

"Yasmin, and she's nineteen."

"Nineteen? No wonder the police don't want to bother if she's done this before. She's an adult. They won't get involved unless there are reasons to believe she could be in danger. Is there a reason you think she may be in danger?"

"I don't know. All parents worry about their children. Do you have children, Mr Raven?"

"I don't but I have someone dependent on me. I know what it's like to worry about someone."

"I just want my daughter home, Mr Raven."

Raven nodded. "I understand. I'll see you at four o'clock, is that OK?"

"Yes, Mr Raven."

"My name is Raven Connor, not Mr Raven."

Raven ended the call and sighed. He hated *MISPER* enquiries, but missing persons had pretty much become his bread and butter, along with matrimonial cases. He had convinced himself that it was a means to an end and that he provided an invaluable service for people just like Mr Patel. This was a job that wouldn't take long to sort out. Raven had another case pending that demanded his urgent attention – one of the matrimonial matters that would need to be actioned within a specific window of opportunity, a case that promised to ease the financial burden that had played on his mind of late. Mr Patel and his daughter could fit in around that.

He jotted notes in his diary and set it aside. Raven opened a file that sat in his 'pending' tray. A wealthy client from the Gower had hired Raven to follow her husband whom she believed was cheating on her. She had supplied details of her husband's car and where and when she believed he'd next be up to his cheating antics. The fee was good, and the case had to take precedence. He read through the case notes and input the postcode for a hotel the client stated would be the venue for the tryst.

The small pile of unopened letters sitting in the in-tray on his desk had to be dealt with. His eyes kept homing in on the unwelcome arrivals. They were innocuous and inert objects that still refused to be ignored. They might as well have been shouting and waving at him. He picked them up, checked the envelopes and threw the ones he guessed to be bills back into the wire receptacle. One of the letters was marked with a frank that revealed the sender was from the local hospital. He sighed and tore it open and fished out the headed letter. He scanned the contents quickly then returned to the beginning and read it again, this time more slowly. The letter was addressed to him but only because the subject of the communication was a ward of his supervision. His sister, Sue, had been born before Raven with many complications. A restriction of blood during contractions resulted in brain damage and other conditions that were now beginning to play out as far more serious than the restricted development of her cognitive functions. To Raven, Sue was fully capable of functioning with a little help from him. But the heart condition was getting critical, and he knew the letter should have been encouraging rather than causing a deep dread. The surgeon had initially told him that Sue's heart was not strong enough to cope with the valve surgery she needed but, after a recent incident in which Sue had been the target of a psychopathic killer, the medical mindset had changed. The resulting stay in hospital after the killer had drugged Sue had been a fortuitous intervention. Raven was not a believer in a Devine power, but he still found himself thanking God for a glimmer of hope that had now presented itself.

Taking his wallet from his desk drawer, he jogged out of the office and across the Mumbles Road, heading for the indoor market that had graced the city for centuries. The market was half a mile away and it took him ten minutes to find the necklace he had seen on a blue velvet card on display in the market jewellery stall a week earlier. He waited another ten minutes for the heart-shaped pendant to be engraved and then jogged back to the office.

Four o'clock came and had passed by ten minutes before Mr Patel knocked on the office door. Raven had hidden the darts and covered the board with a cardboard box he'd cut to fit for such moments and had stuck a poster of Eric Clapton over it. The office wasn't large, about twelve-foot square but large enough for the recycled desk he'd salvaged from the local tip, the rusty metal filing cabinet Raven had rubbed down and sprayed with silver paint and a couple of worn chairs for clients he had recovered in a durable material that he'd pushed back against the wall to make room for his darts practice. A custom Buckeye burl electric guitar, hand-made for him by a local luthier, sat silently in the corner on a stand gathering dust. It had been a present to himself a month or so after his parents had died, and Raven had promised himself that one day he'd learn to play it. For now, it looked good and helped to break the ice on occasions with new clients, but not Mr Patel.

"Take a seat, Mr Patel, tell me the score with Yasmin, and don't leave anything out."

Mr Patel sat on the nearest chair to the desk and turned sideways to face Raven. Patel was a small man, probably in his early fifties and wore a long white robe over what looked like black tracksuit trousers elasticated at the ankles. His open-toe sandals looked new and were made from shiny brown leather but were clearly intended for someone with bigger feet. He sported a thick beard with no moustache and the facial hair had long surpassed the quantity he had left on his head.

"Mr Conner, Yasmin is what you might call a free spirit," he looked apologetic, but Raven knew that most teens doing a runner seemed to be cut from the same piece of rebellious cloth. "We lost her mother to the cancer a couple of years ago and since then, well, how do you say?" He paused as he thought of the words. "She lost the plot. Started drinking, something I do not approve of, of course. And then she started running away from home."

"What do the police say about this latest disappearance?"

"Well, this is the longest she's been gone. Six days now, but they're not really interested. They say she's an adult and she can do what she wants."

"Well, they *are* right, Mr Patel."

He shrugged and nodded his head. "I know, but I want her found. I want to know that she is safe, you understand?"

"Of course, I do, Mr Patel. But you realise that if I find her and she doesn't want to return then there's nothing I can do about that?" Raven searched the man's eyes for understanding but wasn't convinced he *did* understand. "If she tells me she doesn't want you to know where she is then all I will be able to do is let you know she's safe."

"How will I know that you are not just saying so to take my money?"

Raven pointed to the door. "You should leave now, Mr Patel," he said, as calmly as he could. Raven wasn't angry, disappointed perhaps, but not angry. It was a fair question, under the circumstances, but he had to make a point before going any further.

"I don't understand," Mr Patel said, clearly shocked by Raven's response.

"No, you don't. I understand that, I really do. This is the first time you've employed someone like me, isn't it?"

He nodded. "I'm desperate." Raven's frown drew an apologetic rise of the hand. "My daughter is worth the money I will pay you, but I'm a businessman and..."

"As I said, I understand. But *you* need to understand that trust is crucial between us. I'll earn your trust by doing exactly what I say I will do. I'll update you each day, that's how I work. I have ways of proving the safety of people who don't want to be found. I've done it many times before. If you don't like it, you can leave now or even argue the toss with me when it's all over."

"I understand, Mr Connor. I understand," he nodded. Raven noticed tears in his eyes.

"OK, first thing's first. My fee is two-hundred- a day plus expenses. You OK with that?"

"Anything, Mr Connor, just find her."

"You've got her picture?"

"Yes," he removed a photograph from inside his robe and handed it to him.

"She's very attractive, Mr Patel," Raven said, not sure if he'd offended him by saying so but also not really caring either. "I'll do my best for you, but you've got to give me more information."

"Just ask."

"Does Yasmin do drugs or anything like that?"

"Not as far as I know, Mr Connor, but lately she's been so distant. I don't know what's going on in her head," he stabbed a finger at his own forehead to emphasise the point.

"Have you any idea where she may be?"

"No, but the last time the police found her she was in a caravan down in that Trecco Bay caravan place in Porthcawl."

"Who was she with?"

"Some boy that she'd met on the fair-ground."

Raven tried to hide his frustration. He'd dealt with some of the workers down there before. Most were OK but occasionally there'd be some that were less than reputable characters, working on the fair as a stopgap between jobs and often hiding from people in places they could no longer frequent for a multitude of reasons, most being linked to criminal activity. "A name would be helpful."

"No, I can't help. The police didn't say. They just brought her back."

Raven nodded. Made sense. The last thing the police wanted was a disgruntled father heading down to the fair to take revenge on some arsehole. "Look, leave it with me, I'll sort it for you. It may take a few days, but we'll get there, and I'll get your Yasmin back safe and sound," he smiled confidently.

"Shall I pay you now, Mr Connor?"

"No, Mr Patel. I told you I work on trust and that's a two-way thing. If I expect you to trust me then I expect you to be trustworthy too. Pay me when I get a result. Now, you go home and don't worry. It'll all work out."

At least Raven had a place to start. He watched Mr Patel shuffle out on his oversized sandals.

***

Trecco Bay and the fairground had gone through many changes over the last fifty years. Once a favourite resort for local miners and their families to escape the daily toil of the pits. It had suffered a decline in the seventies when cheap oversees package holidays became popular. The fairground had become a run- down attraction, a place where anything and everything existed in some crazy prehistoric equilibrium. Single cell organisms seemed to gravitate towards the fair and usually ended up running them for the wealthy ride owners. Trecco Bay caravan park, however, had recently morphed once more into an attractive escape for those who enjoyed caravan holidays but the same could not be said for the fairground. It was stuck in the past, hanging on to the antiquated 'pay-per-ride' business model that the majority of other tourist attractions had long since abandoned for a single price all-inclusive access ticket.

A missing person case was bread and butter stuff for a private detective and was something that, when it ended well, was extremely satisfying to deal with. It often took long ours of trawling through reports and speaking to lots of people. But Raven already had the infidelity case he had to deal with first, a case that not only would pay well but was limited by time. It was a typical cheating husband case; pretty straight forward, and something that could be dealt with only in the next twenty-four hours. The missing person enquiry could wait that long; it had to. Raven could start the ball rolling for Mr Patel with calls to the last known hangouts of his errant daughter. The money from both cases would at least go some way to settling the outstanding bills that seemed to always outnumber the receipts.

He pulled the necklace he had bought from its box and held it in his hand. He knew Sue would love it. He read the inscription he had commissioned; *'To Sue. What would I do without you? Love you. Raven. XXX.'*

3.

The left rear indicator of the Bentley Bentayga flashed as the intense red brake lights blinked once before remaining on as the car began to slow and pull off the tree-lined road and onto a rough track that would have been more appropriate for a farm entrance than the access road to a four-star hotel.

Out of habit, Raven checked the small analogue clock set into the black vinyl dashboard of his forty-year-old Ford Escort RS 2000. He had checked the clock several times within the last twenty minutes, but he already knew the destination of the flashy motor he had been following for the last hour. *Seven-thirty*; the driver had perfect timing. Most hotels wouldn't allow access to rooms before some ridiculous time in the afternoon. They claimed it was to ensure housekeeping could complete their tasks before occupancy, but Raven suspected it had more to do with money. The hotels sold the rooms on a nightly basis not daily. Seven-thirty would mean most guests would have booked in, eager to squeeze as much time out of their stay as possible, whilst seven-thirty was an entirely appropriate time for a businessman to arrive after a day at work or in time for an evening business dinner – even though this particular businessman had told his long suffering wife that the important dinner was fifty miles in the opposite direction from the Grand Hotel. But the wife had already guessed her husband would be paying the hotel a visit. She just needed hard, indefensible proof.

The old Ford two-litre engine growled as Raven slipped it into third gear as he slowed to match the speed of the Bentley. He stopped the car at the turn off into the lane and waited until the Bentley disappeared over a rise between two expanses of well-manicured fields. Only a line of a dozen or so redundant chimney pots could be seen of the hotel somewhere in the distance.

Satisfied the Bentley was well out of sight, Raven engaged first gear and turned onto the track, slipping the clutch and accelerating to drift the rear end of the car. Raven eased the gas and laughed out loud. He loved the old car. The hard suspension of the RS 2000 could handle the rough terrain as well as the off-road Bentley, but the RS was Raven's pride and joy and the last thing he wanted to do was to ground the thing on one of the many potholes that littered the track ahead. The car might well be old, but it looked like it had just left the new car sales lot and was worth more to Raven than just the monetary value. The car had been his dad's and Raven had kept it in pristine condition after his parents died many years ago.

The black Ford Escort cleared the rise in the track and the Grand Hotel appeared before him. Grand by name and grand by nature, the hotel looked like the great house out of Downton Abbey. A large, pillared porch, supported at four corners by white Grecian columns, sheltered the entrance, probably once considered essential by the lord and lady of the house during inclement weather. The building was perfectly symmetrical, fifteen windows to the left of the portico and fifteen to the right with four large windows that led out onto grand balconies on the two floors above the entrance. Raven wondered whether the architect had simply drawn one side and then flipped the paper. Six floors of accommodation, it looked like no expense had been spared. Huge hand-cut stone lintels surrounded each window, the stone now eroded by weather over centuries but still looking structurally sound. The tan-coloured lintels were a pleasing contrast to the grey stone blocks that formed the walls. Scaffolding was being removed from one end of the building and loaded onto a flat-bed truck. Raven guessed the hotel needed constant renovation at a considerable ongoing cost.

The white Bentley had pulled to a stop under the portico and the occupants had already exited the vehicle by the time Raven's RS cleared the rise and began its descent towards the car park. The man and the woman were standing at the rear hatch as a bellboy was unloading a case from the boot.

The man was a little over six feet tall but stood with a pronounced stoop, chest sunken and covered by a royal blue silk shirt, his hands were stuffed stiffly within the pockets of expensive looking pale blue trousers. Raven knew the man was a year short of sixty whilst the woman was twenty-five years younger. She stood alongside her companion and took two attempts to pull the man's hand from his pocket as they began to follow their case into the hotel. Dressed in a short red dress that complemented her black hair, the pearls around her neck were large enough to be visible to Raven as he parked the Escort in the gravel covered forecourt to the left of the entrance.

Raven killed the engine, switched off the GoPro camera attached to the middle of his windscreen and took a small overnight bag from the boot before he too entered the hotel. He glanced back at his car. The old Escort was probably worth in excess of thirty grand in its present condition – perhaps a lot more. If business didn't pick up soon at least he had the car he could sell. But that would be the last straw. There had to be another way to raise the funds he needed.

Inside, the hotel was just as impressive as the outside. The entrance hall was cavernous and extended twenty metres back to an enormous stone staircase that split into two at a point several feet above the ground and then wound up to the floors above. Raven whistled at the sight. A painted mural of angels and cherubs covered the high ceiling, the colours vibrant and certainly not suffering from age. Perhaps it was a new addition, but Raven guessed it was more likely to be another renovation job.

The couple from the Bentley were at a marble-top reception counter which was supported by dark oak beams and carved panels. Three pendant lights, dressed with stained-glass shades, were suspended above the marble counter and cast a warm, friendly light on the unsmiling receptionist.

Raven held back.

Opposite the reception area was a lounge the size of a tennis court. Every wall was panelled in dark oak, so dark it was almost black, and in the middle of each panel hung a large oil painting of grand looking men and women from another time with horses that Raven thought looked a little odd – the legs seemed too thin to support the mass of the horses' bodies. The enormous gilt frames were not to Raven's taste but seemed to complement the equine subjects with dogs, spoilt looking children and the landowners' trappings of enormous wealth painted to show off the social standing of whoever commissioned the works of art.

Raven dropped his bag next to a green leather wing-back chair and sat with a direct line of sight to the couple doing whatever new arrivals had to do on check-in. Raven watched as he videoed a twenty-second shot of the couple on his mobile phone and wondered what Pauline Phillips saw in the much older, multi-millionaire, Thomas Harland. He smiled as he thought of the well-used, ironic joke.

Four middle-aged couples were sat together on low, comfortable settees either side of a large copper-hooded fireplace. The two low-back settees were of the same style – Chesterfields - but one was a dark red, aged and cracked and the other a worn green, each at right-angles to the feature fireplace. The original fire irons were blackened with decades of baked on soot and a small glow from the embers was being prodded and encouraged back to life by a young woman dressed entirely in black; black tight-fitting blouse over a black leather skirt that looked far too short for someone bending over the fire. Raven noticed the four men seated nearby stealing glances at the young woman's shapely bottom whilst the women with them were engaged in a four-way conversation. The women were laughing at something one of the four had said but the men were too distracted to join in.

Pauline and Thomas had just moved off towards a pair of lifts at the rear of the grand staircase. Raven could only see part of the old iron lift cages that were entirely in keeping with the renovations of a century earlier, if totally alien to the intentions of the architect of the eighteenth-century.

He waited for the lift to begin to rise slowly within the iron grill shaft that reminded Raven of the Eifel Tower – without the sloping sides - and was about to collect his bag from the floor next to his chair when the young woman who had been attending to the fire stepped before him.

"Can I get you something from the bar, sir?" she said.

The young woman didn't smile. Perhaps one of the men near the fire had upset her. Raven thought about declining the offer of a drink but there was no hurry. His room was reserved, and he knew the couple he had followed would not be leaving their room any time soon, not if what Mrs Harland had told him was true, and he had every reason now to believe she was correct. "I'll have a large Irish whiskey, no ice, no water, please," he smiled.

The young woman in black nodded, still no smile, and quickly turned on her heels to head for the bar in an adjoining room. She couldn't be more than sixteen, Raven thought. Probably new to the job, not fully trained, working for a boss who was more concerned with keeping his staff costs down than employing someone who saw the role as a proper career. Most places, hotels, tourist attractions and other service industries in Wales seemed to be employing kids to do this kind of work. It bothered Raven. Contact with the public was a vital part of a relationship between the business and the customer and yet these kinds of places seemed to ignore that in favour of minimum wage employees. But then, what did Raven know and why should he care? He was a private detective, and he wasn't paying the bill tonight. Mrs Harland had already handed him three hundred in cash for the stay and expenses and she had said that the money was the least of her concerns.

The young waitress returned with a circular tray that appeared to be covered in a rubber coating – probably to prevent the glasses sliding – he thought, but out of place in such splendidly grand surroundings. He took the whiskey, handed her a ten-pound note and told her to keep the change. No smile but a definite nod of thanks. That was something.

The whiskey was not his usual. It was a single malt, that was for sure, but a brand he couldn't identify. It was certainly nice and packed a punch – it should do for nearly six-quid for a single shot - Mrs Harland wouldn't mind.

The group of four couples near the fire stood together and followed another young woman dressed like the other. This one did smile at them and asked them to follow her to the dining room as she collected their drinks on another one of those rubber-coated trays.

Raven downed his whiskey and reached

across to a low, oak table where he deposited the empty crystal glass.

Bag and mobile phone in hand, he walked back out into the hall and across to the reception desk. The bag was mainly for show, it did contain notes from a very old cold case he had been working on a few weeks earlier, something that had bothered him and something he was determined to resolve, but it could wait. The case was nearly two-hundred years old already. A few more weeks wouldn't make a difference. The phone he carried was needed for what he knew would happen next.

He paid for the room in cash and signed his name in an old-style register. That was fortunate, he thought. Most places just used computers for booking guests in. Perhaps the Grand liked to keep an air of tradition. Whatever. It was fortunate because no one else had booked in since Thomas Harland and Pauline Phillips and as Raven signed, he could see the names above his were not Pauline Phillips and Thomas Harland. The names above Raven's own scrawl were Mr and Mrs Jeffrey Thompson. They had been allocated room number 10 and a letter 'C' had been written alongside the name. The receptionist took the register from Raven and wrote a 'C' alongside his name. 'Cash,' Raven deduced. Made sense. Harland wouldn't pay by account or with credit card if he wanted to keep the stay secret from his wife. *Another nail in his coffin.* Had the hotel been using a computer system to record the guests then Raven had already covered that base. He had come prepared with a phone app that had been designed by a contact he had made during his eight years with the Special Boat Service. The app had been designed to instantly access low security systems at hotels and other places to locate certain targets. Hotels liked to think their security systems were secure but there wasn't much this app couldn't access. The British Special Forces had some of the best computer minds in the country indirectly working for them and whilst the app was the property of H.M. Government the developer had made a version for him, a version the tech whiz kid sold only to those he had reason to trust – like Raven. Raven had seen it used several times during his time with the service but had only used it a couple of times since he had retired and set himself up in business as a private detective. It was simple to use and gave the operator access to the details of the guests. The original version even accessed personal bank accounts, phone lines, digital communications and even controlled anything else that worked via Wi-Fi, but Raven had not been interested in that. That shit was at a level of risk far above where he wanted to be or could afford.

The receptionist placed the register below the counter and paid no attention to Raven as he pressed a pre-set dial button on his phone and the reception phone began to ring. The receptionist answered as Raven pressed 'end,' and leaned over the counter to take a snapshot of the open page. That would be a crucial piece of evidence for Mrs Harland. The receptionist, frustrated by the deadline, hung up and apologised before handing Raven his key. The Grand still used the old-fashioned mortise type key, none of the new-fangled credit card type of locks for the Grand.

"We've put you into room number 13. I hope you're not superstitious, but that floor has just been renovated and the room is nice," she smiled.

Raven took the stairs. Whilst the lift looked the part it didn't instil confidence in him, and a brisk climb of stairs had never been a chore for him. Room number 13 was on the first floor and to the right of the old lift. The key turned easily and opened into a luxurious room more spacious than Raven's apartment in Swansea. A bed, large enough for four people, occupied one wall to his right. The carpet was a multi-coloured thick pile, soft and luxurious and a door to his left led into a fully tiled en suite with separate bath and walk-in shower. A hundred and seventy quid for bed and breakfast had seemed steep when he handed over the cash, but now he could see why. A large window also doubled as a door onto the balcony he had seen above the portico when he had arrived. Raven closed the door and dumped his bag on the bed. He walked to the window and opened it and stepped out onto the balcony. The balcony was so large it served three rooms, each with a wrought iron dividing fence between them to provide privacy for each room.

Matrimonial cases might well have been Raven's bread and butter, but he didn't particularly like the work. He had to remind himself that it was just a job, a job that often caused a lot of grief for his clients and their partners but also some much-needed closure to relationships that had run their course, for whatever reason. Raven never wanted to know any more about his clients than he had to know to complete his work. It looked like this job was pretty much complete before he even hit the bar.

4.

A club sandwich in the bar was all Raven could bring himself to eat. His client had told him to use the expenses as he saw fit, but he always liked to hand some money back at the end of a job. Most private detectives didn't do that – the expenses were non-refundable – but Raven only used what he needed and never exploited the client. That policy had served to secure more work than he could handle in the past but recently the work had dwindled to a point where he was seriously concerned about the future of his business. Word had got around that he was good at his job, honest and trustworthy but none of that mattered if he couldn't get clients through the door.

He took the stairs again and stepped back into his room and walked to the black and white tiled en suite to freshen up. At thirty-three, he was still fit even though he had left the service four years ago. The life of an SBS Marine had been tough and he had had to be equally tough and fit to survive. Training had developed into a habit that was, for him, impossible to break. His back ached constantly from an injury sustained on active service at sea, fending off Somali pirates, but training and a little meditation and yoga that he had recently become interested in kept him mobile and he believed more balanced than he had been during his service with the SBS. If he stopped training, he knew he would seize up and he couldn't allow that to happen, not whilst he had Sue to take care of.

The shower from a ceiling mounted spray-head was refreshing. He towelled himself dry and sat naked on the floor of the room, next to the bed and crossed his legs. He still couldn't adopt the full lotus position, but he was getting there. He took a deep breath and held it for a few seconds then let it out slowly. He repeated it a few times, concentrating on the breathing and blocking out other thoughts that constantly refused to be ignored. He had been told that he'd eventually be able to block out most distractions but even though he hadn't mastered it yet the process of relaxing for ten minutes was certainly worth the effort. The drive from Swansea to mid-Wales had been tough in the RS but still enjoyable. The car kept him connected to his rally-mad dad. Every time he sat behind the wheel, he could see his smile, smell his aftershave and hear his laughter as his dad would throw the car around dusty corners through the forestry near their home. Raven had loved it and his dad had taught him to drift a car like a pro. He frowned as he realised he had failed dismally in his meditation.

Tomorrow was another day.

A clean, pale blue shirt had picked up some creases in the overnight bag. He contemplated ironing it but couldn't be bothered. Most people at these places would be wearing clothes out of cases and a few would be of the same mind set as him. No one knew him there anyway. He had spent twelve years perfectly ironing his uniform and had sworn the day he left the service that he would never iron again if he didn't have to. His mother would have insisted he iron his shirt, but his mother had always believed that a man's appearance displayed the truth of his soul. If only she knew what Raven's soul had become since she had died alongside his dad in that terrible crash that left Raven alone to look after his elder sister. Sue had never been a burden, but he always worried about her. Sue had developed better than anyone had ever expected but she would never be able to live a fully independent life. Sue had Raven and Raven had Sue and that was how it would stay for as long as possible. Raven knew time was short for Sue. He knew her time was running out and he was determined to make whatever time she had left enjoyable. The letter from the hospital gave him renewed hope. He had promised her that he would take her to France to Disneyland, a place she had always wanted to visit. He had also promised they would go there by boat; the boat he had sworn he would buy specially for her. The dream of the boat now looked highly unlikely. He could barely afford to run his cars. His work took him away from Sue, overnight at times, but he had friends that were always on hand to look after Sue for a short time and now he also had Lynette – a care assistant. She had become a little more than that for him. Lynette had taken to Sue and Sue had taken to Lynette. That was a relief because Raven had also taken to Lynette and, even though nothing serious had happened between them yet, the relationship was certainly flourishing.

There wasn't a moment Raven didn't think of his sister. Sue was no hardship; she was a delight to be around. She kept him sane.

The jeans he was wearing would have to do. They were fresh out of the tumble dryer this morning and, although they were a little creased behind the knees, they were otherwise still serviceable.

He wiped his shoes with the damp towel he had just used and tossed the soiled towel into the bath before he checked himself in the bathroom mirror. *He'd do.* He thought he looked like a blue-collar worker taking an overnight stay and that was fine by him. The less he stood out the better. At a slither over six feet, his fair hair had no colour connection to the name he favoured and it seemed to have a mind of its own, refusing to obey the directions of a brush or comb. He knew many who thought he resembled a well-known recent James Bond actor and that was a curse in his line of business. It was never easy to blend into the background, but he had done enough surveillance jobs during his military service and after to not stand out in a crowd when he needed to.

Phone in his back pocket, Raven waited for the slow and heavy door to click shut and locked it with the key and headed for the stairwell. The lifts were quaint but rattled, squeaked, and were very slow. Both were already in use – not that he would have taken one anyway. The stairwell was between the twin shafts. He walked past room 10 and stopped for a moment to listen at the door. He could hear Pauline giggling but didn't want to stop any longer in case someone saw him there. The last thing he wanted was to be accused of being a voyeur. He smiled at the thought because he knew that the reality of his profession meant that he was often just that – a voyeur, watching others do things that perhaps they shouldn't.

He took a broad, carpeted staircase to the ground floor and walked into the reception area from between the two lift shafts. Several men in dinner suits stood near the reception counter, talking loudly amongst themselves, each holding a glass of some alcohol or other. Raven nodded to one who looked his way and walked into the lounge where a dozen or so more men were dressed the same and downing alcoholic beverages. Another rotund penguin saw Raven and nodded. He nodded back and smiled as he passed them and entered the bar tucked in the large recess of the lounge.

The bar was a long oak structure with copper pipes rising out of the top and curling over to dispense the beers. A mirrored wall behind the bar was fronted with a vast array of bottles of different kinds of vodka, gin and whiskey. Two large wine coolers off to one side were well-stocked and three shelves below the spirits held the hotel's selection of red wines.

More men in suits stood by the bar talking to a smaller group of women in evening dresses. Raven ordered a pint of local beer and overheard a conversation. The men were from a male voice choir and had stopped off for some light refreshments on their journey back to Aberystwyth.

There was no sign of Pauline and Thomas. Perhaps the guy had more stamina than Raven had given him credit for. Perhaps he was being helped by some pharmaceutical friend. It didn't matter. Raven had the evidence he needed, except actual images of them at it and he wasn't keen on going that far on his investigations.

The young, unsmiling waitress appeared behind the bar to help an older man wearing a gold name badge that declared he was the manager. Raven suspected the manager was also the owner of the hotel. It was his manner that gave him away. He was cock-sure, confident and a little arrogant – perhaps too arrogant to be just the manager, perhaps he owned the place. Raven was about to find a seat in the lounge when he noticed the manager pat the bottom of the young waitress who jumped at the contact. She didn't smile and looked away from the man.

Raven leaned on the bar and watched. The manager was clearly also the owner. He seemed sure he could get away with anything – things a manager would never get away with these days, - but then neither should an owner, Raven thought. As the young woman turned to pour a shot of gin for a customer, the manager whispered something in her ear. Whatever he said was not welcomed by her. She didn't smile.

The manager *did* smile though as the young woman carried on with her work. He watched her for a moment too long before serving one of the smartly dressed men. Raven sipped his pint and continued to watch. Was there something going on between them, something that perhaps had turned bad. The manager was at least forty years older than the woman, but it wasn't unheard of for a man in his position to attract a younger impressionable lady, not that she looked particularly impressionable to Raven.

Raven finished his pint and called the glum woman over to refresh his glass. The manager was still serving a large round of drinks to the choir members. "Another pint of the local brew, please," Raven smiled. The woman didn't smile.

The beer from the copper pipes coughed

and spluttered and the woman placed Raven's empty glass on the counter. "Sorry, barrel needs changing," she said - without a smile.

The manager nodded to her. "Put a fresh one on," he ordered.

The woman walked from behind the bar and out into the reception area. Raven watched her and hurried from the bar, past the choir and saw the woman enter a door at the rear of the impressive hallway. He passed the stairs and the lift shafts and caught the closing door before it locked after the woman. Raven stepped into a well-stocked cellar area. Lines of aluminium barrels were stacked on wooden racks and a spaghetti of clear pipes snaked their way from a single point high on one wall to several of the barrels that had been serving the bar. The woman was disconnecting one and moving the fittings over to another.

"Do you need a hand?" Raven asked with a smile.

The woman was startled. "This is not an area open to the public. I'm afraid you must leave," she said. She didn't smile.

Raven held up his hands. "Just wanted to make sure you're OK," he stepped closer whilst trying to force his body language to appear non-threatening.

The woman looked unsure. "It's OK, I can manage," she said sharply.

He nodded. "Look, I couldn't help notice the

way the manager was treating you in there," he gestured back in the direction of the bar.

She stopped her work and stared at the fitting for a moment. "It's OK. He owns this place. He's like that with all of us."

Raven could feel his anger rise. "You know you don't have to let him do those things?"

The woman clamped the fitting to the new barrel and turned to face Raven. "You don't know what it's like. I have no choice, or I have no job."

"There's a law against that sort of shit. No one should have to put up with that kind of behaviour."

She sighed, tears welled in her eyes, but she thrust her chin out and wiped them away. "I'm OK. I can handle it. It's no big deal." The young woman walked past Raven to the door. "Now, you must leave. This is a staff only area and the boss will be furious if he finds you in here."

Nodding his head, Raven followed the woman out into the hallway and the door clunked shut behind them.

"I know this might seem strange to you," Raven said softly, "but if he's giving you a hard time you can tell me. I'll sort it for you."

The woman looked suspicious. "Who do you think you are? Are you trying something on with me?"

Raven laughed. "No. Seriously, I was just worried about you. No job is worth that kind of harassment."

She looked confused. "You have no idea what you're talking about. Thank you but it really isn't any of your business." She turned away and walked back to the bar. Raven watched a moment before he returned through the lounge and collected his now full pint of beer. He handed the woman the money. She accepted it but didn't smile.

The sound of a laughter caught Raven's attention. He turned and looked through the gathered men to see Pauline take a seat in a corner of the lounge. She sank into a soft leather settee as Thomas stood over her and then walked to the bar. Thomas stepped alongside Raven, nodded with a smile and placed an order with the young woman for a bottle of Prosecco. Should have been champagne, Raven thought. Perhaps the Bentley was all show and no real substance.

The young woman popped the bottle, wrapped it in a clean white napkin and placed it into an ice bucket and on to the bar with two elegant glasses. Thomas paid cash for it and returned to Pauline where he sat directly opposite her in an equally sumptuous settee. Raven frowned - the man was obviously incapable of carrying the bottle himself, or thought of himself as too important, and had left it for the waitress to carry for him.

Raven carried his own pint from the bar and found an empty chair amongst some of the choir who had now begun to sing some of the repertoire. Calon Lân was always a favourite with Welsh choirs and it seemed that copious amounts of alcohol hadn't diminished the choir's ability to blast out a decent version of it.

Raven smiled as he listened to the men sing. Just two of the assembled choir looked as if they were under the age of forty. Perhaps it was part of the digital trend. Youngsters seemed to be losing touch with their roots. Male voice choirs were the backbone of Welsh culture. It seemed, in the past, Raven couldn't go anywhere without some male voice choir making an appearance. Those days seemed numbered and he felt sad, not that he was a particular fan of choir music, but he had to admit there was something uplifting about the well-constructed harmonies and golden sounds of the voices singing with controlled passion.

Pauline was wearing a black silky dress that was riding up above her knees. The material held to her shape and Raven could see why Thomas had found her attractive. She had her hair tied back from her face with a couple of loose curls framing her slender face. Her makeup was understated, apart from the bright red lipstick.

Thomas had made an effort too. He wore a suit that looked like it was tailored to his shape. It would not have been Raven's choice, the fine lines of the subtle pattern of grey and brown throughout was still too much for him. It looked expensive. A contrasting pink necktie would never have found its way around Raven's neck, but he had to admit it worked well with the suit. *Who'd have thought it?*

Pauline was still smiling. Raven couldn't see Thomas' face from where he sat but he guessed he was equally happy to be there with Pauline. They looked happy.

Raven thought back to the day Mrs Harland walked into his Swansea office and asked him to take the job. She hadn't seemed unduly upset when she told Raven she suspected her husband of cheating on her. Perhaps she had grown used to it. It certainly hadn't been the first time Thomas Harland had cheated on his wife. This, she said, she knew for a fact but that was several years ago, and it was too late to do anything about that now. But this time she was determined to gather the evidence of his new affair to end the marriage. Thomas had made a fortune from I.T. and other businesses. He had been quick to get involved in the digital revolution back in the nineties and had grown his small one-man business into a leading blue-chip company with over five hundred employees. Two other businesses he owned employed less manpower but were even more lucrative than the I.T. Mrs Harland claimed her husband kept the other businesses from her and suggested he was worth millions and she saw no reason why she shouldn't get a fair chunk of that when they divorced. After all, she had raised their four children and looked after 'the bastard' whilst he grew the business.

Fair enough, Raven thought, though it didn't matter to him. He was paid to do a job and that was all that mattered. He wasn't in the game of moralising the situation. Mrs Harland seemed a strong woman. He guessed she had to be. Many spurned partners were in pieces when they came to Raven and that was understandable but not Mrs Harland. She seemed clear on what she wanted from his services and he was happy to help.

At a little over fifty years of age, Mrs Harland was an attractive woman. Her short blonde hair was gelled into a spiky style at the top and showed no trace of grey yet, perhaps it was coloured. Perhaps it was natural. Her skin looked as if she took care of it and so did her body. She was dressed like a woman far younger. A bright yellow jumpsuit was covered by a black leather biker's jacket – complete with shining studs at the collar and around the cuffs. Not what Raven had expected when she had first called him on the telephone to book the appointment.

Raven watched Mrs Harland's husband reach across the short divide between the two settees and touch Pauline on her bare knee. The hand lingered longer than would have been expected between anyone not comfortable with each other and Pauline didn't look at all as if it wasn't welcome there.

The young unsmiling waitress approached the couple with their bottle of Prosecco and the elegant glasses on the rubber-coated tray, said something to them that Raven couldn't hear, and they stood to follow her to the dining room. As the waitress passed Raven she smiled. It was a sad smile but a smile none the less.

The pint in Raven's hand was finished just as one of the choir began singing a beautiful rendition of Myfanwy, a song of unrequited love best performed by a tenor. Raven loved the way the man effortlessly reached the notes that were challenging and sang it as if he was smitten by the woman in the song. Raven didn't speak much Welsh, but he had made a point of learning the words to the song. It had moved him the first time he had heard it as a child and it still had the power to bring tears to the eyes of even the most hardened of cynics. He listened to the first verse and, although he remembered the gist, he still had to look up the translation on Google.

> 'Why is it anger O Myfanwy
> That fills your eyes so dark and clear?
> Your gentle cheeks O sweet Myfanwy
> Why blush they not when I draw near?
> Where is the smile that once most tender
> Kindled my love so fond, so true?
> Where is the sound of your sweet words
> That drew my heart to follow you?'

Raven's own love life had never been so un-requited, he had never had much time for love, but on the few occasions he had let down his guard he had ended the relationship soon after. He knew some smart psychologist would say he had attachment issues, but his time in the Special Boat Service had taught him to be wary of attachments of any kind. He had seen too many good men die in battle and had been to too many funerals where wives had lost the love of their lives.

The young waitress reappeared at Raven's side. "Can I get you another?" she asked. The smile had gone.

Raven handed her the empty glass and took a five-pound note from his wallet. "Another beer. Here, keep the change," he said. She smiled.

The tenor finished the song and the room applauded. Raven joined in too.

The waitress returned with his drink and she handed it to him and spoke in his ear, "Sorry about earlier."

"No problem. As I said, if you want to talk..."

"Meet outside in ten minutes. I have a smoke break."

Raven didn't wait. He rose and carried his pint out through the front door and stood near a tall stainless-steel ashtray that looked as if it was in need of emptying.

Ten minutes later, the waitress appeared.

She took a cigarette from a pack and offered one to Raven. "No, thanks, I don't," he said.

She lit hers and then held out a small delicate hand. "I'm Justine."

"Raven, Raven Connor."

She smiled. "Raven? That's an unusual name."

"It's my second name. My mother was superstitious and named me Andrew Raven Connor after a raven landed on the windowsill of the maternity ward when my dad and her were thinking of names.

"And you don't like Andrew?"

"Some friends in school found out about my middle name and it stuck. Even my parents started using Raven instead of Andrew."

She smiled. This was a genuine, warm smile. "I'm really sorry I had a go at you earlier."

"No problem."

"It's just that it's awkward."

"It must be," Raven agreed.

"No, you don't understand. Mr Collins, the owner," she explained, "took me and a couple of other girls in some time ago. Gave us a place to live and work. We were all living in bedsits. None of us have families we can rely on. The rooms are nice, and he pays well so it was a no-brainer for us. We don't pay anything for our rooms."

"Very generous," Raven said, although he wondered why.

"Yes, but he's... odd. He expects us to do

things in return."

"What sort of things?"

She looked embarrassed.

"Don't tell me," Raven said. He could guess.

"It started out OK, but things started getting bad when he began to insist we do things for him if we wanted to keep our jobs. What could we do? We had nowhere to go."

Raven seethed. "What about his wife?"

"He's not married. No one would stick him for long... he's disgusting," she said as tears began to well in her eyes again.

"You can't let him take advantage like that."

"What can I do?"

Raven shrugged. "Go to the police."

"Then the bastard would be arrested, and we'd lose our rooms and our jobs. The place would close without him."

"Would you rather live like this or take a chance at finding another job?"

"There *are* no other jobs for people like us."

"How old are you?"

"Eighteen."

"How old is he?"

She shook her head, "Fifty something, I suppose."

"It's got to stop."

She nodded. "What can we do? It's begun to get worse lately, too."

"What do you mean? How could it get worse?"

"He's filming us."

5.

Raven walked around the hotel, past a fifty-two-seat coach that was undoubtedly transporting the choir and kept to the path illuminated by knee-high solar-powered lamps. The grounds were stunning, even in the dark. Low-level lights were hidden within trees and bushes casting coloured light across an expanse of lawn that was half the size of a football field, in the centre of which was a white, hexagonal, stone pagoda that was probably used for summer weddings. He saw a sign for a helicopter landing pad with an arrow pointing towards a concrete circle and some ground mounted lights about two-hundred metres away. He wondered how many could afford to use the facility.

He was angry as he thought about Justine and her friends. How could any man do that sort of thing? Collins was a depraved monster.

Justine had cried as she had told Raven that Collins had warned the girls to keep quiet about his 'antics.' The videos he had made of them would be used against them if they tried to report him for anything.

Collins had to be stopped but Raven didn't

know what to do about it. The obvious thing would be to report the bastard to the police and get the girls taken somewhere they could begin to live their lives again in safety but that was clearly not going to be an option the girls would agree to. He needed to speak to the others, to establish the full facts before he could decide on an appropriate course of action. Justine had told him to walk behind the house and that she'd send the other girls out to speak with him as soon as they could get away for a break.

Raven waited and sat on a low wall, gazing at the serene landscaped garden and wondering how something so beautiful could have been created or maintained by something so ugly. The girls had become captives, imprisoned by a man who was intent on exploiting their dire situation.

It was twenty minutes before the first of the other girls joined him.

Marina was dressed the same as Justine and Raven recognised her as the woman who had booked him in at reception. She too was upset but seemed more upset that Justine had told him about the situation rather than by the situation itself that held the girls virtual prisoners at the hotel.

Tomasina joined him as Marina stomped back into the hotel. Also dressed in black, Tomasina told Raven she was originally from Poland and was terrified of Collins. She wanted it all to stop but, like the other girls, could think of no way to break free from the man who now controlled them.

"You can't carry on like this," Raven said.

"What can we do?" she sobbed.

Raven handed her a handkerchief and gave her a moment to compose herself.

"It's not just us," Tomasina said.

"What do you mean?"

"He films guests too."

Raven was confused. "I don't understand."

"He has hidden cameras in some of the rooms. He's got them in the honeymoon suite and two other rooms, and he checks the bookings as couples come here and makes sure they are put in those rooms."

"What?" Raven was stunned.

"Yes. He films them and posts the videos to some perverted website."

Now Raven had something he could use. The girls were understandably reluctant to do anything even though Collins was abusing them in the foulest way and a criminal offence. The recording of guests was also illegal and would see Collins do time but then the girls would lose their jobs and their home. It was a problem Raven was determined to solve. Somehow.

6.

The choir were leaving the hotel as Raven walked back in through the front door. The men were still singing and clearly the worse for wear as they helped each other to the coach that was now idling with lights on. The driver stood at the door to the bus with a worried expression. "Anyone spewing on the bus has to clean it up," he cautioned each small group as they stumbled aboard. It took twenty minutes to get them all on board before the diesel engine coughed into life and clattered down the unmade driveway to the road.

With the choir gone, the hotel was quiet once more. The four couples Raven had seen earlier were back in their seats near the fire and four bottles of red wine were on the table before them in various stages of consumption.

Raven returned to the bar and saw Justine clearing the empties left by the choir. She was loading the glasses into an automatic glass washer somewhere below the counter. Raven could hear it but not see it. Collins was nowhere to be seen either.

"Another pint?" she asked as she took a

cloth and wiped condensation from a glass fresh from the washer.

"I'll have a whiskey," he said. This time Raven wasn't smiling.

Justine poured the shot and spoke, "I'm sorry, I shouldn't have said anything, but I'm desperate. I just want it to stop," she whispered.

"I understand," Raven said. "You have nothing to apologise for."

She smiled awkwardly.

"Tomasina said something about rooms being fitted with cameras?"

Justine looked shocked. "She shouldn't have said that."

"Is it true?"

Justine checked that Collins was not in earshot. He was nowhere to be seen. "Yes. It is."

"I have an idea. Can you get me in to one of the rooms? If I can find the cameras, I can photograph them and use that to put pressure on the bastard."

It seemed like a good idea to Justine, too. "I'll see what I can do. Meet me in reception."

Marina was not happy. She was angry that Justine and Tomasina had involved someone they didn't even know.

"I'm a private detective," Raven admitted. "I'm here on a job. This is what I do for a living. Trust me."

The receptionist thought for what seemed like an age before she finally relented and showed Raven the register. These rooms here are fitted with the cameras. Each has the letter 'C' next to them."

Raven stared wide-eyed. He had thought the 'C' signified 'cash' not 'camera.' That meant his room was also fitted with them. He had an idea. It was simple for him to search for the cameras in room 13. That was his room, but he needed evidence of other rooms being used in the same way. This could work in his favour. Room 10 was also one of the rooms fitted with cameras and that was the room Pauline and Thomas were staying in. "I'll need to photograph the cameras in each of the rooms. Room 13 is not a problem, but I'll need to get into the honeymoon suite and this room, here," he pointed to room 10.

"The honeymoon suite is vacant," Marina whispered, "but room 10 is occupied."

"Where are the guests now?"

"They are still in the dining room. They are eating dessert. They'll be out soon."

"Can you delay them? Offer them free coffees and a bottle of wine at the table. I'll pay for it."

"I can try," Marina agreed. She handed Raven the master key. "Please be careful."

Raven smiled. "I'm always careful."

7.

Room 10 was identical to Raven's but reversed in its layout. The bathroom was to the right of the door and the bed to the left. It too had access to the balcony. The bed had clearly already been 'slept' in. The sheet was hanging off the end and the duvet lay in a mess on the floor. A trail of Pauline's underwear led from the bathroom to the bed and a pair of spotted boxer shorts lay discarded alongside the pink garments.

He closed the door behind him and flicked the lock. He began the search for the cameras where he thought they would be positioned to get the best, perverted view of the bed. Possibly even the bathroom.

He climbed onto the bed and checked the chandelier suspended above it. The first camera was easy to find. It was built into the light rose, fitted to the ceiling. Raven unscrewed the rose and photographed the camera. He hoped the thing was recording him as he did so but finding the recorder would be the next problem.

***

Thomas and Pauline finished two small

bowls of Crème Brûlée and sat patiently awaiting the return of the waitress to collect the finished deserts.

The meal had been excellent and reasonable, Thomas thought. It was well worth it.

The waitress appeared and collected the empty bowls. "Can I offer you coffees or wine, on the house?"

Pauline looked thrilled.

"That's OK," Thomas said. "We'll take a bottle up to our room," he winked at Pauline who blushed.

Why was she blushing, he wondered? They'd already made love when they arrived. What did she think the waitress would think they were going to do?

"I can serve you here, if you prefer?" the waitress said in hope.

"We'd love a bottle of Prosecco, if it's not too much trouble?"

The waitress smiled and left to get the wine. When she returned, she felt a rising panic. The couple were already standing. How could she convince them to stay longer? The man called Raven had only been in their room for a few minutes. If they left now, they'd surely catch him.

"I thought you'd like to drink it at your table?" the waitress said.

Thomas fished in his jacket pocket for his wallet and counted out enough money to cover the meal and a generous tip. "Time for bed, I think," he smiled.

***

The second camera was installed behind a mirror on a wall next to the bathroom. Raven noticed the edge of the mirror looked laminated. The mirror was fixed to the wall with butterfly screws. That allowed Raven to undo them with just his fingers. That also meant Collins could do the same. The mirror swung away from the wall on a hinge and the camera was set in a recess behind the mirror and pointing directly at the bed. The recorder was also in the recess below the camera on a small shelf. Raven stopped the device and ejected the disc. He slipped it into his pocket and closed the mirror. It was clever. A two-way mirror that allowed the camera to film the room but remain hidden from the occupants.

As Raven began to screw the mirror back in place, he heard a key in the lock.

***

Thomas opened the door to the room as Raven was climbing over the railings on the balcony. He had closed the balcony door as best he could and had ducked out of sight as the room door swung open.

He had reached the second set of railings when he heard the room door close.

***

Pauline entered first and began clearing her underwear from the floor. Thomas pinched her on the bottom. "Leave that for later," he grinned as he swung her around and kissed her hard on the mouth.

***

Raven used his phone to call reception and asked Marina to come to his room to let him in through his balcony window. He leaned against the railings and pretended he was gazing at the view of the mountains in the distance, just in case Thomas and Pauline decided to step out too, but he was confident they had other things on their mind other than taking in the stunning view.

Marina appeared at the balcony window minutes later and let Raven back into his room.

"Thanks," he smiled.

Marina looked nervous. "Tomasina tried to delay them, but they insisted on returning to their room, sorry."

"No problem. No harm done," Raven assured her. He produced the disc from his pocket and waved it before her. "At least he won't be able to use this one," he said.

She sighed. "Good. Now what about the other room?"

***

The honeymoon suite was rigged in the same way as room 10 and his own. It had a large mirror behind which was the camera and recording equipment. The room was much larger than the others and the four-post bed had a camera set discreetly in the corner of each post. Collins was clearly a warped man. At least the cameras couldn't be remotely operated. It meant that Collins would have to set the cameras to record before each time they were used. The honeymoon suite camera was not recording, probably because the room was vacant. That confirmed the fact that it was someone with knowledge of the bookings who was behind the sordid business and Raven had no reason to believe it could be anyone other than the manager.

With all three discs in his possession, Raven slipped the one marked '13' into the DVD player in his room. The disc played and eventually got to the part in which Raven entered and explored the room. There was even footage of him in the bathroom. He searched the shower area where the camera appeared to be filming from and found it set into the condensation vent. He guessed the other rooms would have cameras there too. Collins was a revolting man.

He played the disc from room 10 and if he had wanted evidence to show Mrs Harland that Mr Harland was indeed cheating on her then this was it. It was graphic. He switched it off and ejected the disc. He considered keeping it for his client, but it was too much. No wife should ever see her husband behaving that way with another woman. Raven wanted to snap the disc but thought better of it. Mrs Harland was paying him and if she wanted to see the disc then he would have no option other than to show it to her. She might even need it for evidence in a divorce action. Raven also kept the recording of his own room. That was good enough for evidence for the police if it was needed but Raven didn't want to go that far just yet. First, he would have a 'quiet word' with Collins.

8.

The hotel was empty. The guests had all retired to their rooms and the three young women
were booking off for the night. Raven had another pint and a large whiskey in the bar as the
girls wished him a goodnight. He had assured
them that whatever he did next would not im-
plicate them in anyway. He had enough ammo
to fire into Collins without their testimony. He
checked his phone for updates on Sue. Lynette
was staying over and promised to let him know
if there was a problem. No messages, no missed
calls.

Justine had told Raven the hotel bar would
stay open to residents until one in the morning and Collins would man the bar until then.
It seemed he liked that duty because sometimes
he'd get to chat up a single woman staying overnight on business. One older blonde lady visited
often. It seemed Collins didn't mind how old the
women were.

He sat on a bar stool and wondered where
Collins could be. He hoped the slime-ball wasn't
trying his luck with the waitresses. Raven saw
the night bell on the bar and pressed it. Moments

later, Collins appeared. He looked a little annoyed but forced a smile. "What can I get you?"

"Actually, it's not something you can do for me but something I can do for you."

Collins looked confused. "I'm sorry, I don't follow. Are you a rep or something? If you are, you'll have to speak to me tomorrow. I don't do business out of hours."

"Well, that's not strictly true, is it?" Raven scowled.

"I don't understand." Collins stepped closer as Raven beckoned him near to speak to him.

Raven grabbed Collins by the throat and lifted him off his feet and over the oak bar. Collins screamed and tumbled onto a vacant bar stool before rolling onto the tiled bar floor.

"Jesus! Are you mad?" Collins shouted. "This is my hotel. Who the hell do you think you are?"

Raven kicked Collins in the stomach, not hard but it was enough to stun him. Collins groaned as the air left his lungs and began to pant for breath. Raven bent over and grabbed hold of Collins by the hair. He pulled the man's head up and slapped him across the face, just once. "I know what you've been up to, you pervert," Raven snarled.

The man tried to shake his head, but Raven still had a firm grip on his hair. "I-I... d-don't... know..."

"Shut up!" Raven shouted. "I've found the

cameras in the rooms."

"What cam-cameras?" Collins stuttered.

"The cameras in the rooms. The cameras you use to film guests making love. The cameras you use to post pornographic material on-line, you scum."

Raven let go of Collins' hair and sat back on his stool.

The stunned owner looked up at Raven and shook his head. "I don't know what you mean. Honestly," he pleaded.

"This is your hotel, yes?"

He nodded.

"This is your domain. Who else would install cameras in the rooms? Who else could do it?"

"I don't know what you mean."

Raven stood, bent over the man and punched him in the face, again, not hard but hard enough, a punch less than a quarter of Raven's potential. Collins sprawled back onto the floor, barely conscious. "I'll tell you what's going to happen," Raven said. "You'll clean up your act. You'll stop treating the staff the way you do. I saw you fondling the waitress. Do you understand me?"

Collins nodded as he held his head in his hands. "Yes," he said.

"I'll keep the videos you recorded and use them against you if I hear just a whisper that you're back to your old tricks or even think about calling the cops."

Collins raised his hand. "No more. Please."

9.

Collins was notably absent when Raven booked out of the hotel the following morning. It was what Raven expected.

Raven tried to pay for the drinks he had had during the night, but Marina refused to accept payment.

Justine and Tomasina were not around either. It didn't matter. There was nothing to be said. Raven had told Marina to get in touch if Collins ever tried to revert to his old ways.

The drive home to Swansea was uncomfortable. Raven's knuckles were bruised, and his back ached as the old Ford delivered every bump in the road through to the Recaro seats. The car was lovely, but it certainly hadn't been built for comfort.

He parked the Ford outside the office and greeted Mrs Burton, his receptionist, with a smile. A friend of his late mother, Mrs Burton had offered her services to help Raven out on a short-term basis. That had been over a year ago and she now saw herself as the full-time office secretary until he found someone else. Nothing had ever been agreed but Raven was happy to let things ride. She was a formidable character, a woman who was every bit as stern as she looked. The half-moon reading glasses perched on her curlew beak threatened to slip but never did. She dressed like Mrs Thatcher and Raven wondered if her politics were similar. If they were, she would never divulge. Mrs Burton was also efficient and had made changes to the day-to-day operation of the business that had certainly been effective.

"There's a lady in your office waiting for you," she said.

Raven opened the door to find Mrs Harland sitting in the chair next to his desk. "Thought I'd catch you early, to pay what I owe," she said. She made no attempt to stand or to greet him with a handshake.

Raven threw his coat onto a rack near the door and sat at his desk. He noticed the short skirt that was barely more than a belt, something he thought was brave for a woman of her age. He had to admit she had good legs. "It's all sorted," he said. "I have photographs of them together. It's all you'll need. He might try and talk his way out of it, but it won't wash in a divorce court. Indeed, when your solicitor serves this stuff on his solicitor, I'm sure he'll settle without the fuss."

"That's fine. Thank you," Mrs Harland said.

"Is there anything else?"

"No. I think you took care of it all." She pushed an envelope across the desk to Raven, exposing too much of her ample cleavage in the process. "That's something to show my appreciation. A little extra."

He wondered if she meant the flash of her breasts that were fighting to break free from the thin, low cut top that was losing the battle or the payment. The envelope contained an extra five hundred pounds. Raven whistled. "Wow. There's no need for that."

Raven handed the envelope to Mrs Burton as he watched his client totter on pencil heels out of the office. He rose from his chair and watched her walk towards a red Mercedes SUV parked further along the street. Mrs Harland opened the door and for a brief second the interior light illuminated the smiling face a young woman in the front passenger seat. A young woman he had seen before. A woman whom he thought was unaccustomed to smiling.

***

Collins hadn't wanted to speak with Raven, but he eventually took the call.

"I told you I didn't do it. There's no way I'd risk my business for shit like that," he said.

"I don't believe you," Raven said, "but I'm sure you could try and convince the cops, if you dare?"

"Just leave me alone," Collins pleaded.

"I will," Raven said. "I just need you to explain something that's been bothering me."

Collins said nothing.

"I was told that a blonde, older woman, used to visit you often at night."

"So? There's nothing wrong with that, for God's sake."

"Were you in a relationship with her?"

"What's it to do with you?"

"Look, I'm just trying to understand what's been going on there and something's bothering me."

Collins sighed. "OK. Yes. We were in a relationship... for a short time."

Raven didn't want to ask anything more but knew he had to. "What was her name?"

"I can't tell you that."

"Why, was she married?"

The silence was enough to confirm his suspicion.

"What was her name?"

"I told you it's none of your business."

Raven held back his anger and spoke calmly. "Was it, Mrs Harland, by any chance?"

"Who told you?" Collins snapped. "Was it the girls here?"

"No," Raven said. "Lucky guess, I suppose."

Things were beginning to fall into place. "Did you end the relationship or did she?"

"I don't see what this has to do with anything, but it was me. She was odd. She told me her husband was having an affair, so everything was fine between us. She knew I liked women. I wasn't bloody married so what the hell? But she started getting strange when she found out that two of my waitresses had a thing for me."

Raven scoffed. "A thing for you?"

"Yes. I told them they were too young for me. They took my fooling around far too seriously. They thought I bloody fancied them. Come on. Why would I have anything to do with them? I do very well thank you very much."

"So why did Mrs Harland become strange towards you?"

"The girls told her I was having affairs with them. None of it was true. I swear. And as for the camera stuff you said about, I swear that had nothing to do with me. I've been through the hotel and found nothing in any of the rooms."

"I saw it all myself. You can't fool me. I've even got some of the recordings."

"I swear there's nothing there now. I don't understand. I found the cavity behind the mirrors but there was just a power outlet in there. If that was for the recorder then I swear it had nothing to do with me and whoever was responsible has taken the stuff away."

***

The multi-storey car park was busy, but no one paid any attention to the two young women talking with a smartly dressed older lady. Justine and Tomasina placed the cameras and the recording equipment in the rear of the Mercedes SUV. "That's the lot," Justine said.

Mrs Harland kissed both girls on the cheek and handed over an envelope with five hundred pounds in each. "Spend it wisely," she told them.

"He has no clue," Tomasina said.

"He searched the rooms, but we'd removed the cameras before he even thought about looking for them," Justine added.

"It's been a wonderful couple of days," Mrs Harland smiled, "and I thank you for your help."

The Mercedes SUV roared as Mrs Harland drove out of the car park. It had certainly been a good couple of days.

***

Raven watched Sue as she immersed herself in the latest episode of Eastenders. She sat in a recliner that she had chosen for herself for Christmas and Raven knew it had been a good buy. Sue loved it. He remembered the necklace he had bought and thought about giving it to her but knew she wouldn't be interested whilst her favourite soap was airing. He decided to wait until he told her about the hospital appointment. It would help to distract her from the inevitable fear the hospital always generated in her.

He couldn't begin to imagine what life would be like without his sister. He had looked after her since he left the SBS. He had been pensioned out after being wounded in an operation to stop Somali pirates. The injury had ended his career but, in retrospect, it had been timely. It was during his recuperation that his parents had died in a car crash and Raven had found himself as sole guardian for his dear sister. He had never resented the extra responsibility. He loved his sister and her quirky personality. She made him laugh and there was nothing better than to come home to her smiling face.

Sue's pending operation would threaten everything he had come to rely on. If she didn't make it through the surgery, it would crush the life out of him. It was something he couldn't afford to dwell on. He needed to be positive for Sue. At least he had the distraction of work. He still had the missing girl – Patel's daughter – to find.

10.

The Harland's house was an enormous, modern looking concrete and glass structure that Raven guessed would be referred to as 'architect designed.' A two-storey block of eight windows occupied the main part of the front of the building with a large, recessed glass entry-way and two wings that had been grafted on to each side at what looked like a forty-five-degree angle from the main part of the house. One block housed three large garage doors whilst the other block clearly accommodated a swimming pool; he could see a small springboard through one of the steamed-up windows. *Nice.*

Raven had parked his car well away from the address in a local pub about a mile or so away. He knew that Mrs Harland knew the car he drove. He stood out of sight behind one of the large stone pillars that supported a fancy ornate sliding gate. He peered around the pillar and through the wrought iron work of the gate. A single light was on in the hallway downstairs, but the rest of the house was dark. He checked his watch. 9:34 pm. There should be someone at home, he thought.

The gates were closed but he knew they could be opened using a remote switch somewhere. But did he really want to enter and confront the Harlands – whichever one was home? He knew he was angry; he recognised the signs, he'd been angry many times before and this episode of anger probably only amounted to level-sex out of ten. Level-seven was a clear 'take action' anger and the levels below that were 'response variable.'

The sound of a throaty engine drew his attention to the lane that led to the house from the main road that serviced the south side of the Gower Peninsula, not that it was much of a road, more like a single carriageway barely wide enough in places for two medium sized cars to pass. Access to the stunning Gower was a bloody nuisance, especially during the summer months. Raven always believed that most property owners on the Gower were English – being the only people who could sell a property in London or some equally inflated place and then afford to buy the extortionately priced properties of such a scenic and sought-after location with cash. The Harland's were both English, or at least they sounded English. Perhaps the others around here were Welsh but thought the accent didn't sound posh enough? Whatever! Raven had not come across many Welsh accents in that part of the country.

The engine noise was getting louder. He

ducked back behind the stone pillar and hoped he wouldn't be seen.

The engine tone dropped as the vehicle came within metres of him. Then it stopped momentarily as the gates to the house opened slowly, sliding back silently on unseen tracks. Raven chanced a glance around the gate as the vehicle slowly edged forward between the pillars.

Mrs Harland was sitting in the front passenger seat of the Bentley Bentayga which Mr Harland was driving. What was more, they were both smiling and seemingly chatting happily together.

Stunned, Raven leaned back against the column and wondered what the hell was going on. Anger level had risen to level-nine for a moment but had now slipped back to a five on the scale. Perhaps they had kissed and made up? He wanted to confront them but thought better of it. He was in the dark, both literally and metaphorically. He needed to know more about the couple, to get an insight into their lives, to understand them before he could make sense of this mess he had been dragged into.

11.

Raven drove his Escort to the fairground in Porthcawl and parked it in an hour restriction zone where lots of people would walk past it. He hated leaving it anywhere where some tosser could run a coin down the side or do other mindless nonsense to it. The VW Golf that he used on a regular basis was in the local garage having its first MOT. Raven felt like an expectant dad, hoping his car would be OK. He was still seething about the Harland case. He'd been duped and had given a bloke a slapping when he possibly didn't deserve it. Harland was a cheating husband, that was for sure, but it now seemed like Mrs Harland was cheating on him too.

He locked his car and scanned the immediate area to make sure no one was taking an unhealthy interest in it. The standard locks on the old Fords were notoriously easy to bypass but Raven had fitted a Thatcham security system which included new deadlocks on the doors. Satisfied, he walked into the fairground through gates that made him think that once they got you in, they would never let you out. Was business that bad?

Dozens of families milled around between attractions. Little children were pulling at the arms of parents, dragging them to rides suitable to their age and the excited expressions made Raven smile. He remembered when he too had dragged his parents to the rides many years ago.

Porky Granville stood next to a caterpillar ride that was intended for the younger kids. He was speaking to a lad who wore a leather money bag hanging from a long strap over his shoulder. Porky was in his forties but looked at least ten years older. Raven knew Porky had worked the fairground for years and that he knew everything that was going on in and around the park and Raven also knew he was a nark for the local CID.

"How you doing, Porky?" Raven grinned as he walked up to the pair. "I need a bit of help..." Porky nodded to the young man and took Raven by the arm and led him away.

"What are you trying to do to me? You know I can't be seen talking to cops."

"I'm not a cop, am I?" Raven grinned.

"Just as bad though," Porky said.

Raven let the insult go. "I'm trying to trace a young Indian girl, the local coppers picked her up a couple of months ago. She was dossing down with some shit-bag in a caravan over on Trecco Bay. Any ideas?"

Raven checked no one was watching and slipped him a fiver along with Yasmin's picture.

Porky whistled. "She's a looker, Raven," he said. He knew Raven well enough to call him by his first name. "I couldn't mistake her," Porky continued, "they were over here yesterday, high as kites they were."

"Who's the bloke, Porky?"

"He's a coke-head from the valleys. Bad news he is. Off his head. The boys stay clear of him. Always tooled up. Shanked a few of them he has."

"Got a name and a number for me?"

"Goes by the name of Keanu, from up the valleys."

Raven laughed. "Keanu?"

Porky grinned. "Most of the young 'uns around here are either bloody Kiefer, Beyonce, Shania or some other celebrity nonsense. The world gone to the dogs. Kids are having kids before they've even grown up enough to name them something sensible. Muppets they are. All of 'em." He spat a globule of phlegm onto the tar-mac that Raven was sure would scuttle for cover. "You'll find him in AA12," Porky said as he wiped his mouth with the back of his grubby sleeve. "He's a handful mind."

"Cheers, Porky. Much obliged. Tell the boys not to worry. Tell them that Keanu's had his day. Leave him to me."

"Watch him, Raven, he's got a shiv hidden in his boot."

Raven returned to his car and waited over

an hour until it got dark. He moved his car a few times during the wait to avoid the parking Nazi's and then made his way over to Trecco Bay. The place had changed dramatically from the days when it was flooded with miners and their families down from the valleys for a fortnight. Today it was all yuppies from the Midlands who had probably never seen sand until they'd bought one of the fancy new caravans, or 'holiday homes' as the brochures liked to call them.

He followed the narrow roads that led between the rows and finally parked a short distance from caravan AA12 with a clear view of the only door. No light inside. He assumed Keanu was out somewhere with Yasmin, but that was only an assumption and assumptions often got people killed. Yasmin could have been anywhere, with anyone.

The wait was rewarded when they both came rolling up to the van. Yasmin didn't have a leg under her, and Keanu wasn't fairing much better as he staggered behind her. They were both either worse for wear through drink or high on drugs, or both.

He gave them a few minutes to settle down inside and then knocked on the door.

"Keanu? Got a message for you," he shouted.

"Who the fuck is it?"

"It's the office, got a message for you."

"Hang on a minute."

Keanu opened the door and before he could focus his eyes Raven lunged and grabbed him by the throat. Throwing him back inside the van, he raised his knee into Keanu's groin. A loud moan as the young man collapsed like a sack of dead cats.

Yasmin was lying on the bed, her eyes glazed, her mouth open and emitting a pitiful sound, like a kitten crying for its mother. Keanu had been jacking her up, the gear was on the bed – a syringe, crumpled ball of silver paper and the tourniquet was around her arm. Raven seethed. He hated dealers; there was nothing worse than someone who was prepared to sell that shit to anyone without a thought of the consequences.

He thought about finishing Keanu off with a carefully placed kick but chose to check on Yasmin. Keanu, however, was nowhere near finished by the blow to his nuts and Raven didn't get a chance to check on the prone girl. Keanu had clearly recovered enough to grab him around the neck and put a knife to his throat.

"Who the fuck are you? What do you want?" he panted. He clearly wasn't a physically fit specimen.

"Hang on now, Keanu," Raven said. "You don't want to do this. It won't end well."

Before he opened his mouth to reply, Raven thrust his knee forward and once more connected with Keanu's groin. The man gasped as Raven grabbed his arm, spun him around and punched his wrist as hard as he could. He heard the crack of at least one bone and the scream of pain as the blade dropped into Raven's hand. Furious, Raven jabbed the knife into the femoral artery of Keanu's left leg. The blood spouted like a fountain, and now Keanu squealed like a stuck pig. Raven left the knife embedded in his leg and grabbed him by the throat.

"Your life is in my hands, you piece of shit. I've a good mind to let you bleed to death."

Keanu looked horrified. "Who the fuck are you?" Keanu cried.

"I'm Raven Connor, your worst fucking nightmare."

12.

The man was less than an animal. Raven loved animals, especially dogs. Dogs were honest, loyal and accepting. Few people he'd met possessed anything near the qualities of a dog. Cats were different. Raven never had experience of cats. He had heard cat owners say their pet ruled the home. Cats were perhaps more discerning. Keanu was not a dog or a cat, but he made a good impression of one as his squeals transformed to wails and whimpers as he bled over the caravan floor.

Raven pulled Yasmin off the bed and placed her hard, faux-wood laminate floor. He turned her on her side and positioned her in a classic recovery position he had learned during his military days. Her pulse was shallow but at least she was breathing.

"Get me an ambulance, you mad bastard, or I'll bleed to death," Keanu screamed.

Raven glowered at the scumbag who, just moments earlier, was quite prepared to stick him with his blade and let him bleed to death. Satisfied Yasmin was safe, he grabbed the wailing Keanu by the throat. "What have you jacked her up with, you little scrote? Is it heroin? Tell me or I swear I'll let you bleed to death," he snarled.

Eyes wide, mouth trembling and lips turning blue, Keanu must have realised he needed Raven more than Raven needed him and Raven was in no mood to be messed around. "No, no," he pleaded, "I haven't jacked her. It's 'H' but I haven't jacked her, get me a fucking ambulance for fuck sake... please."

"Put some pressure on it," Raven said dismissively. "You'll live, you little twat."

Yasmin began to moan. Raven turned to check on her as she vomited across the fake wood floor. She began pulling at the tourniquet.

That was a good sign. Raven pulled his phone from his coat pocket and tapped in 999. He asked for an ambulance but didn't bother requesting police attendance. He knew the operator would send them anyway under the circumstances he'd outlined to the operator.

"Yasmin, I'm Raven," he said as he slipped his phone back into his pocket. "I've come to take you home."

The young woman groaned and tried to sit up. Raven held her down gently but with enough force to let her know she wasn't going anywhere. She quickly gave up and closed her eyes.

Apart from the vomit that now decorated the floor, the caravan was surprisingly neat and tidy. A couple of cans of cheap beer and a misshaped, plastic bottle of strong cider stood like silent soldiers on a small worktop in the neat but compact laminate kitchen, but everything else looked remarkably unremarkable. "Your old man is worried to death about you, have you taken anything?" Raven asked the young woman. He needed her to stay awake.

She stirred and shook her head but kept her eyes closed. "Nothing. Just booze." Her voice was weak.

"What the hell are you doing with this clown?"

"He's my boyfriend," she yawned and seemed far away.

"Boyfriend? He was about to jack you up, what's that all about?"

Her eyes snapped open. "Leave him alone, what's it got to do with you?"

"It's got everything to do with me. Your father hired me to find you and find you I have. So, it's back home for you, young lady."

Raven heard the sound of the cavalry arriving and checked his watch. It had taken them less than five minutes. Impressive.

A large shadowy figure blocked out the light from the open door. "Should have guessed," the gruff voice announced.

Raven smiled. His old mate, DS Jake Marler, together with two uniforms and two ambulance operatives were filing in through the narrow door.

"Bloody hell, Raven, what's happened

here?" Marler snorted. Raven could see he was trying not to laugh.

Standing from the girl, Raven stepped aside for the ambulance crew to get to work. "Hi, Jake, this is Yasmin Patel," Raven said as he nodded towards the woman who was now in safe hands. "Her old man hired me to find her, she's been missing for a few days. I traced her here with this twat, Keanu. He pulled a knife on me, we both struggled, and he accidentally jabbed himself in the leg," Raven shrugged, his innocent expression was wasted on Jake Marler. He knew Raven too well. "Look, the syringe and the gear are on the bed. He was going to jack her up, God knows what the outcome would have been."

Marler bent down to take a closer look at the bleeding Keanu who had now fallen silent. "Keanu? He's on licence. It's back to nick for him, toute de suite."

Raven laughed at Marler's pathetic attempt at French.

Keanu was still clutching his leg which was still bleeding but Raven knew he'd live. "He's fucking mad," Keanu cried, he actually cried like a little child whose ball had been confiscated. "He tried to kill me."

One of the ambulance technicians had left Yasmin with her colleague and was now applying a tourniquet to Keanu's leg. "What the hell happened?" She said.

Raven did a double take. The woman had

a large badge stitched to her coverall that declared she was a paramedic, but it was her eyes that took him by surprise. They took his breath away. Dark green eyes were lightly enhanced by a discreet application of makeup, but Raven was sure they didn't need any enhancement. She was petite and he wondered how she would manage lifting some heavier patients into the back of her wagon. He thought she resembled Audrey Hepburn and Raven had always had a soft spot for Breakfast at Tiffany's. Not George Peppard, of course.

Marler leaned over Keanu and whispered in his ear as Audrey rushed out to her ambulance to get something she felt was needed to save the man. "Keanu, if Raven wanted to kill you, you'd be dead by now, so count yourself lucky. By the way, you're under arrest for supplying. I'd normally caution you but you're off your box, so I won't waste my breath. Now... do you wish to make a complaint against this man who has just saved the life of a missing young woman?"

Keanu sighed. He knew he was sunk. "Complaint? Just get me sorted, I'm in agony here."

"Cracking," Marler nodded. "That's the way I like it. Now, you trot off to casualty with the paramedics and I'll see you there once you're sorted. I might even bring you some flowers or some grapes. It's back to the nick and a bit of remand for you, my son."

Marler grinned as he stood and ushered

Raven outside.

"You know him well?"

"Oh aye, he's a Caerau boy," Marler said as he lit a small cigar from a flat tin he pulled from his trouser pocket. "Prodigious supplier," he offered Raven a smoke and Raven accepted and waited for him to offer a light.

"Prodigious? Been reading a thesaurus?" Raven teased. Marler shrugged. Got to sound the part if I want to move up the ladder, mate."

Although Raven had given up smoking cigarettes when he left the SBS, he still enjoyed the odd cigar. He took a long drag and savoured the taste.

Marler added, "I'll do the business here, I think you're right, he probably *was* going to jack her with the 'H', get her hooked and pimp her out on the grounds. Do you think she's dabbled before?"

"Can't see any track marks."

"She's a lucky girl, then."

"I'll give her old man a bell and then go with Yasmin in the ambulance." Yasmin's wellbeing was important to him but was becoming secondary to Raven's desire to spend a little more time with Ms. Hepburn now he was sure the young woman would be fine. "They can check her over and hopefully all will be well."

"Sounds solid to me, Raven. If I need a statement, I'll give you a bell."

"No problem." Raven took a another drag

from the small cigar and almost finished it in one long inhalation. "We'll have to have a pint one of these nights and you'll have to buy some expensive cigars."

"Look forward to it but it's your turn to stand the smokes."

***

"Mr Patel? Raven here. I've traced Yasmin and I need to tell you not to panic and to listen carefully," Raven said firmly. The last thing he needed was a blubbering father on the other end of the call. "She's on her way to casualty. I don't know whether she's pissed or whether this clown she was with has given her something. She's OK but they'll have to check her over."

"Oh, thank you, thank you, I will go straight there."

Raven got in the back of the ambulance. Audrey Hepburn had put Yasmin on a drip, and the young woman was looking brighter. Another ambulance had pulled up to collect Keanu.

"What are you doing with a tosser like that, he could have killed you," Raven said to Yasmin. "Have you done heroin before?"

"Heroin? What are you on about?"

"The delightful Keanu was going to jack you up with heroin, he could have killed you."

"Keanu wouldn't do that, he loves me."

Audrey shook her head, a sad, resigned expression revealing her feelings.

"Yasmin, let me tell you, he's a scum bag. He doesn't give a toss about you. He's using you. Once you'd had the hit that would have been the end of it, you'd have been hooked and he'd have you turning tricks for a tenner." Raven could see Audrey looking shocked by his words. "Your father loves you dearly, don't do this to him, you'll break him. You've already lost your mother don't lose your father as well."

It's difficult convincing a young woman, or man for that matter, that their partner is a waste of space. They generally had to find that out for themselves.

"What will happen to Keanu?" She said.

"He'll go back to the nick and get a stretch for supplying, probably three years."

Yasmin closed her eyes. Raven hoped his words would stick in her mind. He guessed she wasn't a bad girl. She'd just lost her way.

Rushed straight through to casualty, Yasmin was checked over as soon as the ambulance pulled up under the hospital portico. Raven watched Ms Hepburn as she reeled off her observations to a doctor. He also watched her as she reached the doorway to the corridor and turn to smile at him. He felt good. It was a good result.

Another smoke was needed but he knew it was out of the question now within the grounds of a hospital and Marler wasn't around to blag one. The smoking ban was national. Anybody would think doctors knew better.

Mr Patel turned up several minutes later.

His smile was more of a grimace. "How is she, Mr Connor?"

"She'll be OK. I don't know what she's taken but whatever it was she's coming out of it, so I don't think it's anything that will leave a lasting effect."

"Oh, thank you, Mr Connor. Thank you for finding her. When will I be able to see her?"

"I'm a private detective, Mr Patel, not a doctor. I'm just guessing it shouldn't be long. I'll get us a coffee and I'll stay with you."

Raven sat in the waiting room with Mr Patel for over an hour. He hoped he'd see Ms. Hepburn again, but he also really did want to ensure there was a happy outcome for his client. His relationship with Lynette was progressing slowly, but he had a suspicion that most of the attraction for Lynette was his sister. She had grown to love Sue like a sister. And, whilst that was a good thing, Raven wasn't convinced that their fledgling romance would go much further. He believed in fate, in leaving the universe determine his future, whatever that meant.

"Have you any children Mr Connor?" Patel asked.

"No, never had the time." That had been true. Relationships had been pleasant distractions, enjoyable interludes in a life that had rarely had time to devote to nurturing them further than an occasional extended physical need.

"You were a soldier?"

Raven was surprised. "What makes you think that?"

"I think you look like one."

"What the hell does that mean?"

Patel shrugged. "The way you act, the way you talk, the way you walk. You look like a soldier."

A nurse appeared at the corridor door and called them into the recovery room. Yasmin was sitting up on the bed, the top third of the mattress inclined to forty-five degrees. She looked tired and drawn, dark circles enclosed her eyes, and her skin had a hint of grey, but there was still something attractive about her, a natural beauty, the product of lucky genes that refused to be diminished by her near-death experience.

She looked at her father, a tentative, uncertain glance to test the response. He father smiled warmly, not hint of anger or disappointment, just love and concern for her. Then the tears began to run down her cheeks.

"Papa, I'm sorry, I'm sorry, I've let you down."

Mr Patel hurried over to her and held her tight.

Even Raven had a hint of moisture around his eyes that he quickly wiped away.

"How can I ever repay you, Mr Connor? I will never forget this night."

"All I ask is the two-hundred a day plus fifty

for new trousers and a shirt," he joked.

Mr Patel looked at Keanu's blood that had spattered him, smiled and nodded.

13.

Tony Heggerty looked nothing like a singer and stage performer. Forty-five years of age with the physique of a mixed martial arts fighter. His chiselled, square jaw screamed chemical enhancement and his olive skin - with permanent designer stubble - completed the resemblance to Desperate Dan – if the comic book character had been addicted to sun beds.

A Treorchy boy with an unlikely dream, singing had always been Tony's life. With no immediate or extended family ties, he had plenty of time to put all his energy into his unusual full-time profession, a profession that had served him well, a profession that exploited fans of a performer long since dead. Tony was one of the country's best Elvis Presley tribute acts. He performed under the name of *Hound Dog Heggerty,* with the tag line of *the Number One Elvis Tribute Act.* Travelling overseas and the length and breadth of the UK; he would have had more stamps in his passport than the old king, if passport stamps were still being issued in Europe. The Treorchy boy was living his dream and earning far more than most of the kids he had grown up with.

Tony's reputation on the music scene was sealed in a glowing article in the pages of a respected music magazine, having been voted the best Porthcawl Festival Elvis for three years since 2017. He was the first to achieve a hat trick of the awards and his reputation was further enhanced by the fact that he never missed a gig – for anything.

He lived alone in a detached house any winner of the lottery would stop and admire. Situated on the hillside overlooking his hometown where he was treated like a minor celebrity. The acre of land the house sat on sloped gently down towards the mass of terraced houses of the town. A wood and glass balcony spanned the width of the property at the front, taking advantage of the view of the grey slate roofs of the homes of the valley people below. The balcony was not a seldom used aesthetic addition. Each morning, he liked nothing more than belting out Elvis tunes to his well-used backing tracks. He was the star, high above the town on his concrete perch, shining down on the admiring gazes that he knew were watching him at all times, wishing they could be him.

It was two days to the beginning of the annual Porthcawl Elvis Festival, 2020 and Tony lay out his stage costumes on the bed, he was confident that he could take the title for the fourth consecutive year. He was the Arnold Schwarzenegger, or perhaps the Lewis Hamilton of the Elvis world, the determined winners with seven world conquering victories and the men others longed to beat. But he knew there would be stiff competition from the UK and abroad. It was always *Hound Dog* eat *Hound Dog*, no holds barred. Tony also had to watch out for the dirty tricks brigade.

The Porthcawl Elvis Festival had become a major event in the local entertainment calendar. Every September, thousands of Elvis fans descended on the Welsh seaside town of Porthcawl for a celebration of 'the king'. The magnificent Grand Pavilion was always the focus for the main event but there were other shows hosted in the popular 'Hi Tide' pub during the weekend with twenty or so other venues around town hosting tribute events, which formed the fringe festival.

After packing his gear into his silver BMW X5 with its cherished plate ELF111S, Tony drove the twenty-two miles south to Porthcawl. He liked to get there a day or two before the festivities began. Over the weekend, the town would be bursting at the seams with carousers and accommodation would be as rare as hen's teeth. That was not a problem for Tony, however. Tony had a long-standing arrangement with a local hotel and always had his room booked well in advance.

Tony had performed many times at the Grand Pavilion and the Hi Tide over the years.

He liked to visit them incognito, like Clark Kent - without the curl, to soak up the atmosphere from the fans as they arrived in their droves to catch a glimpse of their Superman.

He dumped his gear on the bed of his premier room, hung his costumes up in the walk-in wardrobe and took the lift to the ground floor.

The smell of salt in the air from the breaking waves beyond the seafront road and the sounds of laughter and music from piped sound systems brought a smile to his face as he walked unnoticed amongst the hordes that would soon be swooning over him.

***

Ladbrokes betting shop in John Street, Porthcawl is just like any other betting shop within the ever-growing gambling empire. There isn't a single town or city without some place to lay a bet, to throw away money that was getting harder to earn by the day. Indeed, it was the state of the ordinary person's lot that spawned an increase in businesses that offered a lucky break, a chance to get rich quick and to escape the reality of a life without enough money to cover the ever-present bills. Tony had heard it said that the number of betting, pawn, and charity shops on a street reflected the true declining state of a local community and there seemed to be an increase in all those shops throughout Wales.

Tony loved a flutter, but he would never

admit to being addicted to gambling. Horses, dogs, soccer, rugby or any sport where there was a winner and a loser offered an opportunity to make money - if the punters knew what they were doing. From the moment he got to Ladbrokes, Tony stuck his nose into the Racing Post and ignored the dozen or so other punters doing the same.

Betting offices had transformed considerably over the years and once they became licenced, they had changed out of all recognition. Today's modern shops were a hive of activity from early morning to late at night and if a punter wanted to try their luck at something more niche, then the shop would find a way to exploit that desire.

Decked out with gaming machines, horse racing and greyhound meetings on televisions affixed to every available wall space, it was a wall-to-wall gamblers paradise.

Inevitably, betting shops also became places to launder drug and other money from criminal activities through the gaming machines. It was nothing for some less than legitimate business to pump a grand in to a machine and win three or four hundred with a receipt to boot. Money laundering always came with a heavy price, but anything received with a legitimate receipt was worth the losses. If stopped by the police and asked to explain the cash, they would tell them where they won the money and produce the proof. *Bob's your uncle and Fanny's your aunt.*

It was surprisingly quiet in the bookies, Tony thought, considering the Elvis Festival was due to get underway. He expected the place to be packed, but the peace and quiet to study the form was short lived. His mobile began to vibrate. He checked the number on the screen. It was an incoming call from Rudi, a person not high on his list of favourite people.

"I hope you're not wasting the money you owe us on horses?"

Tony was temporarily dumbstruck. "How do you know where I am?" he said.

"Doesn't take a genius, does it?"

"What can I do you for you, recruiting gamblers now are you?"

"Put it this way, Tony," Rudi grumbled, "If we had to rely on you to make a living from gambling we'd be broke by now, that's a fact."

Tony laughed nervously. "What can I do for you, Rudi? Must be important for you to ring me direct."

"It is. The boss wants what he's owed. Do you have any idea how much it is now?"

Tony snorted derisorily. "Couple of grand, I suppose. Anyway, what's the problem? I'm always good for it."

"You owe three months cash, it's not a couple of grand, it's thirty grand, and the boss wants it a bit sharpish."

Tony knew exactly how much he owed but had hoped Rudi didn't. "Rudi, you know I'm good for it, have I ever let you down? Come on, man, play the game..."

"This is the second time, there's not going to be a third," Rudi warned. "Do you understand? We want the money and I want to collect it now."

"Give me a couple of days, just until I get the festival over and done with, eh?"

"If I don't get the cash, you'll be sorted, do you understand? There'll be no more rocking and fucking rolling for you, no jailhouse rock. You'll be crying in the chapel and washing your own blood off those fancy blue suede shoes you ponce about in, I can promise you that."

"You're not serious, Rudi, you'd get heavy with me?"

"Get the cash today and I won't have to."

"I'm a bit strapped at the moment, mate, give me a week, that's all I want."

Rudi sighed. "I'll give you until Thursday night. If I don't get it then you'll be eating your food through a straw, OK?"

Tony sighed. "Got you loud and clear, Rudi, loud and clear."

Tony had tried to remain calm but was visibly shaken by the conversation. He knew there was no way he would be able to stump up the cash he owed by next Thursday. Who could sort out thirty-grand in a week? Tony knew Rudi didn't take any prisoners when his boss was owed money, he invariably collected by one means or another and in this instance, it would be the other - a few broken bones at the very least. Even though Tony was physically imposing and strong he had never been a fighter. He hated violence. Tony knew all about Rudi. He had been born in Jamaica and Joined the British Army at sixteen after his parents moved to the UK. At six-four and built like a heavyweight boxer, Rudi was rumoured to be a real handful. Tony had heard that Rudi had been dishonourably discharged from the army after beating an officer close to death for daring to tell him he looked scruffy. But Rudi didn't have to hit anyone to get what he wanted. His mere presence: his pock-marked face, his polished head the size and shape of a bowling ball and deep predator eyes were enough to make most men shake at the knees, Tony didn't fancy coming into physical contact with the psycho. Rudi's reputation not only made his knees shake but also sent shivers down his spine.

The urge to chance his arm again on the nags had gone and Tony walked back to his hotel room. He stepped into the en suite and rummaged through his toiletry bag; he needed a release. He found the small plastic bag containing the white powder. He dropped the toilet seat cover and poured out a quarter of the contents, his hands were shaking and some fine grains spilled on the tiled floor.

He took out his wallet from his jacket

pocket, rolled up a twenty-pound note and took two large snorts – one for each nostril. The powder disappeared up his nose faster than a Dyson vacuum cleaner sucked up Shake-and-Vac. He wiped down the cover with a bath towel and slumped on the bed.

The drug did its job in a couple of minutes. Rudi could take a running leap off the pier. Who the hell did he think he was? He was a gofer, a hired hand. He grinned. He knew it was the powder talking. Popeye had his spinach, Tony had his coke. *It was good shit.* He rang his supplier.

"Rose, it's me, Tony. I need some gear as soon as. I've just used most of my stuff and I've got a busy weekend coming up. Can you sort me?"

"Tony my love… you want me to sort you? You're getting no more gear from me until you pay what you owe, it's five grand."

"Shit, Rose, you know I'm good for it, I've always been straight with you, can you sort me out? I'm begging you."

"Why don't you just pay your debts, eh? A little bird has told me you're up to your neck with that bookie mate of yours?"

"No, Rose, I sorted him this morning," he lied.

"Look, I'm not a fucking charity, you used to be OK, but lately you've lost the plot. You're cracking up. Rumour on the circuit is that it's only the coke that's holding you together."

"Bollocks, I don't need the coke to perform, I'm a natural, for fuck sake," Tony snapped.

"If you say so, Tony, then you'd better prove it. You get your act together or it'll all go to rat shit and you can go sing for more stuff off me and you can also expect a visit from a couple of my boys in due course."

Tony lobbed his phone through the bathroom door and onto the bed.

"Tony screamed as he slammed his fist against the bathroom door.

"Control," he told himself and took several long breaths. Singing always calmed him. He broke out into a rendition of 'In the ghetto,' but he knew full well it should have been 'In the shithole.'

It took twenty minutes for Tony to pull himself together, but he knew his world was crashing down around him and he had no answer to it. He had some spare cash but looking affluent was part of the game. He barely had enough left to pay his bills. He knew the drugs were to blame. He was making enough but he was spending it quicker than it was coming in. He certainly didn't have enough to pay what he owed to Rose and Rudi's boss.

It was going to be a very difficult few days for Tony.

***

The Seaview Hotel stood proudly on the

seafront with uninterrupted views of the Bristol Channel. Even though Tony had his usual premier room with views of the sea, things were different now, different from years ago when any old bed and breakfast would do. Tony had come a long way since those days, days when he was only making enough to get by as a pub singer. He couldn't go back to the way things were, not now, not after he had worked so hard to get to the top of his game.

The Seaview staff knew Tony well and were openly admirers of his talent. They treated him like the star he believed himself to be and were never intrusive and, in return, he'd sign autographs for them and pose for selfies. He would even occasionally give them an off the cuff rendition of 'In the Ghetto', a particular favourite of the manager too, and they all loved it.

The sun had begun to enter the downward trajectory towards the darkening western horizon when Tony slipped into a T-shirt and a pair of shorts for a stroll around the town. He needed some air. He needed to feel the fun, the buzz of excitement of others there to enjoy. He reached for the door handle when there was a knock on the door. He jumped back, a reflex action, a primal response – the flight or fight instinct from his reptilian brain that would always take the form of flight for Tony. Tony hesitated. It couldn't be Rudi. He'd already sorted an extension – even if it was something he couldn't honour. He finally opened the door and froze. He couldn't believe his eyes. There in front of him was his old mate, Kenny.

"Hello Lanky, long time no see," Kenny grinned.

Tony felt his bottom lip tremble. He was never known for being openly emotional and the feeling of relief, of joy on seeing his old, trusted friend, moved him more than he would ever have thought possible. Perhaps it was the coke. He grabbed Kenny by the shoulders and pulled him into a hug. "Titch, my old friend."

Kenny 'Titch' Vincent had been the person who had persuaded Tony to go into the Elvis tribute business, God only knew where he'd be without Kenny's advice all those years ago.

Over the intervening years, Tony had lost touch with Kenny, mostly due to the constant travelling. Tony was hardly ever home and then Kenny had moved away to London. Kenny had also been an entertainer chasing the dream of stardom in the early days but, the last Tony had heard, Kenny had married and settled into some manual labour job when the dream of stardom had transformed into a nightmare.

"I was just thinking about you," Tony lied. Lying had become second nature to Tony of late and he had begun to despise himself for it. He felt his fake tan face blush a brighter tone. "It's good to see you, mate," he said with sincerity this time. "Get in here, do you want a drink?"

Kenny said, "That would be great."

Tony poured Kenny a large glass of Bush-mills from a bottle the manager had left for him upon his arrival. The manager knew Tony's tastes and made sure they were well catered for. Kenny walked around the suite. "Smart pad."

"Aye, not bad, is it? Get this down you, butt," he handed Kenny the tumbler of spirit. "What brings you down here? I thought you were somewhere in London."

Taking a sip of the whiskey, Kenny licked his lips. "Yeah, I did a few years in the clubs and pubs, but didn't make it. I had a few agents who ripped me off, the usual story. It got nasty. I couldn't stand it any longer and got a job on a building site."

Tony nodded. "Aye, they're bastards. I look after myself, do it all, book all the gigs, I do every-thing. No Mr forty-per-cent for me. It hasn't been easy, but the last few years have been my best."

"I've followed your career. Fair play, you've certainly done well for yourself."

"Do you still do a bit, Kenny?"

"No, after I ended up on building sites, I realised regular money was more important to me. Fell back on the old trade, but you know what it's like up there in the smoke, it's so expensive. I was living hand to mouth but at least it was regular."

"What about family?"

"Sally passed last year."

"I'm sorry, Kenny, why didn't you get in touch?"

"There was no point, no point at all. Anyway, you could have been anywhere in the world."

"Any kids?"

"No, thank God."

"What are you going to do, where are you living?"

"Got some digs back home, nothing much, but it'll do for a while. Just popped down here for the day. I called around to your house, you obviously weren't there so I guessed you'd be down here at the festival."

"How did you find me?"

"I've done all the hotels, checked them all, then I thought of this place. I asked myself where would 'the great Tony' be staying?" He grinned and was surprised that Tony accepted the mock compliment as if it were commonplace.

"Well, I'm glad you did. Look, you can stay here with me for the week, and then you've got a room back home with me for as long as you like." Kenny tried to protest but Tony held his hand in the air. "Before you say anything, that's final, do you understand?"

"Leave it there, Tony, there's no need."

"Listen, if it hadn't been for you, I wouldn't be where I am today." Tony stood back and made a show of examining his friend. "By the way, you look awful, when did you last have a bit of grub?"

"I had a bacon sarnie this morning, before coming down."

"OK. So, let's get you kitted out," He fished a roll of twenties from his shorts. "Here's a hundred notes, get downtown and sort yourself. I'll arrange a room for you here, the hotel is always full at this time of the year, but I know the manager and he always keeps a room spare for emergencies. When you come back you clean yourself up. You can be my new road manager. I find it hard going on my own, I can't pay you wages just yet but that'll come if you want it?"

"What can I say?"

"Say nothing," he smiled warmly. "From here on in, it's just me and you. You'd better prepare yourself for a bit of travelling. I take it you've still got a passport?"

Kenny laughed. "You're joking, Tony? London is the furthest I've been."

"We'll sort that Monday. Now you get down the town. I'll see you later and we'll have a bit of grub, you can fill me in on everything."

14.

The sun had set, and the bright orange glow had begun to take a crimson hue when Tony and Kenny entered the hotel restaurant. Kenny had shaved and was decked out in some clothes, courtesy of Tony. Not exactly a caterpillar to a butterfly but he looked different to the man who had knocked Tony's door a few hours earlier. It had been a long time since Kenny had worn a pair of Chino's and even he had to admit that the pale blue shirt looked good on him.

They sat down at a reserved window table overlooking the road and the sea beyond. A hint of breeze was the perfect evening conditions for festival visitors to take a stroll along the promenade and hundreds were making the most of the good weather.

Tony picked up the menu.

"What do fancy, Kenny? You loved a steak in the old days, is that still the case?"

"Those days have long gone, Tony."

"Order what you want. Have the works. It's not every day friends reunite after so long. Everyone said we used to be joined at the hip."

Kenny laughed. "Yes, they were good days,

Tony. Look at us now, eh?" He sighed and smiled. "You've done really well for yourself."

"Hasn't always been like this, Kenny. Since I won my first festival, things have taken off. Took my breath away, it did. I haven't looked back since. Making a cracking living now, I am."

"So, no regrets, Tony?"

"Only family, Kenny. But that's all in the past. I've moved on, got no one really." Now he sighed and smiled. "Got no one, full stop. Anyway, what are you having to drink? Fancy a Guinness?"

"Oh aye, it was nearly my downfall back in the day when things weren't working out. Luckily, I got together with my Sally. She kept me on track through the rough times."

"I want to know all about Sally."

Tony beckoned over a young waitress.

"Good evening, Mr Heggerty, are you ready to order?"

Tony ordered a pint of Guinness and a jug of still water. "I'll have the Welsh lamb cutlets and Kenny here will have the Rib Eye, medium rare, Kenny?"

"That'll do me."

"We'll have all the trimmings as well, my love."

A few minutes later the waitress deposited the Guinness and water on the table.

"Your meals will be about ten minutes, Mr Heggerty."

"There's no rush my love, we've got a lot of catching up to do." He watched the waitress walk away. "That's a nice arse. If only I was ten years younger."

"Just ten?" Kenny joked.

Tony laughed. "Now, Kenny. Tell me about Sally."

"Not much to tell really, Tony. You knew her," he took a sip of his Guinness.

Tony was confused.

"Sally from the home?" Kenny explained. "She moved to London with adoptive parents during our last years at the home?"

"Ah, yes," Tony said, as he blushed. His reaction wasn't lost on Kenny.

"I only had her two years, butt. I came home one night and found her on the bed. There was an empty bottle of vodka on the floor. She'd taken a load of pills. Things had been good, I thought. I have no idea why she did it."

"That's terrible, you must have been devastated."

"It was ironic really. She had been the one to keep me sane and then she…" he left the words unformed. "When I lost her, I hit the bottle again, went really off the rails. I eventually pulled myself together, more for Sally's sake than mine. I remembered how she told me life was worth living. Joke, eh?"

Tony shrugged.

"I was so fucking angry, Tony. I kept asking

myself why it happened to us."

"So, no note or anything?"

"No, nothing. She had a few mental health problems, but the medication seemed to keep her on an even keel."

"Was there an inquest?"

"Yeah, the coroner was good. Sally had killed herself, I knew that, but fair play to the coroner, he classed it as accidental or misadventure or something like that. It was all a blur."

"Well, I suppose that's something."

"It cracked me up, Tony, brought things flooding back. I nearly topped myself, too."

Tony reached across the table and patted Kenny's hand. "Listen, that's all in the past, this is now, and the future looks good. We must never lose touch again. I'll make sure of that," he smiled.

"Cheers, Tony, it's much appreciated."

Tony shook his head dismissively. "It's nothing. We can go for a stroll after the grub, take in a bit of sea air, good for the old pipes."

They talked for hours, reminiscing about their lives growing up in the Rhondda. They were comfortable in each other's company. It was as if they had never been apart.

Tony signed a few autographs for some of the staff and a handful of residents as they left for the evening stroll.

They began walking towards the golf club in Rest Bay, a mile or so away.

"Remember the outings we used to go on with the home, it was down here mainly. Got fed up of it in the end."

"Oh aye, they were happy days though, Tony. And the talent contests in Trecco Bay were a blast."

Tony laughed. "We never ever won, but we enjoyed."

"Aye, we must have done it about six or seven years on the trot?"

"Six," Tony confirmed.

"Hegs and Vince. We put the King to shame, eh?"

"We did him justice, I reckon. That was the start of my love affair with Elvis." Tony jumped up onto one of the promenade benches and began belting out a few verses of 'Love me Tender'.

Kenny sat down alongside and laughed. He closed his eyes. It was as if Elvis were there in person. Tony really was that good.

A small crowd of people gathered, clapped and sang along.

Tony finished and signed autographs for the fans. "What about all this, Kenny? It'll be like this for the whole weekend, so you better get used to it," Tony grinned.

15.

Midday. One day to go to the main event.

Tony and Kenny arrived at the Grand Pavilion for the afternoon press conference.

Opened in 1932, initially intended as a Palm Court to host tea dances, grand balls, civic functions and numerous entertainment events throughout the year, the Pavilion had gained an international reputation and one of the highlights for the town had become the weekend Elvis Festival. The main event would be hosted at the Hi Tide pub at the fairground, but the Pavilion had more space for other events like the press conference.

Crowds had gathered along the promenade, the majority dressed in Elvis costume. Even some women were sporting Elvis sideburns or dressed in fifties style clothes. The drink was flowing openly on the streets in disposable pint pots and the party mood enhanced by renditions of Elvis's greatest hits blasting out from speakers in open doorways for revellers to sing along.

Tony was the star of the conference. It took him and Kenny nearly ten minutes to get through the crowd of admirers and Tony spent an age signing autographs for everybody, even those who had not asked for them.

"What do you reckon, Kenny, do you think you'd enjoy all this adoration?" Kenny didn't answer, shocked by what he'd seen. Tony grinned at his friend as they finally cleared a way through to the hall. "Just go with the flow, brother. Just to warn you though, there's a lot of jealousy within the tribute scene, so just watch our backs. I've had a few run-ins over the years and have made a few enemies, nothing heavy, sticks and stones really."

Tony left his friend at the front of the stage and sprang up several wooden steps.

The hall was packed with press and noisy admirers and Kenny stood in awe. He had no idea the festival was internationally acclaimed. It was crazy. How the hell could a tribute festival to a long-dead American singer in a town in South Wales get to be so big? It didn't make sense, but Tony had clearly made the most of it.

Taking his place in the centre of the stage, Tony was the king of kings amongst the twenty or so Elvis tribute singers. They were from all over the world; American, Dutch, German, Spanish, Scandinavian, Indian, Chinese, Japanese, and there were others Kenny struggled to guess at their origins.

The press conference lasted for over an hour with a lot of impromptu singing and press questions punctuated with some 'uh-uh-ing' thrown in for good measure. All the singers were playing to the audience who cheered and clapped enthusiastically.

It was the same every year and Tony loved it. He had come to depend on it, it was like the drugs, no, it was better than the drugs. If only he could bottle it and sell it as an elixir for others to feel the high he got from it.

After the conference, it was more of the same. Lots of selfies with the fans and scribbled autographs.

"Tony, they love you. I didn't realise how popular you are," Kenny laughed.

"Well, you better get used to it, Kenny-boy, it's like this everywhere I go. Always sell out audiences. They can't get enough of me, and you're a part of it now," he patted Kenny's shoulder just as another Elvis, a very large version in a full white suit resplendent with sequins and a chest of thick, black hair grabbed Tony from behind and threw him to the floor. Tony grappled with the other Elvis impersonator. Two Elvis Presley's were rolling on the floor, taking wild shots at each other with neither making contact. The reporters were in a frenzy, sharks circling the fighting fish, waiting to snap at the remains of the loser, and no one was intervening to break it up. Kenny felt he had no choice. He had to do something. He was Tony's new manager. He couldn't let his charge be injured prior to the main event. He dived on top of them both, wriggling between the two sequined gladiators and pushing then apart.

Blood seeped from Tony's nose and threatened to drip onto his formerly immaculate white jumpsuit. Kenny pulled a tissue from his pocket and held it to Tony's nose. The other Elvis had a gash over his right eye.

Kenny led Tony out of Pavilion and on to the promenade to amazed glances from the crowds outside.

"What the hell was that about, who's that bloke? He's a monster, what the hell are you doing brawling with him?"

"I think he's done my nose, Kenny," Tony moaned. "He's always at it, every year he performs like this. But this is the first time there's been an actual fight. He goads all of us, he caught me on the hop this time."

Kenny stood open mouthed, shocked by the events that were more at home at a pre-boxing match than a tribute festival. "Who the hell is he?"

"He's a German, Fritz Mueller. He's big in Europe..."

"He's bloody big everywhere. Did you see the size of him?"

Tony sniggered. "But I put him in the shade every year. It's just jealousy."

"Let's get you to casualty," Kenny said as he produced another paper tissue and tried to dab at Tony's nose.

"No, I'll be OK."

Kenny shook his head and ushered Tony into the car to drive him the short distance back to the Seaview.

They sat in the car for a moment. "Tony, do you want me to sort out Fritz? I know he's a massive twat, but nothing a length of two by one wouldn't cure. I'll make sure he doesn't start his nonsense again."

Tony was amused by the suggestion. "No, leave it, let's just get cleaned up. Don't think the old snout is damaged, just a bit of blood, I'll be fine."

Kenny shrugged. "Whatever, but he needs sorting." He locked the car and they walked towards the entrance.

"Aye, he needs sorting, but leave that to me." Tony added. "He'll be runner-up again this year and that's good enough for me. Let's get up to the room. We'll give room service a bell and have a bit of grub."

"Aren't you worried about the press and what they'll say tomorrow?"

"Nah, in this game there's no such thing as bad publicity. I'll milk it, you watch. There'll be more interviews, and the more publicity the better for us all, adds a bit of life to the festival," he led the way and walked in through the main door.

Kenny stopped, stunned by his friend's attitude. "If I didn't know any better, Tony, I'd swear you and the German staged it," he shouted after him.

Tony turned and winked.

***

Fritz Mueller was built like a brick out-house. Six-two, with shoulders like a heavy-weight boxer, he was facially similar to Elvis. However, he also knew his American accent needed a bit of work before he was the full package. He sounded more like Arnold Schwarzenegger than Elvis.

Sitting on the bed in his hotel room, his manager was dabbing his right eye with some cotton wool and antiseptic. It wasn't a deep cut, more of a scratch.

Ingrid Bauer was a smart woman, not tall, below average for a woman and proportionately built. Her short blonde hair was cut in a precise bob and her blue eyes were enhanced by subtle makeup. Dressed in a white silk blouse and grey pencil cut leather skirt, she looked more like a vertically challenged catwalk model than a manager for a tribute act. "What the hell got into you, Fritz? Why did you attack him, are you back on the steroids?"

"No, I just hate the bastard. He's up on stage, lording it over us, as if we're nothing and the contest is already won. I just snapped. I'm sorry, look I'll apologise in the morning."

"Yes, you will, Fitz. This doesn't bode well

for the weekend. I can imagine the headlines now and none of them will show you in a good light, you stupid bastard. I'll call a press conference in the morning, I'll get in touch with Tony and see if he'll agree to be there, you can apologise publicly."

"Whatever you say, Ingrid, you sort it. I'm going to have a sleep now," he waved a dismissive hand.

***

Tony and Kenny picked at their room service meal in awkward silence. They both thought it best to stay out of the public eye for a while, let the fuss blow off with the warm south-easterly wind. There was nothing more to be said on the matter. The meal was a selection of sandwiches hidden beneath a growth of leaves masquerading as a fashionable salad. Tony sipped from a large carboard cup of coffee Kenny had brought from a machine in the reception area, when the room phone rang.

Tony answered.

"It's Ingrid. I'm just ringing to say I'm sorry about earlier. Fritz is sorry, too. He was out of order…"

"Yes, he certainly was," Tony said as he struggled to not sound smug.

"…But you must admit you do like to think you're better than anyone else."

"Ingrid, dear Ingrid, you know only too

well that I am better, darling," he laughed at his own arrogance. "Now you haven't rung just to apologise have you, what do you want?"

"This needs to be sorted. It doesn't look good for any of us..."

"Doesn't look good for Fritz, you mean?"

There was a brief pause and Tony pictured Ingrid taking a deep breath and counting to ten. It wouldn't be good for her to lose her temper just now. Tony knew Fritz would come out of the situation worse than he would. "

If I call a press conference for the morning. Will you attend? Fritz will make his public apology, are you OK with that?"

Tony had heard enough and had no inclination to make things worse than they already were for her. He liked Ingrid, they had history. "I see no problem, what time?"

"Say... midday, at your hotel?"

"No problem. I'll be here, sore snout and all."

"Is it broken?"

"No, thank God. Mind you, may stop me snoring, you always complained about that, didn't you?"

Ingrid sighed. "See you tomorrow, Tony, goodbye."

16.

The sound of excited voices drew Eira Pritchard's attention away from the packet of dry roasted peanuts as she sat quietly in the corner of the lounge of the Seaview Hotel stuffing handfuls of the snack into her mouth. The bastard had arrived. She saw him waltz into the reception area with another man like he was a celebrity. What made it worse was the fact that the hotel staff also treated him like he was some superstar. Tony might well be a successful Elvis tribute act, but he was also a bastard.

At least Tony hadn't seen her yet. She had hidden her face behind a copy of the Western Mail she had borrowed from reception and Tony and his friend had gone up in the lift to their rooms.

Eira loved the real Elvis. It was her love for the singer that brought her to Porthcawl three years ago. The festival had surprised her. It was well organised, and the thousands of people enjoying the acts were from all over the UK. Everyone seemed to be in the mood for a good time and Eira had certainly been having fun on the first occasion she met Tony.

Hound Dog Heggerty had just finished his act. She had been impressed. His voice was very close to that of the King and, in his costume, he did look like Elvis in the last years of his performing life. Tony was a few pounds lighter than Elvis had been during the years leading up to his terrible demise in 1977 but even though Tony clearly worked out he had used padding around his waist to recreate the image of the king's decline. They had first spoken when Tony was signing autographs and disc cases of a compilation album he had recorded of the King's best-known tracks.

Tony had been charming, so much so that Eira had woken up the following morning in bed with him. She had to admit that he'd been an attentive lover and his charm was clear for all to see. By the time she left for her home in Cwmtwrch on the Monday following the festival she knew she was in love with him and he had told her he felt the same way. They promised to call each other, and Tony said he would visit – depending upon his busy work schedule. He never did. As soon as she got home, she discovered that the telephone number he had given her was false. She thought, at the outset, that she'd written it down wrong but when she didn't get a call from him, she soon realised that Tony was not what she had hoped he would be. Why had he been so horrible? It wasn't because she was ugly or anything. Eira was not classically attractive, her face, like most people was asymmetrical, not by a lot, but enough to add character. Her face was slim, and her large eyes were dark and twinkled with life; at least that's what Tony had said. He also said he loved her boobs and her bum, which he said was like two puppies in a sack. He had been funny and told her he loved her. The bastard.

She had booked herself into a small B & B just down the road from the hotel and she had already spent weeks plotting her revenge. The bastard would get his comeuppance. Now all she had to do was wait.

17.

Kenny stood at the back of the grandly decorated hall of the hotel as Tony sat alongside Fritz on the stage. The cameras clicked like machine guns, the rapid flashing lights creating a strobe effect that made movement akin to watching an old black and white cine film restored to full colour. The reporters were firing questions at Fritz about his behaviour the previous afternoon. Tony sat silently with a smug expression on his face as he listened to Fritz mumble an apology for his behaviour. Kenny checked his watch. Any publicity was good publicity and Tony was right, it was working in his favour, Kenny could see that. His friend was a lot smarter than he had remembered him.

Tony began to shift uncomfortably in his chair. The movements exaggerated by the strobing lights. Kenny could see him looking at someone at the front of the crowd, captured within the lights from the cameras. Along with the reporters, another fifty or so fans had clamoured to be present and were smiling, waving and bustling to get close to the star Tony clearly had become.

The lights made Kenny feel sick as he craned his neck over the heads of the fans to see what Tony was looking at.

***

What the hell is he doing here? Tony wondered. He was the last person he wanted to see. Lenny Stone was a loose cannon, someone who could mess everything up. He was standing in front of the line of photographers just staring at him.

"What do you think of Fritz's apology, Hound Dog?" a reporter asked.

Tony nearly missed the question. Having a stage name took some getting used to. Even though he'd been Hound Dog for many years it still took him by surprise when someone called him that.

"Er, I think it's great," he finally said. "No hard feelings."

"Do you think it will have any bearing on your performance Sunday night?"

Tony shook his head. He wanted to be confident, to be the cock-sure performer they all expected but the arrival of Lenny scuppered that. "No. I don't. I'm a professional, so is Fritz. May the best Elvis win. Now if you'll excuse me, I have to go and rehearse."

Tony pushed his way through the crowd towards the exit. He ignored the fans who he would normally spend time with. He hurried outside and turned to head for the hotel when he heard the call from behind.

"Tony. I hoped to catch you," Lenny shouted.

Tony stopped and turned slowly. This was a nightmare. Lenny was even dressed in a blue Elvis costume. "What do you want, Lenny?"

Walking slowly towards him, Lenny smiled. "Just the usual."

He had hoped this was all behind him, but bad pennies had the habit of turning up just when you least expected them to and Lenny was certainly a bad penny. "OK," he sighed. "Meet me down on the pier tonight about eleven. Now stay away from me."

"Don't let me down, Tony. You know what will happen if you do?"

Tony said nothing.

18.

Double back shifts, from evenings to days, were a thorn in DS Jake Marler's side, at least that's how it felt to him. They seemed to drain the life out of him, leaving him exhausted. It wasn't natural, the body wasn't meant to be subjected to such soul-sapping exhaustion. But he knew he was a slave to the job and thrived on everything it threw at him, even the stupid shift system.

It had been an eventful couple of weeks. Raven Connor had done it again, managed to stab a scrote - almost in the scrotum - and Marler had let his old friend get away with it. Old bonds ran deep, and Raven Connor was not a man anyone would want to cross. The last thing Marler wanted was for anything else to deal with. He was sinking under an ocean of pending case files. All he needed was a quiet couple of days to clear what he already had on his plate, but his hopes of that were soon dashed. The internal phone on his desk rang.

"CID. Jake Marler." He barked and instantly recognised the voice of the Operations Room duty Inspector on the other end of the line.

"Jake, they've got a body on the rocks down at the pier. White male in his thirties. He's got some injuries, so they want you down there ASAP."

"Is he in the water, Inspector? Do I need my wellies, or is he really on the rocks?"

"He's on the rocks, Jake, well above the tide mark at this time, but I haven't checked the tidal times yet. A local fisherman found him. He'll probably know all about that sort of thing. Lifeboat crew is also in attendance in case the sea water starts to pose a threat, just to be on the safe side."

"Tell them I'll be there in ten minutes, boss. And just to be on the safe side, get the FME and CSI's down there."

"Leave it with me, Jake, It's all in hand."

The pier and surrounding area had been cordoned off and the local bobbies were keeping the rubberneckers well away from the scene when Marler arrived twenty minutes later. He finished the last bite of a Cornish pasty he had picked up from a local bakery on his way to the scene. He had to change his dietary habits. The odd hours were never conducive to healthy eating.

Ducking under the blue and white tape barrier, Marler yawned and nodded to the old gnarled uniform copper that stood guard.

He reached the end of the pier and clambered down a rusty ladder set into the wall, the short struts set into the old stone had worked loose over many decades of weathering and the ladder felt like it might break free from its mounts at any moment. Jake reached the bottom and scrambled over the wet, black rocks towards the body. It was obvious from initial view that the victim hadn't been there long. He also noticed what looked like a swollen lip, a swelling under the left eye and marks to the deceased's scrawny neck. Something else caught his attention - a trace of white powder under the victim's nose. Dressed in a blue Elvis costume from the superstar's latter days, there was nothing on the body to provide identity, which Marler thought was odd. Everyone had some form of identity on them these days; credit cards, driving license, something with a name on it. Marler was sure this wasn't an accident and called it in from his mobile phone and asked for the major crime team to attend.

Another one for his growing stack of case files, he sighed and clambered back up the slippery iron treads of the ladder and lit a cigar.

The sky was a clear, bright pale blue without a wisp of cloud. He puffed on the cigar and walked over to a plaque that had recently been set in the stone wall overlooking the small dock. The brass plate was inscribed with a memorial tribute to a local woman Marler had known. She had been called 'The Bag Lady' and her murder some months ago had shocked the local community. Terry McGuire had led the manhunt for the killer, but he had failed to catch him until the psycho had returned to practice his dark arts on Raven Connor's sister. Thankfully, Raven and McGuire had caught up with him at the Meridian Tower in Swansea and Raven had seen the madman fall several floors to his death. Marler grinned as he thought about that incident. If he knew Raven at all, he knew his old military pal had had some hand in the demise of the killer. McGuire had substantiated Raven's statement that the killer had fallen without the assistance of a third party and that was all that mattered.

He checked his watch as he saw the marked police estate car arrive and park near the cordon. It had been less than thirty minutes since he had placed the call and both CJ and Glyn Walcott had arrived. Both were carrying aluminium cases, full of what Marler knew would be their essential equipment; cameras, tape, brushes, fingerprint powder, plastic bags, labels, pens and just about anything and everything a Crime Scene Investigating Officer might need to gather and preserve evidence.

They gathered at the ladder, Glyn climbed awkwardly down to the rocks and CJ and Marler passed the aluminium cases down onto the rocks.

CJ was an efficient medical examiner but looked more like an actor auditioning for the part of Doctor Who. Tall and slim, dressed in a full-length leather jacket, even in the heat of a September morning, with platform boots and a hint of black eyeliner that was clearly a nod back to his Goth youth. "What have you got?" CJ asked Marler.

"White male. I'd say in his thirties. Looks like he's taken a dive, but I don't know for sure. He's got injuries to the face and neck but they're not consistent with a fall from this height. I haven't turned him over. I'll leave that to you and Glyn."

"OK, we'll take it from here."

"The lifeboat crew will be on standby, just in case, and I've requested major crime to attend."

"Excellent, the quicker we get him on the slab the better." CJ frowned as he flung the end of his now trademark scarf over his shoulder and tucked it into his coat.

"I know Julia's on this morning," Glyn shouted to Marler. "She'll be here double quick."

"I'll hang on here and bring her up to speed."

Julia arrived behind him as he finished speaking and tapped Marler on the shoulder. "Your arse looks good in those trousers." she smiled and pouted her lips.

Marler laughed. "I'm sure that's a sexist remark."

"What's a bit of banter between colleagues? Anyway, you know you're not my type."

"That's not the impression you gave me at the Christmas piss-up."

Now Julia laughed. "Dream on, Jakey."

Marler gave her a minute to view the scene from the advantage point high on the pier and watched as CJ and Glyn opened their cases and began their examination.

"What have you got boys?" Julia shouted.

CJ stopped what he was doing and smiled up at her. "Morning, Jules. Pop down and have a closer look."

"No thanks, CJ, this'll do for me. I'll observe from here."

CJ smiled. "The marks to his face are very recent, they are certainly anti-mortem, probably just minutes before he died. The swelling of the lip and the contusion in the area beneath the eye are in the early stages of formation. I'd guess it was just minutes before death, but we'll get a better idea down at the morgue. There's also the powder on his philtrum... the dent bit here at the bottom of the nose," he said as he pointed to his own.

"I know what a bloody philtrum is, CJ..."

He nodded and offered an apologetic grin. "...that could be anything, tox will enlighten us."

"Surely, there'd be bruises all over him if he'd just taken a tumble off the pier?"

CJ nodded. "He's also got finger marks around the neck, Jules. If I had to make a guess, I'd say he was dead before he hit these rocks."

"Shit!" Now it made sense, Julia had wondered why Marler had called it in as suspicious. When someone keels over from a heart attack or falls off something when drunk it's normally just a case of paramedics getting stuck in and whisking the victim away for treatment. This wasn't such a case. This now looked like murder.

"I'll give the boss a bell and bring him up to speed," she shouted. "A murder, when the town will be inundated with Elvis fans, is going to be a real nightmare," she added quietly just for Marler's benefit. "She shouted to Glyn and CJ again, "I'll leave you to do the business. I'll get the room opened and see you down at the mortuary later."

"I'll give you a bell once the PM is scheduled, Jules," Glyn shouted back.

Julia turned from the edge and stared back towards the gathering mass of inquisitive bystanders at the entranceway to the pier. A television news team had just arrived and were setting their camera and lights up on the other side of the cordon. A fresh face anchor woman was checking her appearance in a window of the BBC News van. She had seen her on the telly many times but looked much slimmer in real life. "Well, Jake, looks like you made the right call."

"Thank you, Ma'am," Marler nodded. He had attended enough serious incidents during his career to know what to do.

Julia pressed the direct dial link to call

Terry McGuire. McGuire had only recently made Julia one of his Detective Inspectors and she was grateful to him for the opportunity, especially after she had recently begun to recover from the problems that had threatened to derail her career. McGuire was a man she respected, not because he had seen something in her that others hadn't, but because he was a bloody good detective and treated everyone fairly.

"Morning, boss, looks like we've got a murder in Porthcawl," she said as she watched the tv crew and the female reporter. "White male, no ID. It was thought, at first, that he'd fallen off the pier, however, Jake Marler wasn't happy with it and looks like he was spot on. CJ thinks it could be strangulation and the victim was dead before he took the tumble."

McGuire sat up in his office chair, he'd been in since six am to sort out the ever-growing piles of files that littered his office floor. Once again, he'd found something to distract him from the task he was dreading. "OK, Jules, I'll get the room opened. I won't go to the scene. I'll meet you at the nick and we can prepare a press release. Get as much information as you can, and I want Jake Marler in the room. He'll be useful with his local knowledge."

"I will. But Jake doesn't think the victim is local, boss. As you know, it's the Elvis weekend. The bloke could be from anywhere."

"We'll cross that bridge when we come to it,

Jules. For now, I'll just call out the troops."

19.

The local midday news was broadcasting from the flat screen television on Kenny's hotel room wall as he poured himself a cup of instant coffee. The coffee tasted like dishwater but at least it was better than the tea.

He had not seen Tony since his friend left the press conference in a hurry. Something was wrong with him. He'd practically run all the way back to the hotel, got changed quickly and then drove off somewhere. Kenny had asked him if there was anything he could do to help, whatever it was, but Tony had said nothing. He was certainly not the Tony he had been before the conference. Perhaps the fight had upset him more than he had let on.

Tony's absence had at least given Kenny some time to himself. He had taken a walk to clear his head and to think about what he could do to help his friend. If Tony was going to continue to be successful, he'd need to watch his back. There was always someone who would gladly spoil things out of spite or jealousy. Kenny was now his manager, whatever that meant, but he knew it was his duty to look after Tony.

Eyes drawn to events on the small screen, the scene was familiar. It was the Porthcawl harbour. Police tape had been strung across the walkway to the end of the pier. Two officers were turning people away as the reporter delivered her report. Kenny turned up the volume and sat closer to the television.

"...a man aged in his thirties has been found dead on the rocks below Porthcawl pier. Police have confirmed that the man appears to be one of the many thousands who have descended upon Porthcawl for the annual Elvis tribute festival. Police have yet to confirm the cause of death. A witness told ITV news earlier that the man, dressed in a blue Elvis costume, was found by a local fisherman. With so many people drawn to Porthcawl for the Elvis Festival anything like this could..."

Kenny reached for the off switch on the remote.

Deaths were not unusual in events like this. The excitement, overeating, overindulgence in alcohol, it was a recipe for heart attacks or falling off the bloody pier whilst pissed. Easy to fall and crack a head against rocks.

20.

There's no other job like it. McGuire thought as he poured a third cup of coffee into a chipped and stained mug. When detectives got the call to a murder on their patch, the adrenalin rush was akin to that of an athlete taking to the field of play. They all knew only too well that the first 24 to 48 hours of the investigation were critical. Statistics confirmed the fact that murders that went undetected after that time period were far less likely to ever be solved and McGuire's strike rate was up there with the best. He had no intention of letting his batting average drop now in the twilight of his career.

His team were well drilled and, setting up the Incident Room quickly and efficiently was something he didn't have to worry about, it was now second nature to them. Each detective knew their role. They left no stone unturned, even the slightest, seemingly irrelevant piece of information would be logged; nothing would ever be dismissed out of hand. McGuire had worked on too many murders in the past where SIOs - Senior Investigating Officers - would disregard information and opinions of seasoned detectives only for it to come back and bite them on the arse when disclosure questions arose at the Crown Court in front of the old, wigged overseer. Even seasoned senior officers would, metaphorically, and on occasions, literally, shit themselves.

Detective Inspector Julia Johnson had already issued a press release regarding the victim, even though there was nothing to identify him at that moment in time. All they knew was that he was in his thirties and wearing a replica blue Elvis suit. The victim could have been from anywhere in the world. The town was inundated with Elvis fans. McGuire knew that until they posted some pictures of him there wouldn't be much by the way of identification coming into the room. The quicker he got detectives on to the streets the better.

"Listen up, ladies and gents. This is what we've got..." he waited a moment for the gathered officers to settle and fall silent. "We have a white male in his thirties. He was found earlier this morning on the rocks just below the pier. At first, the uniforms thought it was a straightforward fall. However, this is certainly not the case. I'll let Jake fill you in. Jake, in your own time."

Marler stood and faced the assembled group of a dozen detectives. "Like the boss says, initially the uniforms thought that the victim had fallen on to the rocks, possibly under the influence or as a result of a heart attack. However, when I arrived, I took a closer look and noticed he had injuries to his face and neck, certainly not consistent with the fall. He was decked out in the Elvis suit but there was no wallet or anything to identify him. The FMO examined him more thoroughly and says these injuries are anti-mortem, caused minutes before he expired. Also, he says that the marks around the neck were finger marks. There was also residue of a white powder around his nose, possibly cocaine. The PM won't be until later this afternoon. The FMO and DS Walcott are down at the morgue waiting for the Home Office Pathologist as I speak."

McGuire stepped forward and patted Marler on the shoulder. "Cheers, Jake," he looked at the others. "Any questions?"

DI Colin Boulton sat with his legs crossed in the front row. "Any idea as to time of death?"

"Looks like within the last twelve hours, boss," Marler said. Probably, say, from ten last night. Luckily, the victim wasn't actually in the water, so he hasn't been munched on by the fish."

Colin nodded. "Good, at least we've got some kind of timeline to work with."

"Obviously we'll know more later this evening after the PM," McGuire said. "The main priority is to identify the victim and try to establish a motive. Was he involved in some random argument, or was the killer known to him? You all know what it's like during most festivals, sex, drugs and rock and roll. Anyone have any ideas who he could be?"

"No, boss," Marler said. "I know all the locals. He certainly isn't one of them. I'll start putting feelers out with a couple of my narks, they'll soon put us straight if they know him."

"OK, we'll action that out to you and you crack on, time is of the essence."

Marler nodded. "I'm on it, boss."

McGuire nodded at Colin. "Colin, you'll be running this one with Julia. I'll make my way to the mortuary and confer with the boys. Hopefully we'll have the full picture of how the victim died. I'll get Glyn to take a few snapshots and we can get them out there later on this evening."

"No problem, boss, we'll start with house to house around the pier area and collect any CCTV footage. I just hope there are a few cameras in that area."

"Excellent," McGuire smiled. "We'll call a conference around ten o'clock. Let's get cracking."

McGuire checked his watch as the other senior officers present tasked the detectives with jobs. Molly, his wife, needed to know he wouldn't be home for the foreseeable.

"Put the dinner in the dog, love. It's going to be a long one, I'm sorry."

McGuire's wife was well used to such news. "I heard it on the news earlier, poor man, any idea who he is?"

"No, not at the moment."

"I'll expect you when I see you."

"It'll be about eleven, after the conference, sorry about this, love."

"Terry, how many times have I heard that? Trouble follows you like a bad smell, and it looks like you've got plenty of suspects to get your teeth into, the town is teaming with Elvis fans."

Molly had put up with a great deal over the years and McGuire knew that many wives of detectives would have packed up and left years ago, but Molly was not like most others. She was a different breed and McGuire was always grateful that he never had a hard time from her when he had to work late. He ended the call and kissed his phone.

21.

The glossy photograph was creased and dog-eared, and the signature had faded from countless caresses. The smiling photograph of Tony made up to resemble Elvis went everywhere with Eira and had suffered from its time in her purse, but that didn't matter. It was a memento of a wonderful time, the best time of her life when no one else had mattered to them. She had felt honoured that he had chosen her. Out of all the beautiful women in the festival, Tony had chosen Eira Pritchard. Eira from Cwmtwrch. Eira who had never had a real boyfriend in the whole of her thirty-three years. Eira who had devoted her life to her pets. She had been Tony's Pricilla.

How could a man who liked to dress up as a dead singer possibly win her heart? Indeed, she had fallen completely for Tony and his promises of a life together with her pets.

Her dogs had always been her life. From before she could remember, she had always been around dogs. Her parents had owned a boarding kennel in the little village where the houses had been built over decades with no obvious building plan; seemingly scattered randomly into any vacant parcel of available land. At one time in the distant past, Cwmtwrch – the valley of the bore – the pig variety not human - like many other villages in the area - had more pubs than chapels. Things had changed and the pubs had become restaurants and then, in more recent months had suffered the fate of many small local pubs and closed their doors for the last time.

The kennel was opened on the Pritchard family small holding in the village forty years ago, before Eira was born. The smallholding was another planning anomaly, set in perpetual shade at the bottom of the valley. With just over an acre of land squeezed between a row of terraced houses and the river. It was just enough land for the handful of wooden buildings her dad had built to house the dogs with enough room for them to run free within the fenced enclosure that sloped down to a shallow stream. Only when the sun was at its zenith would bright sunlight reach the enclosure for just over an hour or so but that had never seemed to bother her dad.

Educated in the village primary school and later in the local comprehensive – Maesydderwen - Eira had been a bright student and had been offered a place at university, but that was a career path she had never wanted to follow. The dogs meant everything to her. Apart from the animals that would be booked in for a stay at the kennel, Eira's family had sixteen dogs of their own, big, small, medium, hairy, fluffy, furry and bald, they had them all and Eira loved them all equally. She had been happy. Never one to socialise much, Eira devoted her time to the kennel and could never envisage a time where any man would ever upset the status quo. That was until she met Tony. Tony had offered something she thought she would never experience and now he had also taken it away.

Eira stared out of the small window that overlooked a side street off the main drag. The streets were busy; she could hear the revellers on the main road singing along to Elvis songs playing loudly through speakers set up in the local bars. She loved the music of Elvis Presley but now it stirred some other feeling inside her, one she had never experienced before – hate – not for the music but for a man who would always be associated with it, a man who had sung the King's love songs with such emotion but now she knew that emotion was fake, an act that was intentionally misleading, an act that promised much but delivered nothing but pain.

22.

There were much better ways to spend a Friday afternoon than watching some poor soul being sliced and diced on the slab. Twenty-four hours earlier the victim was probably enjoying himself on the booze in one of the town's hostelries, McGuire thought. Such was life and death, *who knows what tomorrow brings?* As old Joe Cocker would sing.

McGuire wondered what possessed someone to become a pathologist, spending their life surrounded by cadavers and body parts requiring testing.

He walked along a white-walled corridor smelling of chemicals that were probably common to hospitals around the world. The mortuary door opened as he reached it and CJ and Glyn Walcott greeted him, both were grinning. McGuire wondered what could be funny, but he knew that those who dealt with death on a regular basis had strange ways of coping with the situations. Then he saw, behind them, a woman doing the post-mortem, she was so focussed on what she was doing she didn't even look up from behind her full Perspex face mask as he entered the disinfected environment. McGuire hated the smell in the mortuary. He dipped his fingers into a jar of Vick that was kept by the door and smeared some beneath his nose, a routine he had adopted many years before.

"Selina is about halfway through. Do you know Professor Selina Hamilton?" CJ said as he stepped back into the room with Glyn.

"No, I haven't had the pleasure."

Selina paused a moment and looked up. She placed the scalpel she had been wielding on to the stainless-steel slab and pulled up the facemask.

"Ah, Superintendent McGuire," she smiled pleasantly. "The boys said you were on your way. Please excuse me for not shaking your hand."

"Pleased to meet you, professor."

"We'll have a chat later. I've been called in to do this one as first reserve, so to speak. Shouldn't be too long," she grinned.

"What's in it?"

"Definitely foul play. I'd say he's been dead a minimum of twelve hours. He's got injuries to his face and lip together with what appears to be a finger mark bruise on the side of his neck. He's also got a hairline fracture to the base of the skull."

"Do you think that was from the fall?"

She nodded her head. "I'd say that was post-mortem, the other injuries are definitely anti-mortem."

"So, it's a murder?"

"Without a doubt. His hyoid bone is fractured, and he was probably dead in minutes. I'll be writing this one up as manual strangulation."

"Well, that's put the damper on the Elvis weekend," McGuire said. "Any other anomalies on the body?"

"We've done a quick test on the powder residue from the nose and that's positive for cocaine. There's also evidence of anal penetration, however, there's no bruising or tearing, which would suggest that he's probably a consenting adult."

"That might put a different perspective on it, a gay, cocaine sniffing, Elvis impersonator, that's a first for me."

Glyn smiled. "I've taken a few facial shots, boss, before Selina got to work; they're not too bad, ideal for identification purposes. Also, he's got a few prominent tattoos on his arms. One is a heart with an arrow going through it with the initial's TH and LS and looks relatively new... the colours are still quite vibrant. The other tattoo is a full-blown Elvis over the entire length of the arm."

That was great news. Someone would recognise the tattoos. McGuire nodded. "Excellent. Glyn, get back to the Incident Room and bring Colin up to speed and get the pictures out there as soon as possible. With a bit of luck, we can get something on the evening news."

It took Selina another half hour to wrap up the P.M. McGuire watched as she immersed herself in her work.

"Give me five minutes. I'll put the poor bugger on ice and then get cleaned up, bear with me."

CJ tapped Terry with his elbow. "Impressed or what, Terry? Nice to see a vision of beauty doing the business for a change, eh?"

"When I first saw you, CJ, my breath was taken away, but for different reasons," McGuire grinned.

"There's a shortage of pathologists at the moment, retirements and holidays."

Selina appeared, clean and wearing a figure hugging, white fluffy turtleneck sweater over blue jeans that looked as if they were tailor made for her. A pair of tan knee-length boots also looked expensive. McGuire had to admit that she was an attractive woman. Made a change from the grizzly old pathologists he had dealt with in the past. He thought she was about five foot eight tall and her face radiated warmth. She looked more like a wealthy landowner than a pathologist. Her hair was blonde, cut into in a bob and her body looked well-toned. McGuire guessed her age at mid-forties even though she looked ten years younger.

Selina held out her hand, a firm grip, not what he expected from someone of her diminutive build.

"I'm very pleased to meet you, Terry. I often

wondered what you'd look like in person."

"I hope you're not disappointed?"

"Not at all," she smiled.

"Flattery will get you everywhere, Selina," McGuire laughed. "How did you get into this game?"

"Don't I look like a pathologist?"

"Honestly? No."

She laughed, "It's in the genes, Terry. My dad was a pathologist in Pembrokeshire. It was either this or become a vet."

"So, are you living locally?"

"No, still down in Pembroke. I'm on-call at the minute. I'm actually based in Glangwilli Hospital where I do a lot of lecturing."

"I'm well impressed. I'll have to put you on speed dial for the future."

"Likewise," she smiled. "Perhaps you could pop down and give some input on my lectures? I'm sure my students would love to hear from a real detective of your prowess."

McGuire blushed. "When can I have your report?"

"The next couple of days. If I'm not too busy, I'll drop it down to the Incident Room. I should have the toxicology results back tomorrow. I've told the lab it's a priority."

"That'll be great, you can meet the team and get to know them personally. I've no doubt we'll be doing business again. Anyway, we'll leave you to it. Are you sorted for transport? If not, I'll get one of the traffic boys to take you home."

"No problem, Terry, got the old banger outside."

CJ walked with McGuire as they left the mortuary.

"Felt a bit of electricity there, Terry," CJ teased. "Never seen you like that before."

"What are you fucking babbling about now, CJ?"

"Well, you know, she's a bit of a looker."

"Get lost, CJ, leave it there. I'm very happily married... mind you, she's in better nick than old Doc Powell."

23.

McGuire had already briefed the team about the post-mortem results during the Friday night briefing. Nothing much by way of information was coming into the room from the public. Hopefully, with the victim's facial photograph and pictures of his tattoos having now been circulated both via TV and the Saturday papers, there was a good chance the team would have more luck.

It was a little after midday, and McGuire was on his third cup of coffee when he saw DC Roger Bailey take a call and wave at him.

All eyes turned toward the young DC as he switched the phone to speaker.

"I've just seen the photograph of the person found dead on the pier," the caller said. "I recognise him. He's my brother... Lenny. The tattoos... that's Lenny."

Bailey raised his eyebrows and looked at McGuire for guidance. McGuire nodded and waved his hand for him to continue.

"What's your name and address please, sir?"

"My name is Phillip Stone." He told Bailey

his address in Pencoed.

"Are you at the address now, sir?"

"Yes I am. I can't believe it. It *is* Lenny, I'm sure."

"Just hang on the line, sir. I'll get the Senior Investigating Officer to speak with you."

McGuire nodded at Colin Boulton. Boulton had recently been promoted to acting Detective Chief Inspector at the same time McGuire accepted the rank of Superintendent. It was not a rank Boulton really wanted but agreed to it whilst a new DCI was selected. Boulton loved the cut and thrust of policing and was happy to remain a DI. He picked up the phone.

"Mr Stone, this is Acting Detective Chief Inspector Bolton. Are you certain that the picture is that of your brother Lenny?"

"Yes, I'm certain."

"When did you see him last?"

"Not for some weeks. We don't really get on. He pops in the house now and again. He lives his life and I live mine."

"Where did he live, Mr Stone?"

"In a bedsit above the Spar, here in Pencoed. We're from the Rhondda originally. I moved down to Pencoed when I started working in Fords."

"OK, Mr Stone, stay where you are. I'll get two of my officers to come and see you. Do you have a key for your brother's bedsit?"

"No, I've never been in it. I think the shop

owner will have one though, he's the landlord."

"OK, my officers are on their way."

Boulton grinned. It looked like the break that the team had been waiting for.

"Julia. You and Caroline go and see Mr Stone," he said.

McGuire was happy to let Boulton run the investigation. He knew he was more than capable and the soon he got his feet beneath the table the better.

Boulton continued. "Marigold, you and Duggan go to the bedsit and give it the once over. Bag and tag anything that you think is relevant."

***

Caroline drove the pool Vauxhall as Julia checked the briefing notes. Julia was happy to work with Caroline. As DI, it wasn't always possible to have a comfortable relationship with an officer of a lower rank, but Julia had never been the type of person to pull rank on anyone, unless there was no other option. Caroline had already proved herself to be a good DS and Julia had no doubt she'd soon be promoted to DI. They didn't have a lot in common, other than a sense of humour that often bordered on the dark side.

It didn't take Julia and Caroline long to get to Pencoed where they met Mr Stone.

Julia said, "We know that this must be distressing for you, but are you certain that it's your brother?"

Stone thrust his large square chin forward. "Without a doubt." Julia thought the man looked like the real-life version of the animated character Buzz Lightyear.

"Can you give us a bit of background on Lenny, his age, where he worked, anything?"

"Where do you want me to start?"

"Just give us a picture of his life," Caroline chipped in.

"We were both born in the Rhondda but moved to Pencoed with our parents in 1996. I was eighteen and Lenny was seventeen at the time. Sadly, we lost our parents through the cancer a few years later. We both got jobs in Fords and lived here together, just the two of us. We earned good money; everything was OK until Lenny got sacked."

"Why was he sacked?" Julia said.

"It was the dope. He was working on the line when they did a random check on his locker. They found some pot and a little cocaine, and they got shot of him. He then went from bad to worse."

Caroline scribbled notes into her pocketbook. "Did Fords report the matter?"

"No, they just sacked him on the spot."

Julia was intrigued. "What do you mean he went from bad to worse?"

Stone shrugged his shoulders and walked to the window overlooking the quiet street. "His behaviour spiralled out of control. I put up with it for years, but I'd had enough, so I bought him out. I gave him thirty grand and he signed the house over to me; it had been left to the both of us by our parents just before they passed." Stone stood still, staring out the window at nothing.

Caroline stepped alongside him and gazed in the same direction. "So, how long has he been living in a bed sit?"

"A couple of years now," Stone said as he turned his head to look at the detective. "He didn't have a job. I think he's been living on benefits." He turned back towards the street and sighed. "Do you know how he died? The news said he'd fallen off the pier."

Caroline touched him gently on the shoulder. "I'm sorry to say, it looks like he's been murdered."

Stone turned quickly to face Julia standing behind him. "Murder? Who'd want to murder Larry? He wouldn't hurt a fly."

"What about his private life," Julia asked, "girlfriends, that sort of thing?"

"Girlfriends? Never!," he scoffed. "He was gay. Never hid it, not even from my parents. He was proud of it and wasn't shy of flaunting it too."

"What about male friends, can you give us any names?"

Stone shook his head. "Not really. I never really met any of them."

"What about the tattoos, can you tell us

anything about those, the lettering?"

"No, I can't help you there, sorry. Never had any when he lived with me."

Caroline continued to scribble notes. "When your brother's body was found, he was wearing a blue Elvis Presley suit," she said.

He nodded. "I'm not surprised. He was a big fan. I know he always visited the festival."

"We'll take a full statement off you now and then take you to the mortuary for a formal identification, is that alright?" Julia said.

He sighed and nodded. "Not a problem."

Caroline began taking the statement while Julia stepped outside to make a call to sort out the mortuary visit.

It took Caroline over an hour to extract all the information for the statement and then the detectives drove Stone to the mortuary where he positively identified the body of his brother Lenny.

"For the benefit of the record," Julia needed to be sure. "Are you positive, Mr Stone?"

"Yes," he nodded as he wiped a solitary tear from his left eye, "that's my brother, God bless him."

"Mr Stone, I know this may seem a touch indelicate, but can you account for your movements from... say... from midday Thursday to midday Friday?"

He shrugged his shoulders. "I understand. I've got no problem with that. I worked afternoons on Thursday and then worked a night shift. I got home around eight in the morning on Friday. You can easily check. I would never have anything to do with Lenny's death."

Caroline walked outside and tapped in the number for the Incident Room and spoke to McGuire. "Boss, positive identification on the victim. Lenny Stone, aged 39, lived on his own in a Pencoed bedsit. We've taken a full statement off his brother, Phillip. He seems genuine enough. Doesn't look like there's any love lost though. Bit of background there, I think. The brother has no idea about the tattoo initials. Perhaps the boys will get something from the bedsit."

"That's good work. Now get back here, sharpish," McGuire said. "We'll sort out a press release and see if that will throw a bit of light on things."

24.

"Looking good," Tony said to his own reflection in the mirror affixed to the tiled wall of the bathroom. The sparkling white costume was snug around the waist thanks to the padding strapped around him. It just made him look more like the original Elvis in his later years.

He smiled; his whitened teeth had begun to yellow at the gums. Another visit to the technician would be needed soon. Eighteen hundred quid to get a shiny smile. Who'd have thought that Tony from the valleys would be paying that kind of money on his teeth, even if he didn't have it to spend?

"Where is he?"

Tony turned and walked to the door to listen to the raised voices in the sitting room. He wasn't expecting any visitors but had become used to fans discovering his room and attempting to get a selfie with him.

"I need to see him, now," a woman's voice said.

"He's about to go on in under an hour," Tony heard Kenny reply.

"I know he's here. I just need to see him for a

moment."

Tony recognised the voice. It was Erika or was it Eira? Yes, it was Eira. He remembered because she told him it meant snow in Welsh. Tony had never learnt Welsh much past a handful of words in school. Shit! What the hell did she expect from him? One night of passion – however good it must have been for her – didn't make him responsible for her. He checked his smile again and stepped out into the bedroom and opened the door to the sitting room.

"Eira, what a surprise. So good to see you. I've been trying to call you, but I must have the wrong number," he blustered.

Tony could see the moment of confusion in Eira's eyes. He knew she was doubting herself. Was he being straight with her? Was there still a chance of rescuing the relationship? How stupid some people could be, he thought.

"I don't understand," Eira muttered. "You said…"

Tony saw his chance to quell this potential explosion and grabbed her by the shoulders and pulled her to him, his teeth still gleaming by average standards. "It's so good to see you again. I thought I'd lost you," he lied.

Eira pushed him away. "I called you, lots of times. I left messages…"

Tony feigned shock. "But I didn't get them. There must be something wrong with my phone."

"You're a lying bastard. How could you do this to me," Eira screamed.

The fuse was clearly still burning and looked close to ignition.

Kenny stepped between her and the rapidly retreating Tony. "Shh, please. Enough!" Kenny pleaded.

"Cool down, babe…" Tony said.

"Don't call me babe, you… you… snake," she fumed.

"How can you say that to me," Tony shook his head sadly. "I loved… love you. It's just a mistake, that's all," he attempted an appeasing smile.

Eira's shoulders sagged. She didn't believe Tony for a minute, but this wasn't what she thought it would be like. She didn't feel anywhere near as angry as she thought she should. Tony had talked her into his bed, promised her everything and then taken off. She knew she wasn't the first woman to be caught in this way and certainly wouldn't be the last, but it still hurt. How could she have been so gullible? She slumped down into a chair next to the bed.

An exchange of uncertain glances between Tony and Kenny galvanised the singer into action. He stepped closer to the distraught woman. "Come on. Let's go for a spin. We'll talk in private and work this out. I'm horrified by my actions. I should have driven to your home in… Cwm-scut?…"

"Cwmtwrch," Eira said flatly.

"Yes, Cwmtwrch, that's it. I should have come down to you, but I've been so busy. I was only thinking of us, how I could earn enough to keep us happy together..." he glanced again at Kenny whose expression told him he was overdoing it.

"A talk, yes," Eira nodded. Defused, defeated. "We need to talk."

Tony led Eira down the emergency staircase, 'to avoid the fans,' he explained, and clicked the auto lock on his BMW. "Go on, run for it," he told her. Eira didn't see the need for it, but she did as she was told. Tony waited until she had settled in the passenger seat before he too ran to the car. He clambered into the little sports car and started the engine. He smiled at Eira. "Let's go somewhere quiet."

25.

Uptight, Tony had been taken completely off guard by Eira's arrival, just what he didn't need. Eira's behaviour was unsettling, ranting and raving and verbally aggressive. Tony wanted to throttle her but knew he had to stay in control.

"Look, Eira, I'm really sorry for messing you about, but it was all a big mistake. What have I got to do to get things back on track?"

"You know what I want, I want you," she seethed. "I want you all to myself. I want it to be like it was. I want you to care of me, like you promised."

"Bloody hell, Eira, are you sure that's all you want?"

"Yes," she said, confused. "All I want is for you to treat me like you promised. I know when you're on tour women throw themselves at you. I can understand that, and I don't mind, honest, as long as you come back to me."

Tony was shocked. He expected an earful from her but not this. "That's a bit full-on, Eira, you'll be asking me to marry you next," he laughed.

"Well, would that be such a bad thing? At

least it would scotch the rumours that are circulating," she said.

"Rumours, what rumours?"

"The ones that you like a bit of both," she said.

Tony laughed nervously. "Bloody hell, Eira. I'm as straight as they come. That's a load of bullshit, you know that first-hand."

"What about Lenny?"

Tony gripped the steering wheel tightly, Eira had hit a nerve.

"Who the hell is Lenny?" he bluffed.

"Lenny Stone. I've seen you with him, Tony. I've followed you. I've seen you both in the back of your car up at the quarry, the place where you made love to me too."

"This isn't right, no way is this right," he blustered.

"I'm sorry, Tony. If this gets out your career will be at an end, do you understand?"

"Please don't threaten me, Eira, please don't do this. Even if I was... you know... it wouldn't be a problem. Not that I am. No one has a problem with being gay these days."

Eira snorted. "You know he's dead? The police will dig into his relationships."

That was true. He had pretended to ignore the news of Lenny's death when Kenny broke it to him earlier. But fooling Kenny was one thing, fooling the police was an entirely different matter. They would want to know everything and there was things Tony wanted kept quiet.

"Take me to the quarry, Tony. Let's put it all right. Forget about Lenny. He's going to be old news."

"Eira, this has got to be sorted, one way or another."

Tony drove out of Porthcawl and headed to the quarry in Cornelly. He followed the route he knew well. Eira wasn't the only lover he had brought to this place and parked the car on the quarry's edge.

Eira got out and stood with her arms spread wide like a scene from Titanic. Tony snorted a line of coke before he followed.

"I wonder what the headlines would be in the morning, Tony... if I jumped? The publicity would destroy you."

Tony grabbed Eira and pulled her towards him. "You were always on my mind," he said then sang the words again. "You were always on my mind." He held her tight as she laughed, and Tony led her back to the car.

They got into the backseat and began to kiss.

"I love you so much, I've never been with anyone else, you know that, don't you?"

"I know, just relax."

"I've got something else to tell you, Tony."

"Later, Eira, later, just relax."

The car windows began to steam-up.

"Tony, this is important," Eira insisted. "I

don't know how to tell you."

"Tell me what, Eira? Look, we'll start from scratch, it'll go back to the way it was."

"Tony, you've got a daughter. Her name is Grace, I named her after Graceland, and she's three months old."

"What? You're joking?" Tony said, stunned by Eira's words.

"It's true. I caught the first time we did it. That's why I've been trying to contact you. You've got a beautiful daughter."

Tony had no idea how he was supposed to feel. He pulled his clothes together and stepped out of the car. He leaned on the door and stared at the water way below. "This can't be happening."

The sound of footsteps behind him.

"Did you enjoy your shag, Tony?" A voice behind him said.

"What the hell are you doing here?"

"It's payback time, Tony. Your days of taking the piss out of everybody are over. Have a bit of this."

Tony's body went rigid as a high voltage, low current charge entered his body at his neck, just below his right ear. The 6 kilo volts sent his body into spasm. His muscles began to dance independently of his brain; the uncoordinated rave brought a smile to the assailant's face as Tony crashed back into the car, his head thumped against the roof, and the woman occupant inside. Tony bit into his own tongue and lost consciousness immediately. The shock was over in a second and a blow to the right temple with a baseball bat ensured he went out like a light.

Eira was barely conscious. Her face bled from where Tony's head had struck her during his seizure. She had no idea of what was going on. She had just told Tony he was a father and things should have been happy.

Eira wiped the blood from her face and clambered out of the car over the still body of Tony to meet the same fate. The blood in her eyes prevented her from seeing it coming, a crushing blow to the back of her head, she dropped like a sack of coal.

The attacker sat on the bonnet of the car.

"You deserved it. You've had it coming for years. Well, this is it, no more festivals for you, end of."

The attacker stood and struggled with Tony's limp, lifeless body as it was bundled out of the back and into the driver's seat and then Eira's partly clothed body was crammed into the passenger's seat. The car was put in neutral and then pushed over the edge. The killer watched it with a satisfied smile as it bounced and tumbled into the ice cold, quarry water far below. The attacker bowed and clapped gloved hands.

The attack was over in less than a minute and the baseball bat, hidden beneath the run flat tyre in the boot, had gone down with the vehicle.

Eira was just collateral damage, but Tony

had it coming.

26.

Lynette looked radiant as Raven opened the rear door to the company VW. The RS was back in the garage at last, secured and on ice for the winter. The VW Golf would serve its purpose as a workhorse for the agency and as Raven's social domestic and pleasure mode of transport. At least if that was damaged Raven wouldn't lose sleep over it.

"Why, thank you, kind sir," Lynette said as she sat in the rear seat and Raven closed the door for her.

He opened the front passenger door and waited a moment for Sue to come bounding out towards him.

"Can't wait. I love Elvis," she said.

"It's not the real one, mind," he said. "The real Elvis died in nineteen seventy-seven."

Sue stopped and shook her head. "I know that, silly. It's joking Elvis and it's still going to be good."

Raven strapped his sister in and closed the door before getting into the driver's seat.

"You take this stuff seriously," Raven said as he started the engine.

"Got to make the effort," Lynette agreed. She was wearing a fifties style lemon coloured dress with white sneakers.

Raven had tried to fit in, too. He had fished a well-worn black leather jacket from his wardrobe, which he had paired with faded blue jeans and trainers and a white T-shirt under the jacket. To complete the look, he had also slicked back his thick black hair.

"You look like the Fonz," she giggled, referring to the cool character from the US hit comedy 'Happy Days'

"Heeey!," he said in his best impersonation of the character.

"I loved Happy Days," Sue agreed. She too had tried to fit in with the theme and was wearing her late mother's dress that was the closest Raven could find to being in keeping with the fifties. He had never found the time nor the inclination to throw his parents things out. He had promised Sue he would do it one day, but that day had not yet come. He would often open the wardrobe containing his mother's clothes and just smell her perfume still lingering after all these years. Then, as time went by, the smell began to fade along with his memories, but there was still a hint of her each time the wardrobe door was opened.

Porthcawl was buzzing with fun; Raven thought he'd driven back in time to some town in the States. More than half the visitors to the festival were dressed in homage to the King of Rock and Roll and several period American cars, behemoths of automotive engineering, were cruising the seafront. Raven smiled, at least he wouldn't look out of place.

He managed to find a space to park the car in a back street and checked the nearby posts for restriction signs. No doubt the parking wardens would be in force for an event drawing so many to the town.

The queue into the Hi Tide was snaking along the sea front, past the fair and onto the main road. Raven and Lynette joined at the tail, about two-hundred metres from the entrance. He guessed there must be at least three hundred people in line ahead of them.

Nearly forty-five minutes later, they walked hand-in-hand, with Sue between them as they entered the building and followed the crowd into the lounge where an Asian Elvis, with what sounded like a real American accent, was going through his routine as the crowd sang along and danced.

"Sounds good," Raven shouted.

Sue nodded and smiled. "Wait until you hear Hound Dog Heggerty, he's the best."

Raven laughed. "Hound Dog Heggerty?"

"He's due on after this chap," Lynette added.

"Wins the Best at Festival every year," Sue said.

"Looks like Elvis and sounds so much like him, even has the moves," Lynette agreed.

"How the hell do you both know all this?"

The two women looked at each other and grinned.

If this Hound Dog fella was better than the Asian guy currently performing then he must be good, Raven thought.

The set came to an end and a local comedian stepped onto the stage and took the microphone.

Raven grinned. "That's Owen Money. Saw him do a set in the local social club. This should be fun."

"Ladies and Gentlemen, let's hear it once more for Elvis Wesley, all the way from Nashville, Tennessee." The crowd cheered and clapped enthusiastically.

Money waited for Elvis Wesley to leave the stage and for the noise to die down before he began to smile. "I've jetted in from sunny Merthyr today," he said. "Hell of a journey it was. Booked the flight through Thomas Cook. Paid for first class. Like to travel in style, I do. Got to Merthyr International Airport and went straight into the lounge reserved for first class passengers. Great it was. Widescreen tellies everywhere, coffee machines, those games consoles for the kids. The Brains bitter was free and the Peter's pies were cooked to perfection. 'Help yourself to anything,' the waitress said, so I did.

Hell of job carrying an X-Box and widescreen telly onto the plane. Anyway. Then the stewardess tells us over the tannoy that the company had gone broke and the flight was being diverted to Ton Pentre International Airport. Special kind of thieves up in Ton Pentre. Before the plane had even stopped, half a dozen of the little buggers were out of the terminal and had stripped the wheels off quicker than a formula one pit team."

"I had a girlfriend once," Money said seriously. "And we stopped at a well-known burger place just outside of a little North Wales town called Llanfairpwllgwyngyllgogerychwyrndrobwllllantysiliogogogoch…" the crowd cheered at Money's pronunciation. "The girlfriend wasn't from Wales," he continued. "She was a Texan and didn't believe I pronounced the name correctly. Couldn't believe it, she couldn't. It's right, I said. I'm Welsh, mun, from Merthyr, I am. We're always right in Merthyr. Anyway, she made me bloody mad so I called the waitress over and said to my girlfriend, listen now, will 'ewe? She's local. She'll tell 'ewe. Excuse me Miss, I said. How can I help you? She said. Can you settle an argument? I said. My girlfriend here is from Texas and she didn't believe me when I told her where we are. Can you tell her, very slowly, the name of this place? Aye, she said, no problem, bach. You're in Burrr…gerrr…King."

Raven had heard the joke before but laughed anyway. The man was infectious.

Money waited for silence then held up his hand for silence. "And now, ladies and gentlemen, the moment you've all been waiting for, the star attraction for the last three years, the winner of the Best in Festival 2017, 2018 and 2019..." the crowd began to cheer again. "Yes, you know who I mean... put your hands together and let's give a big Porthcawl welcome to... Hound Dog Heggerty..." Money pointed to the wings and the crowd roared in anticipation, but no one appeared. The true professional, Money began to crack more jokes as he waited for the star, but Hound Dog was nowhere to be seen.

27.

"Another?" Raven asked, as he pushed through the customers standing around the bar. Lynette looked flustered. Squashed between dozens of revellers, she grasped Raven's hand and let him drag her and Sue through to the bar.

"This is crazy!" she yelled over the noise – a mix of some Elvis song she didn't recognise and the toneless yelling of those who were trying to sing along.

"If you'd rather go somewhere quieter?"

She held her ear close to him and mouthed, "What?"

"Let's go somewhere quieter," he shouted just as the song ended and the noise died down. Faces turned towards Raven and Lynette then a loud cheer erupted. "Someone's getting a leg over," they began to chant good humouredly. Sue shook her head and grinned. "Not with me with them."

"Shit!" Raven mumbled. Lynette laughed and pulled him after her as she pushed through the crowd back towards the exit, Sue in tow.

"Make way," Sue yelled, "man in need of a shag."

Raven allowed himself to be led out of the cheering bar with a big grin on his face.

They burst out through the door like an exploding champagne cork and Lynette turned to face Raven, giggling, her hair blowing in the light breeze. "That was fun," Lynette chuckled as she began to walk back towards the pier. She made no attempt to let go of Raven's hand and Raven was happy to keep hold of hers.

The smell of fish and chips wafting from a nearby shop triggered a rumbling in Raven's stomach. "I'd like to treat you to a nice meal."

Lynette smiled. "That would be lovely. I haven't had a nice meal out in an awfully long time."

Sue stopped suddenly and pulled at Lynette's other hand. "Don't let him fool you. He's tight. He's talking about the chippy."

Lynette shrugged. "Sounds good to me. I love fish and chips." She kissed Raven on the cheek and hugged Sue.

"He moans when he buys me a McDonalds," Sue mumbled in the huddle.

"Hey! Mr Connor." A voice shouted from behind them. Raven turned to see the old man from the stage running towards him. Out of breath and hobbling, it was more of a stumble than a run.

"Slow down!" Raven shouted. "I'm not going anywhere."

The old man raised his hand and panted his

thanks.

"What can I do for you, do I know you?"

"No… I… know… you," the old man puffed.

Raven was intrigued. "Oh?"

"You're… the detective…"

"Private investigator," Raven corrected him.

The old man nodded and coughed. "Not as fit… as I used… to be. I used to run… the eight hundred metres… as a lad… in one minute fifty-nine… that was good… I'm not as old as I look… sixty-three… but had a stroke a few years back…"

Raven could see the man was struggling to speak. "Take a breather. I'll wait for you to get your breath back."

He nodded gratefully. "Thanks."

Lynette held Sue's hand as they waited for the man to recover.

"OK… thanks," he finally said. "I'm OK. I know you. You helped a woman I work for. Husband was cheating…"

Raven nodded. "Do a lot of that sort of thing."

"I need to speak with you about the Hound Dog…" the man continued.

"The singer?" Raven said.

"That's him. Never missed a show in years, especially if he's celebrating another win."

"Disappointing. I'd heard about him and was looking forward to hearing him. Perhaps he's been delayed?"

The man shook his head. "No way. He'd call, he'd never let down his fans."

Raven laughed. "Fans, seriously? He's a tribute act..."

"Don't laugh. Tributes are big business and a singer who's as good as Hound Dog probably makes more than you and I combined."

"Wouldn't take much to earn more than me," admitted Raven.

"Anyway, something's happened to him. His friend came to see me backstage and said Hound Dog had gone off somewhere with a woman, a mad woman. She was clearly mad with him. He drove off with her to cool her down and disappeared."

"Nothing worse than a woman scorned," said Raven.

Lynette pulled at his arm and grinned up at him. "Remember that, eh?"

Raven laughed. "Look, Mr...?"

"Dafydd, just call me Dafydd."

"OK, Dafydd. He's probably trying to appease her. Perhaps they've gone for a meal or perhaps his luck's in?" Raven squeezed Lynette's arm. She nudged him.

"No way. She's done something to him. Perhaps she's stabbed him or cut his goolies off or something?"

Sue grimaced.

"Why would you think that?" Raven said.

"Woman scorned, as you said."

"Scorned is one thing, murder or mutilation is something else. Anyway, he's an adult. You won't get the police interested. People disappear for a day or two then turn up again. If the police actioned them all they'd be doing nothing else."

"I know the police aren't interested. Already tried them. That's why I'm speaking to you."

Raven nodded. "So, just leave it a few days. If he doesn't turn up then, give me a ring. I don't want to waste your money."

"It's not my money and it'll be too late then. He should be on stage now."

"So, you're only worried about the show?"

Dafydd looked angry. "That's unfair. What if he's lying in a pool of blood somewhere?"

Raven handed the man a business card and turned away. "Give me a call in a few days if he's still missing."

"Something's happened to him... mark my words..."

Raven held up his hand as he walked away. He led Sue and Lynette across the street to a short queue of people standing near an open shop window selling fish and chips.

"So, this really is your idea of dining me, eh?" Lynette pretended she was hurt.

"Told you," said Sue.

"Trust me. You can't beat a good portion," Raven whispered in Lynette's ear.

"Oh er, Missus," Lynette joked.

Raven laughed. "It's good. You'll love it."

"And the chips?"

Raven pulled her close to him. "I like your sense of humour."

"Me too," agreed Sue.

Sighing, Raven shot his sister a withering glance. "You've got ears like a bat."

28.

July 2017.

Kenny sat in a red, leather high-back chair, staring out of the floor-to-ceiling bay window that provided unspoilt views of the Cotswolds countryside.

The big house would never be found by anyone without the latest updated satnav. Situated in forty acres of land with its own lake and riding school, Lakeside House was built in 1870 for the Member of Parliament for Witney at the time. A half mile of unmade driveway snaked through manicured trees from the secluded village of Swerford and onto the far side of the valley. The house had been purchased by a mental health charity a decade ago and it was still extending and updating facilities to cater for its clients. Kenny had been referred to Lakeside by the mental health team at the South London and Maudsley NHS Foundation. After six months at the Maudsley, Kenny had been deemed well enough to benefit from the care programme offered at Lakeside.

The drive out of London to the little Oxfordshire village had taken over an hour and

Kenny had watched the taxi metre clock up the enormous fare that, thankfully, he didn't have to pay.

Swerford is a village somewhat removed from the main arterial route. Set off the A361 Banbury Road, the village reminded Kenny of the mythical village of Brigadoon. Like the Scottish community of the Gene Kelly film, Swerford seemed to exist only for those who knew it was there. With a population of a little over 130, including a well-known bestselling crime author, the peaceful hamlet seemed an ideal place for a Lakeside retreat.

In 2013, a stable block for six horses was added to the complex. The horses were, for some patients, a great way of spending time in the fresh country air and provided distraction from their troubles. The horses were part of a small menagerie, including a dozen dogs, two goats and a small flock of sheep. Kenny had quickly found an affinity with the animals and spent most of the day either mucking out the horses or riding them whenever he could.

He stared through the window at a bird of prey, probably a hawk of some kind, as it swooped high above, carried effortlessly on thermals. He heard voices behind his chair but chose to ignore them.

"Kenny?" the male voice was more insistent.

Kenny turned his head and spared a single

nod for Eric, the nurse.

"It's time for your chat with Mr Anand."

"Already?"

Eric nodded more enthusiastically and smiled.

Kenny rose slowly from the comfortable chair and followed Eric out of the lounge and into a carpeted hallway. Each end of the hall was secured by a heavy door with a combination lock, but Kenny and all the other residents knew the numbers. They were free to come and go as they saw fit and had been told the locks were there to keep unwanted visitors out rather than keep them inside.

Mr Anand's office was at one end of the corridor. Anand was originally from Iran but had left the country in the late seventies when the political situation in Iran began to take a turn for the worse. He still had an accent, but Anand saw himself as a true Brit and had no intention of ever returning to the land of his birth. Recognised as a leading 'alternative' psychotherapist, Anand had snapped up the opportunity to leave the Health Service to work at Lakeside.

"Come in, Kenny," he smiled warmly as Kenny knocked and stuck his head around the partially open door. Kenny stepped inside the office and took a seat he had occupied many times over the past few weeks. "Looking good, how are you feeling?" The psychiatrist asked.

"I'm OK," Kenny nodded. "I feel much better. It's the horses, I think. They take me away from the things I can't control. As you said, I can't change the past, but I can have a say in my future."

Anand rubbed his hands together and nodded. "Excellent. It's easier said than done, I know. It takes a big effort to alter your mindset and, whilst that is not the answer to everything, it certainly is a step in the right direction. So... tell me... what about your brother?"

Kenny stared at the ceiling for a moment, gathering his thoughts. "I know there was nothing I could do. I almost died too."

"And your friend?"

"Tony?"

"Yes, Tony."

"Nothing he could do either. We were all caught up in the mess."

"He was the eldest and you said he wanted to go to what you call the feeder?"

Kenny nodded. "I guess I was just as much to blame for that..."

"You can't be at fault for something you had no idea would happen."

"OK... fair enough. It's a lifetime of blame I've carried. It's hard to reprogram my thinking."

"It's a lot easier when you accept what you have no control over."

"But I was all my brother had and I felt I let him down."

"Do you think you should have died instead

of him?"

Kenny's face flushed for a moment. His eyes glazed as he nodded slowly. "Yes. But then I wouldn't have met my wife, would I?"

"And she clearly meant a great deal to you."

He nodded and sniffed back a precious memory that threatened his composure.

"Would you like to talk about her?"

He shook his head. "Can't."

Anand sat back in his chair and watched Kenny as he shifted awkwardly. "Loss is never easy to deal with. It often causes deep psychological issues that some people try to overcome on their own but not everyone can do that, and it's nothing to be ashamed of."

"I know," Kenny said quietly.

"You lost two people who you clearly loved deeply in circumstances that shocked you. You weren't expecting either and that takes its toll."

Kenny nodded. "I understand that."

"But you can't speak to me about your feelings?"

"I don't really know you. You're here to assess me..."

Anand held up his hand. "Stop! I'm here to listen to you and to help you. That's my overriding remit. Assessment is secondary. Of course, I have to report on your progress but unless you help me to do that then it's difficult for us both."

"What do you want me to say?"

The psychiatrist sat forward again and

leaned on the desk. "Just start by telling me how you met your wife," he smiled warmly.

Conflicted, Kenny knew the doctor was there to listen to his troubles. He also knew that talking about problems often helped ease them, but there was also the fact that Anand had his own agenda. Perhaps Kenny could turn things around and make that agenda work for himself. "OK," he said reluctantly. "My wife, Sally, was my world. She helped me when I was down. I had always struggled with the loss of my brother, the realisation that I was partly to blame for his death ate me up inside. How can a kid be expected to deal with something like that?"

The doctor sat quietly, he said nothing, not wanting to break the flow.

"I left the children's home at sixteen to work for a construction company... only labouring, you know, but it was a job. I moved with the company to London to work on a sewerage job, big job it was too. Then I started drinking too much. It was innocent enough, to begin with, you know. Out for a pint after work, then two pints, then pissed. I started losing shifts, not turning up, and was put on a warning. Then I met Sally. She saved me."

"How did you meet?"

"It's a long story... Sally was also in the children's home. We met as kids then she was adopted by a family who moved to Staines, and I didn't see her again until I moved to London.

We met up in a pub in St Catherine's Dock. Pure chance. We talked for hours. She was with a few friends, and I was on my own. She spent the whole evening with me."

"That must have been good for you?"

"It was. It was great to meet up again."

"What happened next?"

"We saw each other every week for a month or so, then began seeing each other every night. We lived half an hour away from each other, but we made use of the tube. It changed me. I was happy. I was even turning up for work on time and not missing shifts."

"Sounds good."

"It was… on the whole…"

"Oh?"

Kenny shuffled awkwardly. "I was her second choice. She loved someone before me. She said nothing had ever happened between them, but he was her first true love."

"Anyone you knew?"

"Yes."

29.

Finding a replacement for a high-profile job in the police is never easy, especially when the replacement is for your own role. With the demise of the bent Superintendent Myers, and his own promotion to Detective Super, McGuire had been pondering a suitable replacement for himself as the Detective Chief Inspector. Colin Boulton would do a fine job but had made it clear from the outset that he wasn't interested.

A few senior detectives came to mind, but he had to be a hundred per cent sure. He had to pick the right one. The job was going to rat shit at a rapid rate of knots. There were no detectives coming through the system. Young Duggan was the exception to the rule within the lower ranks. McGuire had encouraged Duggan to experience life in the CID and the lad had taken to it well. But to select a DCI was a different proposition. It had to be someone who knew how to manage serious crimes. A Senior Investigating Officer had to make decisions that directed a serious investigation to a successful conclusion. This meant that he or she had to determine the policy – the way the investigation should proceed and the allocation of resources. One name came to mind.

Early Monday morning, McGuire called in to Headquarters in Bridgend to speak with ACC Chambers.

"I guess you haven't solved the Elvis look-alike murder yet?"

"Bloody hell, boss, give me a chance," McGuire laughed. He felt comfortable in the ACC's presence and had no issue swearing in front of him. ACC Chambers was once a 'real' police officer before he reached the heady heights of senior management. He had done the hard yards and McGuire respected him and he knew the feeling was mutual. Ever since Chambers asked him to investigate corrupt detectives, things had become far more comfortable between them. They had even played the odd round of golf, something McGuire had discovered he was a natural at, but not as good as his boss. "We'll sort it, don't worry."

"Have you made your choice for your replacement yet, Terry?"

"Yes, boss. That's why I'm here. I want Bryn Rowlands. I believe he's still a DCI down the bay," McGuire looked at Chambers for affirmation. Chambers nodded. "Bryn's got a good track record. He's well respected and gets the job done. He'll do for me."

"You didn't have a lot of choice, Terry. But I understand why you want Bryn. I think he's the best of the bunch. He won't let you or the team down. Do you know his full background?"

"Oh, yes. He joined the job in '92, born and bred in the Garw. Most of his family were colliers and he was the first of his family to go to Uni'. A solid background. He got a double first but has never used it to get on. I like that. He started on the tools and worked his way up the ranks within the CID. I think he'd be perfect, if you're in agreement?"

"I've got no problem, Terry. It's your call," he smiled. "I'll get hold of him later and break the news. When do you want him to start?"

"Tell him to call into the Incident Room Thursday morning. I'll introduce him to the team, and he can crack on with them sorting out the Lenny Stone killing."

"I must say, Terry, Bryn's got big shoes to fill."

McGuire didn't like compliments. Compliments made him feel uncomfortable. "Thank you," he could feel himself blush. "He'll fit in nicely and, to be fair, it'll give me a bit of a breather," he paused and shifted awkwardly in his chair. "Can I tell you something in confidence?"

Chambers nodded. "Of course."

"I'm thinking about putting my ticket in. Life's too short to do this for much longer."

"Terry, pigs will fly before that happens," Chambers scoffed. "You're a dying breed. We can't afford to lose you, not yet. Now get out and do the business."

McGuire frowned. "I'm serious, boss. Can't go on forever."

"None of us can, but I need you here, at least for a while longer. I'm retiring in fourteen months, three weeks, six days and..." he checked his watch, "...six hours and eleven minutes."

"Not counting then, boss?" McGuire laughed.

"I've had enough too, but there are things we have to sort before we hand over the baton. You and me, we make a good team."

McGuire nodded. "Cheers, boss, I'll keep you up to speed with the enquiry."

It was ten o'clock when McGuire got back to the Incident Room. The phones were ringing off the hook and most of the team were out on the actions. McGuire called Colin aside for an update. There hadn't been any solid leads regarding the demise of Stone, but it was still early days.

McGuire said, without preamble, "The new DCI will be Bryn Rowlands, he runs the office down the bay. Do you know him?"

"Bryn? Of course, I've been on a few serious incidents with him, he's a cracking bloke. I haven't seen him for a few years, he's a good choice, proper detective, he'll fit in well. I must tell you the team were worried. They thought we'd be landed with some dodgy highflyer, you know, here today and gone tomorrow."

"No, the ACC knows my feelings on butterflies, there's got to be stability. This is a good team and I want it to stay like that. You can let the team know tonight in the briefing."

McGuire poured himself a hot cup of coffee and stared at the pile of files stacked around his office. It was time to do something about them. He took a sip of his coffee and picked up the first file just as his phone rang.

"Can I help you?" he said, relieved to be distracted once again from the filing task he had put off for far too long. He knew he could delegate the task, but it was his fault they had mounted up and he was embarrassed by it.

"Is that Mr Terry McGuire?"

"Yes, who wants to know?"

"My name is George Callard, I'm a solicitor dealing with the estate of the late Mr Edgar Bridges."

"Oh? He was a very good friend of mine, what can I do for you?"

"Well, Mr. McGuire, it's more like what I can do for you," he chuckled. "Can you call into my offices? I think you'll be presently surprised."

"What do you mean? Don't tell me Ed's left me that fifty quid I lent him when we were in training school?" McGuire laughed.

"Not quite, Mr. McGuire, but I suggest you bring some identification with you. You'll find my offices just down the road in Esplanade Avenue. Shall we say around two o'clock, if that suits?"

McGuire checked the time on his watch. "I'll be there, Mr. Callard, no problem."

There was still time to clear the office and McGuire got back to sifting through some files.

Two o'clock came and McGuire walked the short distance to the solicitor's office. He was welcomed personally by George Callard, a pencil thin man with dark, sunken eyes and a five o'clock shadow. Callard reminded McGuire of the villain – Captain Black – out of Captain Scarlet.

"Mr. McGuire, so pleased to meet you. It seems I've known you all my life," he smiled warmly. "Edgar and I discussed you on many occasions before his sad demise."

Surprised, McGuire shook Callard's hand and followed the thin man into the main office.

"Take a seat, Mr. McGuire"

"Call me, Terry," McGuire said.

"Thank you, Terry."

"What's this all about?"

Callard donned a pair of John Lennon spectacles and peered over the rims at McGuire.

"Terry, this is the last will and testament of Ed. It was made a short time before his death and you are the sole benefactor, so I'd strap myself in if I were you."

McGuire was shocked. "What do you mean?"

"Ed has left you everything, the business, the house and all other possessions, plus over £250,000 in cash, that's about it," he smiled. "Ed was a perfectionist when it came to business and he thought the world of you. You were the only person he actually trusted. I don't think he even trusted me, to be honest."

McGuire sat like a stunned ram. He had heard the words but couldn't comprehend what he'd been told. "You're telling me that Ed's left everything to me?"

"Yes, Terry, everything. His main concern was the business, he had hoped you'd retire and go into partnership with him. I even drew up the contract, obviously you never had the chance to sign, but now there's no need is there?"

Callard leaned over his desk and shook McGuire's hand. "Congratulations, Terry, bit of a life changer, no doubt?"

"Fuck me, George, life changer? That's an understatement."

"I've got all the documentation relating to the business and bank accounts, there'll be no problems, it's all straightforward. The will has been executed, so it's signed and sealed."

"Look, George, give me a day or two to get my head around this and I'll give you a bell. Perhaps, to save any problems, you can act for me, is there any problem with that?"

"No problem, it will be my pleasure."

"I'd better pop home and tell the missus, God knows what she'll say." McGuire shook Callard's hand again and left the office in shock.

Edgar Bridges had indeed been a good

friend to Terry over the years. They had joined the police together many years before and both men had become detectives. Ed had resigned from the force after a run-in with a senior officer who had taken a dislike to him. It was a sad fact of the service that personality clashes could often result in the junior officer coming a cropper and no longer being a copper. It was unfair but a fact of life that no doubt played out in a similar way in many other career paths.

Ed had recently been involved in a case that had resulted in his death at the hands of a serial killer. Run through with an ornamental sword, McGuire had discovered his body in a high-rise flat along with Raven's sister Sue who had been drugged and abducted by the killer. Thankfully, McGuire and Raven had saved Sue, but it had been too late to do anything to help Ed.

The journey home was a blur. On autopilot, McGuire, if asked, would never be able to recall anything about the drive home.

Molly was surprised to see her husband so early in the day. It was rare since he had been promoted to Inspector several years ago. Since he had become Detective Chief Inspector it had become almost unheard of. She hoped the new rank of Detective Superintendent would allow more time with her husband, but she had doubted it. "Well, what do I owe this pleasure to? Home before four o'clock, that's a first. Have you been sacked?"

McGuire's vacant smile had Molly concerned. "You OK? You look half soaked. Have you been on the booze already?"

He shook his head. "Sit down, Molls, I've got something important to tell you."

Molly's face drained of blood as if a plug had been pulled. "What's happened, is it the children?"

"No, Molls, it's not the children. It's Ed."

She sat. "What about him?"

"He's only gone and left me everything in his will, the business, cash and even the house."

Molly laughed. "Terry, you're joking? Stop winding me up."

"No. it's true," he said as he leaned over her and held her shoulders. "I've just come from the solicitor's office," he stared at Molly and pulled her to him. "This is a life changer, Molls. He's left me a quarter of million in cash, too."

"M-my G-God," Molly spluttered. "I can't believe it."

McGuire sat on the edge of the table.

"Get off there," Molly said. "You'll break it."

McGuire laughed. "I think we can afford a new one now, Mol."

Molly began to weep gently, her lips trembled and she shook her head slowly, unable to grasp the significance of the news. "Bless him" she finally said.

30.

Sitting at his desk, Raven thought about the weekend. At least his love life was now going in the right direction, even if it was still early days.

The phone on his desk rang and he answered after the first ring.

"Raven Investigations, can I help you?"

"Is that Mr Connor? A friend of mine told me to give you a call."

"Yes, I'm Raven Connor, what can I do for you, and who's your friend?"

"My name's Kenny Vincent. Dafydd told me that you could probably help me."

"Help? Help you with what?"

"My mate Tony Heggerty. You might know him as Hound Dog the Elvis tribute act?"

"Oh yes, Dafydd spoke to me last night. Tony didn't turn up for the finale, he went off with some woman, didn't he?"

"Well, yes, but I haven't seen hide nor hair of him since."

Raven sighed. It was hard to get concerned family and friends to understand that adults often disappeared for a while without telling anyone. It was a privilege of being an adult. Raven understood that sometimes there were good reasons to be concerned but ninety percent of the time there was an innocent explanation for the disappearance. "Look, Kenny, he's a big boy, he can look after himself, he'll turn up."

"I'm not so sure, Mr Connor."

"Call me Raven." Raven sat back in his chair and thought for a moment. "What do you want me to do for you?"

"Find him, obviously. He's the best Elvis in Europe, he'd never leave his fans down. There's something wrong. Can I meet you somewhere? Can I hire you?"

"I'm not cheap and I don't want you to waste your money."

"That's really noble of you, but you've just got to find him, please?"

"Where are you now?"

"I'm in the Seaview Hotel lounge."

"OK, I'll be there in half an hour. You can tell me what you know. Does that suit you?"

"Brilliant, Mr Connor."

Raven could hear the relief in his voice. He knew that sometimes all it took was a chat, for the client to know someone was listening and taking them seriously.

"Like I said, call me Raven."

***

Arriving at the Seaview in less than thirty

minutes, the road from Swansea to Port Talbot had been surprisingly quiet and only the fifty-speed limit at Port Talbot had delayed him from being in Porthcawl in under twenty minutes, Raven had chosen to drive the Ford instead of the VW. The VW was a great work horse, but the RS was more fun. The RS Escort had powered through the Porthcawl lanes and Raven smiled as he locked his beloved car and walked into the hotel.

A man sat alone in the corner of the lounge, he looked small with dark hair thinning in typical male pattern baldness. His eyes were dark, and his brow seemed heavy. His skin was pale, and he didn't look healthy. Worry for his friend could do that. He was dressed in jeans and a white T-shirt and was sipping from a pint of light beer or lager. It had to be Kenny, there was no one else there.

"You're Kenny?"

Kenny got up and shook Raven's hand. His grip was weak and his hand cold.

"Yes. Can I get you a drink?"

"No, let's get down to business, shall we?" Raven said as he sat opposite the man. "Time's money, as they say," he smiled.

"Where do I start?"

"From the beginning. First, tell me your connection to Tony. Why is he so important to you?"

Kenny took another sip of his lager and

placed the glass on a cardboard drip mat. He shrugged his shoulders and tilted his head to one side. He stared at a painting on the wall of the bar – a seascape. A ship rode through a breaking wave and the artist had somehow managed to capture the sense of terror the crew must have felt on the turbulent ocean. A bit like his life to date. "He's been like a brother to me," Kenny said quietly. "We drifted apart, like most friends do, but this weekend had been a chance for us to catch up again. We used to have a great time together and this weekend was like we'd never been apart. He even gave me a job to manage him."

"Have you any idea where he may be?"

He shook his head and took another mouthful of his rapidly diminishing drink.

"Where was he staying?"

"Well, here. But the staff haven't seen him since late yesterday either. Then he never turned up for the Elvis finale at the Hi Tide," he leaned forward, his brow creased, and his dark eyes revealed his concern. Raven could see his eyes were sunk in the sockets, giving his brow a false appearance of dominance. "Look, I'm telling you, this isn't right."

Raven nodded slowly as he watched the man. "I'll have a chat with the manager later, check any CCTV, that kind of thing."

"I'll leave all that to you. You're the expert."

"OK, let's start from the beginning, and I mean the beginning. When did you first meet

Tony?"

Kenny talked Raven through the events of his childhood, his younger brother who died in the feeder and of Tony, his best friend, their love of music and in particular their love of Elvis, and how they had gone their separate ways.

"So, when did you see Tony last... before this week?"

"Oh, years ago. I hit the bottle, got married, got sober..." he said in a matter of fact way - no emotion, Raven thought he'd told that story many times before. He seemed used to telling it.

"Why did you get in touch with him after all these years?"

"I recently lost my wife," this statement was less confident, probably not talked about his wife as much as the drink. "I suppose I've been at a low ebb. I knew Tony would be at the festival, so I took a punt and found him in the hotel."

"And everything was normal?"

"It was as if we'd never been apart. I told him about my situation and, like the Tony I knew, he offered me the job as his road manager, straight away, just like that. We were back together as if nothing had ever changed."

It didn't make sense. "If everything was so cool, why the hell has he just disappeared without a word?"

"You tell me, Raven," he shrugged. A hint of acid in the words.

"Sounds bizarre to me."

Kenny leaned forward and nodded his head vigorously, as if punctuating a moment of realisation on Raven's part. "That's what I'm telling you."

"OK, is there anyone who had it in for him, anyone who might want to hurt him?"

"Well, only that German Elvis impersonator... Fritz or Franz or something."

"Why?"

"Fritz Mueller... that's it. Fritz. They had a bit of a set-to during a press conference, he gave Tony a clip. The bloke is so jealous of Tony, all the success and money he's earning. Anyway, he apologised publicly the next day. It was nonsense. I didn't think so at the time, but Tony said it was all cool."

"Anyone else?"

"No, I don't think so. Everybody loved Tony, just ask the staff."

"What about this woman he went off with, who is she?"

"Her name is Eira, some bird from one of the valleys, somewhere near Neath or Swansea. She was in a real rip with Tony. He calmed her down and then left with her. He was going to take her for a run in the car to talk things through."

"What did you think of that?"

"Woman scorned and all that," he shrugged. "Perhaps she's done something to him?" Then Kenny gave a little laugh, the idea was ridiculous.

"Many a true word spoken in jest, Kenny. Who knows?"

"Sorry, I didn't mean to seriously suggest she has."

"OK, so let's see what we've got, eh? Successful Elvis impersonator is assaulted by a German rival. A woman scorned named Eira and nothing else." he looked at Kenny and Kenny nodded his head. Raven sighed again. This was not going anywhere but if the guy really wanted to pay him then who was he to argue? "Leave it with me, Kenny, I'll see what I can do. I'll give it a few days and then get in touch. Give me your mobile and the address where you'll be staying."

"Tony gave me the keys to his house in Treorchy. I'll stay there for the time being and then head off back to the smoke if he can't be found. There's nothing down here for me now without Tony."

Talk about a pessimist? Raven had met many with a similar attitude. Tony was probably OK. Probably got drunk. Probably had sex with the woman and was probably sleeping it all off somewhere. Lots of probable's and Kenny really needed to lighten up. "Just one more thing... what's the name of the home? If I can't find Tony, I'll have to dig a bit deeper."

Kenny nodded. "The Bryn Bach Children's home in Treorchy, but it's probably closed now. I haven't been back there for years."

"OK, leave it to me, I'll be in touch. I'll start with the hotel manager. There's not a lot you can do, if you hear anything, give me a bell."

They shook hands and Raven watched as Kenny finished his pint and strolled out of the bar. His shoulders were hunched, and Raven had to admit that he did look worried.

Raven headed for the reception and spoke to the young woman with the black plastic badge that revealed her name as Hazel - in gold letters – not silver or bronze. Perhaps she was a golden receptionist? Hazel had to be good at her job because she also had four gold stars under her name.

"Ah, Hazel," Raven smiled. "Is it possible to speak with the manager? My name's Raven. Can you tell him it's a matter of importance?"

"I hope it's not a complaint, Mr Raven? Is there anything I can do?"

"No, no complaint," he leaned on the counter. "It's just Raven." He smiled and Hazel blushed and picked up her phone.

"Thank you," he smiled again.

She pressed a button and waited a second before speaking. She stole a glance at Raven and quickly averted her gaze. "Mr Horgan, there's a gentleman, Mr Raven, would like to speak to you. He's at reception, there's no complaint but he says it is important."

Hazel put the phone down on the desk and smiled at Raven with even, white teeth framed with bright red lipstick. "Mr Horgan will be here in a few minutes, Mr Raven," she smiled again, this time awkwardly.

"Thank you, Hazel. My surname is Connor, but everyone, especially my friends call me Raven. I'm looking for Tony. Did you know, Mr. Heggerty, the Elvis tribute singer?"

Again, Hazel blushed.

"He's been staying here every year for years, but just when the festival's on. He's the best. We love him in the hotel."

A door behind the reception opened and a serious faced man walked through it. He was average height, whatever that is these days. Average for Wales is probably five-nine. Welsh were never bred to be tall, not like the Dutch. He wore a navy-blue suit with a waistcoat and a name badge that boasted five gold stars. "I'm Andy Horgan, manager of this hotel, how can I help you?"

"I'm a private investigator," Raven said as he shook the manager's hand. I've been hired to find Tony Heggerty, seems he's gone missing. I was wondering if you know where he might be?"

The manager didn't seem at all concerned. "Oh, don't worry about Tony, this is nothing unusual. If I know him, he's probably shacked up somewhere with someone."

"What do you mean?"

"He always pays in advance, never books out and usually turns up a few days later to pick up his odds and ends and to pay his bill."

"But he didn't turn up for the Elvis finale, is that something he would do?"

A serious expression took on an even more severe countenance. "No, it's not," the manager looked at Hazel and stepped out of the reception. He led Raven back into the bar. "Mr. Raven, I know Tony intimately," he said in hushed tones. "He's a good man, but recently he's been a... troubled soul."

"What are you saying, Mr. Horgan?"

"Well, gambling, cocaine. He's not the Tony I met a few years ago, let's just say that. I wouldn't worry about him, he'll turn up, I'm sure of that."

Raven picked up a connection between Horgan and the missing man. Horgan's stance and voice were very effeminate. If he wasn't gay he was certainly doing a good impression. So, was Tony into men and women? That was what he assumed from Horgan's demeanour. Raven knew lots of gay men and women and lots who liked both. That wasn't any reason to be harmed, but it did mean that he might have lots of ex-partners who might hold a grudge and, that coupled with gambling and cocaine could be a recipe for disaster.

"Mr. Horgan, are you saying you were in a relationship with Tony?"

It was the manager's turn to blush. "Not a relationship, as such..."

"You had sex?"

Horgan looked to the receptionist and could see Hazel's eyes twitching between them. Horgan turned his back on her. He knew she couldn't hear the conversation and now she couldn't see his lips. "Yes, a few times."

"OK. Can I view your CCTV for yesterday... say... from four in the afternoon onwards?"

"Of course, Mr. Connor. Step into my office. The cameras record twenty-four-seven and we keep all the video on memory cards for twenty-eight days, as per the police instructions, you know, what with all this terrorism business."

Horgan showed Raven into the office and played the data card for the relevant times. Raven stopped the action at the first point in the recording where he saw Tony accompanying Eira to his car and then drive out of the rear car park of the hotel. It was just the two of them.

"What do you make of that, Mr. Horgan?"

"Knowing Tony, probably going for a quick shag. He was never fussy," he said.

"So, having been his lover, this doesn't bother you?"

Horgan snorted. "Not in the slightest, Mr. Connor. We were just... casual. It was never anything more than just a roll in the hay, kind of thing."

"I see."

"Did I tell you I'm in the business, Mr. Connor?"

"The business?"

Horgan puffed out his chest. There wasn't much to puff out. He was a little under five-ten in height and weighed not much more than Hazel behind the counter and Hazel was an average sized girl – whatever average for a Welsh woman was these days.

"Well I've been in a few local dramatic productions, played the lead a few times, still hoping my chance will come. Don't get me wrong, I enjoy my job here but..." he stopped speaking and sighed. He stuffed his hands in the pockets of his trousers and shuffled on the spot for a moment. Embarrassment clear. "I met Tony and he encouraged me... and that's when we... you know... stupid really, isn't it?"

"Not really," Raven said. "We all have dreams. Nothing wrong with that."

The manager nodded, deep in thought and then forced a smile.

"OK, can I have the memory card? I'll keep it safe. If the police want it you can tell them to give me a bell. They know me. I know Terry McGuire one of the top men."

"Mr. McGuire, yes. We know him here. I can't see any harm."

Something was clearly amiss, there were plenty of circumstantial motives but nothing concrete yet. Perhaps a trip to Tony's home in the Rhondda would reveal some answers.

31.

Raven had watched television with Sue and drank a four-pack of beer before he went to bed. He woke the next morning with the sun and lay in bed reading a book on his Kindle before he checked in on Sue. He could hear his sister snoring and grinned. She never believed him that she snored. He often teased her about it. Sue was ten years older than Raven, but Raven knew she would never be able to live an independent life. He didn't mind the responsibility. Since his parents died Raven had gladly accepted his duty to his big sister. It had not been easy, but he couldn't imagine life without her. It hadn't been long ago when he thought he would have to learn to live without her. A serial killer had drugged and abducted Sue, and Raven had felt totally helpless. As a former soldier, he wanted to face the killer, but whilst he had searched for her he dreaded the outcome. It was only thanks to his quick intervention – along with the help of his new friend, Detective Superintendent Terry McGuire, that Raven was able to save his sister and the killer 'fell to his death' from the top floor of the Meridian Tower in Swansea. McGuire had not actually seen the killer's last moments alive. Only Raven really knew what happened in those last moments and that was how it would always remain.

Sue had been unconscious during the whole incident and thankfully remembered nothing at all about it. Thank heaven for small mercies, Raven thought.

He checked his watch – six-thirty am. He closed the door gently behind him and quickly scribbled a note for Sue and Lynette. Lynette would be due to call at eight to spend the day with Sue. A trip to Joe's ice-cream parlour was promised for her and Raven wished he could go with them.

Raven had met Lynette several weeks earlier when he had been employed to research a historic murder and links to a serial killer plying his trade in the United States. Part of his work required him to travel to New York, where he became a target of the killer – the same psycho who then followed him back to the UK and abducted his sister.

During his time in New York, his client, the owner of a news agency, had hired Lynette to look after Sue whilst Raven was away in the States. Since then, Raven and Lynette had become close and he had decided to keep Lynette employed three days each week to ease the pressure on himself. There was also the added attraction of seeing her more often. However, the money problems were not easing. He knew Lynette would help out without payment, but Raven knew she needed the money too. Perhaps the arrangement would change in the future but for now he felt duty-bound to keep the two aspects of the relationship separate. That would perhaps hurt Lynette but he needed more work to cover costs but with more work meant more time committed to jobs and it was impossible for him to earn more without hiring extra investigators and paying for more care. More staff meant more costs, but he was between a rock and a hard place and he knew he either had to hire someone else to help him or close the agency.

He checked the lock on the apartment door as he left and jogged down the stairs to the VW Golf parked in the street. The car had flown through the MOT and the garage had dropped the car off for him. The RS was tucked up in the garage and he thought about the money he could get for selling it. The car had to be worth at least thirty grand. That was money he could use to keep the company afloat for a few months, but it would be a last resort. The car had belonged to his dad – how could he sell it? He clicked the lock on the Golf and thought about returning it to the dealership. He had it for business and was paying for it on a lease contract agreement. It wasn't cheap.

Raven drove the Golf through the streets of mis-matched buildings of Swansea and onto the coast road before cruising past the new university campus, a place that somehow reminded him of Disneyland Paris. The complex had been built relatively recently from European grants and he wondered if the city would ever see any development like it in future now the UK had pulled out of Europe.

The M4 was thankfully quiet and he checked his speed as he drove through the fifty-mile-per-hour limits through Port Talbot and floored the accelerator at the first opportunity. Tuesday morning was a good day to travel. The rush of Monday was a nightmare, but Tuesday's always seemed quieter.

The journey to Treorchy took an hour and Raven checked the satnav for the lane he knew would lead to the Bryn Bach Children's home. The lane wasn't marked on the system and neither was the post code. He'd have to think of something else.

Raven didn't really know why he was wasting his time. Of course, he wasn't going to turn down the money. God only knew how much he needed it, but Tony was a grown man, a bit of a 'playboy' who swung both ways. He'd spend a few days on the case, make a few shillings and let it die a death. He was confident that Tony would turn up at some stage.

Kenny would be at Tony's house, so he knew there would be no problem with a bit of rummaging, and he could get directions to the children's home from Kenny.

Raven parked the car on a block paved driveway and rapped on the front door of an impressive house. Built in the Art Nouveau style, the white walls were coated in a textured stucco and the curved windows must have cost a fortune. How on earth did they curve glass like that? Raven wondered. Someone, probably the architect, had designed a full width balcony across the front of the house that must have been a great vantage point over the valley below.

"Come in," Kenny said as he smiled through the open oak and glass panelled door. "I've just boiled the kettle. Do you want a coffee or something?"

"No, I've got to get on. I just want a look around to see if there's anything that might give us a clue as to where Tony might be."

"When I arrived yesterday, there was a pile of mail that was days old. So, he hasn't come back here."

"Have you had a look around?"

"Not really. I didn't like to. I've checked the rooms, stuck my head in to make sure he's not lying dead somewhere," he laughed nervously, "but that's all. I'm hoping he'll just walk in as if nothing has happened."

Raven nodded. "That's what I'm expecting. I'll just have a little skulk. I know what I'm looking for. You just sit there and finish your coffee."

The house was impressive. Large rooms were decorated in keeping with the style of the property. The staircase was cast from con-crete and curved in a sweeping ascent from the ground floor to the first floor level. Each stair tread was capped with marble and the wrought iron balustrade was clearly a custom-made item that probably cost more than Raven made in several months. He left the bedrooms until last. Raven knew from experience that bedrooms hid many secrets and on this occasion Raven was right. He opened one of the free-standing ward-robes where Tony kept his tribute act costumes. One side of the wardrobe was bare. Raven stood back and gazed for a short while, something wasn't right. The bottom seemed higher than it should be.

He tapped the interior panels with his knuckles, the plywood bottom sounded different to the side walls. Raven ran his hand around the edge and found a small hollow between the panel and the frame. He squeezed his fingers into the small space and prised up the base board. Tony clearly was a complicated character. Inside the small space was a black plastic bin liner contain-ing silver foil, a small packet of white powder and pictures of Tony partaking in sexual activity with partners that the pictures suggested were unaware of the presence of the camera.

Raven called out to Kenny. "Kenny, get in here and have a look at this lot."

Raven lifted the bag out of the wardrobe and tipped it all out on to the bed. "What's all this?"

"What the hell's going on?" Kenny said.

"Well it seems your mate Tony is an addict with a varied sexual appetite to boot."

Kenny looked genuinely shocked. "I don't know what to say, I can't believe it, I honestly can't explain this. This isn't the Tony I used to know."

"Have a look at the pictures. Do you recognise anyone?"

Kenny gathered the photos off the bed and flicked through them, about thirty in all.

Raven had already taken a quick look and recognised one of the participants as being Andy Horgan, the hotel manager.

"I recognise at least three, Raven." He pointed to a couple of the images. "That girl Eira, the manager of the Seaview, and the German Elvis' manager, a woman named Ingrid. She was there when they had the dust up. What the hell's going on?"

"I've no idea. I'll take all this. You stay here, just in case Tony turns up. If he does, give me a bell. I'm off to the children's home. Tony may have stayed in touch with them."

"Shall I come? I feel helpless here."

"No, you sit tight. Leave it to me."

Kenny drew a map of the road and lane leading to the home and explained the best way for Raven to find it. Bryn Bach Children's home was a twenty-minute drive away.

The lane had recently been resurfaced but the home needed some TLC. The white plaster had been mostly chipped away and the mortar between the stone blocks had cracked and fallen into small piles at the foot of the walls. Raven parked the VW and found the entrance door was locked. He rang the bell, a black button set into chipped, white plaster remaining around the door frame. A man appeared in the hallway and stared at Raven through the glass panel for a moment before opening the door.

In his late sixties, the man was medium height but carried a little extra padding – nothing excessive - but his bottle green sweatshirt was tight around his waist. His blue jeans looked a size too large for him and were displaying the stains of a recent paint job. Perhaps he was a decorator, Raven thought.

"I'm making some enquiries into the disappearance of a man called Tony Heggerty. He was once in care at this home. Do you know him?"

"Tony? Yes. Missing? Bloody hell. I hope he's alright," he said as he looked to Raven for a confirmation that didn't come. "I remember him well. As you can see, this is no longer a home for children. I just keep the place tidy now, but I worked here and bought the place when it closed. I still have the memories. Good times. Good kids. They were all treated very well here."

"You said you used to work here?"

"Yes. I'm Ivor Pickett. I was one of the

carers. Saw many youngsters pass through here over the years. Many were troubled souls with horrendous family backgrounds."

Ivor stepped aside for Raven to enter the hallway. The place was a real contrast to Tony's home. Raven could imagine it had once been a grand house. Sections of ornate coving had dropped from the ceiling. Plaster had fallen from the walls iside too, revealing the old lath timbers behind. The parquet floor was in the process of restoration, small piles of reclaimed blocks were ready for relaying in the herringbone pattern that had begun to reappear.

Raven stood in the middle of the hall. "Must have been impressive once?"

"It was. Sad to see it like this now, but I intend to renovate it, restore life to the old place. It's expensive work but I'm doing it a bit at a time. I'll get there," Ivor's earnest expression left Raven in no doubt that he probably would realise his ambition for the place.

"What do you remember of Tony?"

"I still see him regularly. He often pops in for a chat, but I haven't seen him for a few weeks."

"Oh?"

"Yes. Likes to call in because he once told me this place was the only real home he ever knew."

"What about his mate, Kenny?"

Ivor scratched his head. "I haven't seen him

for years. Like brothers, they were. Mind you, we called them Lanky, Tiny and Titch. Tony was the big boy, the driving force there. Titch was late growing and his little brother, God rest his soul, was even smaller."

"Well, like I said, Tony's gone missing, Kenny's worried about him."

"You've seen Kenny?"

"I have."

"How is he?"

Raven pursed his lips. He had never been the best at judgment calls on what others were feeling. "Seems OK. As I said, he's worried. He told me he had only recently caught up with Tony and now Tony's disappeared."

"Lucky to be alive they are," Ivor pushed his hands into his trouser pockets, his shoulders pushed forward as he leaned closer to Raven. He looked around as if he was about to reveal some gossip to a neighbour across a garden fence.

Raven took a small step back, maintaining his personal space. "What do you mean?"

"They nearly drowned when they were here. Went swimming in the pit feeder, the three of them. Only Tony and Kenny survived. Kenny's younger brother drowned. It was horrific. Kenny wasn't the same after that."

"I'm not surprised. But Kenny didn't tell me about his brother."

"I think he blocked it out, truth be told. Like I said, he wasn't the same after. Became withdrawn. Started wetting the bed, but we felt sorry for him. What an ordeal it must have been. I think he blamed himself."

"What about Tony? Was he affected by it?"

"Not really. Don't think so. He was always the stronger of the three. They looked up to him. Tony was like their older brother. He saw himself that way too. They were close."

"Were the police involved?"

"Oh yes. There was a big row, an outcry about safety, and all that. There was no blame apportioned to anyone though."

"Can you remember who the officer was that dealt with it?"

"Of course I can. It was Ralph. Ralph Crane. He dealt with it. He was one of the best. Retired now, obviously. He spent a fair bit of time with the boys after the drowning. He's the man to speak to. He'll know everything about it."

Raven handed Ivor his business card and headed back to Swansea. He thought about calling back with Kenny to question him about his brother's death but decided against it. It would be prudent to get the facts from someone who knew the full story before broaching it with Kenny.

***

It was early afternoon when Raven got back to the office, he still wasn't really concerned about Tony, but his gut feeling insisted something wasn't right. The drugs and the sexual behaviour were certainly possible motives for his disappearance, perhaps a jealous lover or a dealer wanting to collect, and Tony taking off to avoid them. But whilst there was still no sign of Tony, it was simply speculation.

The phone rang.

"Raven, it's Terry McGuire."

"What have I done?" Raven joked.

"Apart from throwing a killer out of the window of Meridian Tower?"

Raven almost choked. "He fell…"

Raven relaxed when he heard McGuire laugh.

"How can I help?"

"How's business?"

"Up and down with some crazy shit sprinkled here and there. I'm working on a missing Elvis at the minute, bit of an odd character, but he'll turn up, I've no doubt." Raven decided against telling McGuire about the drugs and the sex images. If Tony appeared, as Raven expected, then he'd consider his options again. Likewise, if Tony didn't turn up then Raven would have to divulge his information but, for now, things were best left unsaid.

"OK, so I'll cut to the chase," McGuire said. "My old pal Ed's left me his whole estate, the whole shooting match, house, investigation business, the lot."

Raven had only met Ed a few times. Ed had

been a private detective in the Bridgend area and had passed some work over to Raven when he had been too busy. Ed had been a good man and he didn't deserve to die such a horrible death - run through with a sword by the same killer who had later fallen from Meridian Tower. "Lucky you, Terry. I liked Ed."

"I've got a proposition for you, just say if it's not a goer…"

Raven was intrigued. "Hit me with it."

"I haven't got time at the minute for the business Ed left me in his will. Ed was always banging on about me jacking the job in and becoming a partner with him. He even had the contract drawn up. I've got some cases I'd like to top and tail before I'm ready to retire. Someone has got to run Ed's business until I can. I'd like you to take it over… fifty-fifty with me, and when I retire, I'll come in with you. It's a thriving business, top end clients, it's a gold mine. To be honest I could do with your help. There's not a lot I don't know about policing and detective work, but private investigations are your thing. What do you say?"

Raven was shocked. "Give me a minute, Terry, it's a lot to take in." Raven thought about how the offer could be the answer to his money problems. He'd still need to take on another detective – perhaps two, knowing the workload Ed had. But did he really want to give up his control? Did he really want to be a partner? Did he really have the choice? At least Terry McGuire knew his stuff and had connections Raven could only dream of. "Fifty-fifty in the business, you said?"

"That's what I said."

"I can only just handle the work in my diary, so we'd need someone else to help out.

"I was thinking the same thing."

"OK. I'll do it. What do you want me to do?"

"Excellent. You'll have to move offices to Bridgend."

"No sweat. I'll sort the remainder of the rent here and I'll empty it tonight and meet you tomorrow. How does that sound?"

"I'll see you around ten at Ed's office with the contract. The will won't be finalised for several weeks yet but just sign my contract and we're off and running, and I promise I won't interfere... not yet" he laughed.

"Can I ask one favour, Terry?"

"Go on."

"Can you get me the address of a bobby named Ralph Crane, worked the Rhondda back in the day?"

"And the reason, Raven?"

"It's to do with my missing Elvis, there's something about it that's bothering me, and Ralph Crane might be able to join up some dots for me."

"OK. Can't see that being a problem, see you in the morning."

32.

Squeezed between high street shops, Ed's place of work didn't look like much from outside, indeed, if a prospective client didn't know where the office was located, they'd probably just walk on by.

A half-glass aluminium door set between a barber's shop and an electric goods store led up a flight of steps to a solid oak door at the top of the stairs. A small brass plaque was the only thing that revealed the occupation of the former owner.

Checking the digits on a notebook, Raven had tapped in a combination of numbers into a keypad affixed to the oak door and the lock clicked open. The bright interior anti-room was clearly the reception with a single desk and a large screen Mac computer. A name plate on the desk read Joan James P.A. Sitting behind the receptionist's desk was a smiling Terry McGuire. "You're late," McGuire said.

"Bloody Port Talbot traffic," Raven explained. He didn't have to say any more. The traffic across the raised section of the M4 past the steel works was horrendous either side of rush hour. The local authority had, in most of the public's view, totally cocked up the stretch of road. Extended fifty-miles-per-hour sections had been added on the pretext that the slower traffic would reduce the air pollution. Anyone and everyone using the road could not fail to see the horrific clouds of pollutants billowing out of several tall chimneys across the three-mile steel works site. Raven failed to see how the reduction of pollutants from vehicles by dropping the speed would make any difference to the quality of life of the thousands who lived locally. But then again, any reduction had to be better than nothing.

A pair of doors stood open from the antiroom. One led into another, this one the size of the reception area and full of cardboard file boxes, a photocopier, aluminium filing cabinets standing to attention along one wall and shelves of various stationery. Raven walked past the desk and through the second open door. McGuire said nothing, seemingly happy to let his new partner explore the new business premises.

The rear office was once Ed's domain. It was a large square room with an equally large window to the left of the door, occupying the entire wall and overlooking the high street below. The desk was also large and made from what Raven guessed was some kind of white hardwood. The desk sat at a right angle to the window and a high-back, white leather chair was positioned behind the desk with a clear view out on to the street below. Another large screen Mac occupied the white desk alongside a phone and a note pad. It was a stark contrast to Raven's own office. All the furniture looked new and still had labels attached. It looked like Ed had just had a total refit before his death. That was nice of him.

Raven sat in the chair and swivelled around like a child on a 'bring your kid to work day'. He saw another troop of filing cabinets against the opposite wall. The cabinets were also made from the same coloured wood as the desk and each was numbered from 1 to 10.

McGuire had given Raven the key code to visit the office and to check the case files that might be still active. If they were going to make a go of the business, they couldn't afford to let cases slip through the net. The last thing they wanted was for disgruntled clients demanding repayment of their fees.

It was a new chapter in the life of both men with, hopefully, exciting times ahead. Raven was looking forward to working with McGuire, he knew they would make a good team, but that was all in the future and this was the present. McGuire appeared in the doorway.

"Nice to see you settle in, Raven, you're looking good, you've put on a bit of timber," he teased.

"You cheeky bugger, I'm the same weight as when I joined the Marines," Raven frowned.

"Didn't think they let fat bastards into the Marines," McGuire joked.

"It's lucky I've got a sense of humour."

"Let's get all the formalities out of the way, shall we? Here's the contract," McGuire dropped several sheets of paper on to the desk. "Like I say, it'll be a fifty-fifty partnership, with you running the show until I call it a day, and even then I may not fancy it. I might just remain a silent partner."

"That's a laugh, it's in your blood, you'll never leave it, even when you retire. Anyway, we'll make a good team, me the brains and you the brawn," he said, straight faced.

McGuire faked offence. "I don't think so, I've seen you in action first-hand. Window and skydive comes to mind."

Now Raven feigned offence. "He fell and he deserved it, no loss there," he held out his hand. "Just give me a pen."

Raven signed on the dotted line, without reading the document.

"Aren't you going to read it?"

"Terry, if I can't trust you, who can I trust?"

McGuire handed Raven a set of keys for doors Raven would have to figure out and shook hands with his new partner.

"I must say, Ed had good taste, makes my office look like a shithouse."

"Ed was a sharp cookie, he had some high-end clients, you'll need to be getting in touch with them. My brief has already had a few of them contact him to find out what's going on."

"Yes, when I've got five minutes I'll start sifting through the live cases."

"By the way, Raven, now you've shut the Swansea office, how are you going to manage the commuting?"

"Well, I hadn't really thought about it. I suppose I'll have to suck it and see."

McGuire stared out the reception window at the shoppers below. It was a surprisingly busy street. "I've got another proposition," he said. "Ed left me his house, why don't you move in? I know the situation with your sister, Sue. Perhaps a change of scenery will do her good and there's a lovely big garden there for her to enjoy."

"Jesus, Terry, I think you've already done enough."

McGuire shrugged. "I think it makes sense, rent free, what's the problem?"

"The problem is, Terry, it would be like owing you and I don't like owing anyone, never have."

"We're business partners. Just call it an investment. If the business carries on as it is, you'll be buying your own in no time, I guarantee it."

Raven was moved and lost for words. No one had done anything for him since his parents had died. "Terry, what can I say?"

"Say yes. Ring Sue and tell her to get packing."

Raven offered his hand.

"What have you got planned for the day?"

"I've got to get on with the missing Elvis. How's it coming on with the body?"

"Slow. The victim was strangled and pushed. So it's a murder. No leads at the moment. We'll get there, eventually."

"Bit ironic, Terry, I'm still trying to find that Tony, the Hound Dog. God knows where he is, and I wonder if there's a connection between him going missing and the body on the pier. Bit of a coincidence?"

"I won't rule anything out. As you say, bit of a coincidence. There's nothing to suggest a connection at the moment. Your man isn't even in our thinking at present, but I'll keep it in mind. That reminds me. That address you wanted for DS Ralph Crane? He lives in Pencoed," McGuire fished in his pocket for the address he had written on a Post-It. He's in his seventies now."

"I'll take a spin out there after we lock up, see if he can throw some light on it. Tomorrow, I'm off to sunny Cwmtwrch. Looks like Tony was pegging a woman from down there and she was with him at the time he disappeared."

Raven turned to leave but McGuire stopped him. "There's only one thing I'll ask," he warned Raven. "Do things by the book. I know your reputation and if you have any problems you let me know. I'll declare my business interest, so no nonsense until I finish, got it?"

"Got it. So no more flying villains, eh?" he

grinned.

"What happened in Swansea is done and dusted and that's the way I want it to remain. Does that answer your question?"

Raven shrugged.

"I also want you to be trained up to the level of a proper detective."

"I've done a course…"

No, not the certificate shit. I want you to think like one of my team."

"How am I going to do that?"

"I'm going to teach you. You'll be my apprentice and I'll be your Jedi Master."

Raven laughed.

***

Raven pulled up outside the address in Pencoed, a well-appointed corner plot bungalow, with beautifully manicured lawns and a colourful border yellow and white blooms. He walked along the short block path and knocked the front to be greeted by a white haired, well dressed lady in her seventies.

"Can I help you?"

"I'm a private investigator. Does Ralph Crane live here?"

She wasn't convinced. "I'm Ralph's wife, have you any identification?"

Raven produced his business card and handed it to the lady who read it carefully.

"What do you want Ralph for? Ralph

doesn't live here anymore, he's been diagnosed with dementia. He's in Bryntirion, the nursing home," her eyes brimmed with tears and she swiped them away with her sleeve. "I can't see him ever coming home."

"I'm very sorry, Mrs Crane. I'm sorry to have bothered you."

Raven turned to walk away.

"Mr Connor," she called after him. "May I ask what it's about? Maybe I can help you."

It was always worth a try. Ralph must have told his wife about the young boy's death in the feeder. "I'm trying to locate Tony Heggerty, he was a youngster at the Bryn Bach Children's home, his friend Kenny is concerned about him, I thought Mr Crane could help with their background."

"Come on in, Mr Connor. I knew the boys well. Ralph told me about them. The young kid was drowned."

Bingo!

Raven followed her into the living and noticed the photograph of a group of young police officers in three lines, smiling at the camera. Raven guessed it was Ralph's passing-out parade photo from the time he first joined the police. Raven took a seat in a worn leather armchair. The green dye having worn at the arms and cracked with age.

"You knew the boys well?"

"I came to know them. I would go with

Ralph sometimes when he visited the home and then started volunteering there. Ralph was devastated for the boys after the death and did what he could to help them, but couldn't do much because of his job. I know he was delighted that I helped out there, never said as much, mind. He didn't like to talk about his feelings. Kenny and Tony were lovely boys. It was very sad... what happened. Ralph dealt with the inquest file, very upsetting because our two boys were around the same age at the time."

"I understand it was Kenny's younger brother that drowned in the feeder?"

"Yes, that's right."

"Kenny never mentioned this to me. I was speaking to Mr Pickett yesterday up at the home. He told me about it."

"Ah, dear Ivor. He loved the kids. I haven't seen him for many years."

"What about Tony and Kenny? How did it affect them?"

"More Kenny than Tony, of course. He became a bit withdrawn, kept very quiet, he wasn't the same after the drowning."

"And Tony?"

"Well, Tony was older, a different kettle of fish. He had no fear, seemed to cope with it better than Kenny, but they were both joined at the hip. I always told Ralph the tragedy brought them closer together."

"When did you last see them?"

"They must have been in their mid-teens, I gave up the voluntary work about that time, but Ralph would see them and keep me up to date. The drowning did affect Ralph, that's why he kept an eye on the boys until they left care."

"Do you think Mr Crane would be able to speak with me?"

"Well, his short-term memory isn't very good, but on occasions, his long-term memory seems to kick in. He couldn't tell you what he had for breakfast but will often talk about his police service as if it were yesterday."

"Would it be asking too much to speak with him?"

"I don't suppose it'll do any harm. Won't be much help though, I think. I was just popping down to see him, when you called. Come with me. Perhaps a fresh face may do him the world of good"

"Brilliant, I'll give you a lift."

***

Raven didn't know what to expect, how could he know? Neither of his parents had had the chance to live into old age, but he knew only too well that many people alleged the standards at some nursing homes were far below the well-being guidelines. He also knew that other homes excelled at looking after their patients. He wondered which Ralph was experiencing in his time of need. It often seemed like a lottery and that gamble had been one of the reasons that made him promise himself that he would never let his sister enter one.

He signed in at reception at Bryntirion and watched as Ralph's wife did the same. He felt sorry for the woman. He just couldn't begin to imagine what it must be like to lose your life partner in everything except body. Ralph Crane's room was on the second floor. The facilities seemed good to Raven. The place was clean, and all the staff seemed to be wearing smiles that appeared to be genuine. Perhaps this was one of those homes that did things right? He hoped so, for Ralph and his wife. The smell of lavender reminded Raven of his nan. Mary Connor had been a strong woman. She lived into her nineties and would never have allowed anyone to take her from her home in Godregraig, not even when a well-documented landslide in 1963 nearly wiped her home down into the bottom of the Swansea Valley.

Ralph Crane's room was small but well equipped. He was sitting in a comfortable armchair watching a flat screen telly attached to the wall with one of those angle-adjustable arms that allowed him to see the screen from anywhere in the room. A black and white episode of Dixon of Dock Green was playing, and Raven wondered if the old programmes helped Ralph, or, indeed, did the opposite and kept his mind locked in the past.

"Hello, Ralph," Mrs Crane said as she kissed him on the forehead. Ralph smiled and pulled her close, his face was alive at the sight of his wife and the smile was heart-warming. It was obvious that Ralph recognised his wife, so that was a good sign.

"Ralph, this is Mr Connor. He's a private investigator. He does what you used to do, years ago."

Raven shook Ralph's hand. "Pleased to meet you Mr Crane, how are?"

"He's a joking detective," Ralph grinned wickedly. "I'm not too bad," he said. "I'll be going home tomorrow. I've been here long enough now."

Mrs Crane smiled warmly at him. She squeezed his hand. It was moving to see, and Raven felt another rush of sympathy for the couple.

"Ask him whatever you want, Mr Connor and call him Ralph."

"OK... how long were you in the force?"

"Did my full service. Thirty years."

"I bet you could tell a tale or two?"

He smiled. "Aye, I was a detective, like you, but a real one. Where do you work?"

"I'm from Swansea, but, as you pointed out, I'm not a real policeman. I'm a private detective."

Ralph nodded. "Never knew any good one's in my time. Are you like Sherlock Holmes?" he began to laugh.

"I wish, Ralph. Not as clever as him, I'm afraid."

"So, what do you want?"

Raven sat on the end of the bed. "Do you remember Tony and Kenny, they were two boys in care at the Bryn Bach Children's home up the Rhondda?"

Ralph's smile vanished. He looked at his wife and screwed his face. It looked like Raven had hit a nerve.

"Ask him again, Mr Connor, he looks like this when something's triggered, go on, ask him again."

"Tony and Kenny? They went swimming in the feeder and Kenny's brother drowned, yes?"

"They were silly boys, silly," Ralph muttered.

"Then you *do* remember them?"

"They were good boys, really, like ours, but they were very silly boys that day."

"What was Tony like?"

"The ringleader he was..." he paused and looked at his wife. "Have we had dinner yet?"

"Not yet darling, a bit later," his wife said softly. "What about Kenny and his brother, love?"

Now Ralph beamed "They were all good boys; all the kids were good. I remember them all."

"Well, Tony's gone missing and Kenny's concerned about him," Raven said. "I'm just trying to fit all the pieces together."

"Kenny was always upset, he was always crying after the accident."

"Must have been hard for him, Ralph?"

"All of us were upset. Silly boys, they were always told about the feeder. Is it still there?"

"No, long gone, since the pits closed."

"When was that?"

"The eighties, Ralph, no mines left at all now," Raven explained.

"Where's my dinner?"

Raven could see Ralph was beginning to shut down, to retreat to that place where he would once more lose his grip on the present. "You've been a great help, your dinner will be here shortly."

Ralph smiled again, it was sad for Raven to watch him. Raven had never seen anyone with dementia before and he knew it often got far worse. He wondered how it happened to some and not others. It was probably not so long ago this man had a mind like a scalpel, now he was just a mere shell barely able to function.

"Mr Connor, Ralph mentioned Kenny crying all the time, there's no doubt that the loss of his brother affected him more than Tony. When you see the boys next give them our best wishes, is there anything else we can help you with?"

"No, Mrs Crane, I'm very much obliged and I hope Ralph stays well," he said as he stood to leave.

Mrs Crane followed him out into the corridor. "I've lost him, Mr Connor. He'll not get any better, but at least I can be with him whenever I like."

Raven shook her hand and stepped inside the room once more. "I'm off now, Ralph, you look after yourself."

Ralph smiled and nodded. "Can I come home with you, son?"

"I'll wait here with Ralph for a while," she checked her watch. "There's a bus that'll take me home in a little over an hour. Ralph will have had enough of me by then,"

"I can give you a lift, if you wish?"

She shook her head. "Got to make the most of our time together while we still can," she said grimly.

33.

Raven couldn't help but smile. The constant worry of the last few weeks had eaten away at him and now he felt like the sun had dawned on a new day full of hope. He was delighted with McGuire's offer and knew he could get used to this new direction. He had to do his part and make a start on Ed's files. He returned to the office after visiting Ralph, the former detective.

A small stack of drawers under Ed's desk contained a small, metal petty cash box. Inside was a little over a hundred pounds in cash. Another box contained a new pack of business cards and a handful of assorted pens lay alongside.

He laid everything out on the desk and watched a cyclist weave through pedestrians below. Someone shouted abuse at the young cyclist who responded by laughing and raising his middle finger. Raven laughed too.

He stood from the desk and walked to the filing cabinet marked '1'. It seemed as good a place to start as any. The cabinet was open, the keys were on the top. Raven pulled the top drawer out and looked inside. The drawer was crammed full of case files, some thin but most several inches thick. He pulled the first file from the collection and looked at the information typed neatly on a label affixed to the brown card cover. 'Davies v Davies. 10/01/92.' Scribbled below it was a note in blue pen; 'Case completed 17/01/92.'

The next dozen or so files were all dated and marked up as completed. Indeed, all the files in cabinet 1 were either completed or resolved as much as it was possible to do so, and it had only taken Raven forty minutes to work through them all.

Raven found a mug and kettle in the storeroom off the reception and brewed a mug of coffee. He carried the drink back into the office and found a small slate coaster to prevent the mug leaving a ring stain on the new desk.

Cabinet 2 was much the same as cabinet 1 but all the cases were dated in the noughties – 2001-2009.

Cabinet 3 covered cases from 2010-2018. The rest of the cabinets were empty apart from one marked up as 'Outstanding.' "Shit!" he moaned to himself. "Why didn't I notice that before?"

Just one drawer contained a dozen or so case files. Raven pulled them all out together and dropped them on to the desk.

The top file caught his attention. Written in blue pen was the name 'McGuire.' Coincidence?

He opened the file and began to read the contents.

34.

McGuire sat wrapped in a thick coat on a wooden recliner. He stared at the weeds pushing up between the boards of the decking and promised himself that he'd sort them out when he got five minutes. The cold autumn air had no chance of penetrating through the coat and the old grey suit he wore beneath it. He had risen early, as he always did, and Molly had cooked him a full English. The Lady Grey tea he sipped was Molly's latest preference, but it would take time for McGuire to adjust to its delicate flavour. Molly had nagged him to cut down on his consumption of coffee. He knew caffeine was no good for him – everybody knew caffeine was no good – but it was his only real vice – apart from Jameson's whiskey.

McGuire wanted to get into the office early, to introduce his new DCI, Bryn Rowlands to the rest of the team. He knew they would all know of him - that was the good thing about a force of no more than a few thousand officers - but not many would have worked with him. McGuire had read Bryn's personnel file and memorised it all.

Bryn had joined the Met at twenty-four

after his degree at Oxford and served in Kennington, part of the Met's L Division with its divisional HQ at Brixton. McGuire wondered how Bryn had managed to get by in the Met, especially in that division. After the riots in 1981, the Met had taken stick for being 'institutionally racist,' an allegation that McGuire knew was a serious insult to the majority of the rank and file, but McGuire was also a realist. He knew all organisations had officers who should never have been allowed to don the uniform of constable – McGuire had met a lot of them throughout his career. But that didn't mean the majority could be tarred with the same brush. Bryn was a young black recruit taking to the streets where the coppers were labelled as racists and the majority black population in his new patch saw black coppers as traitors. It couldn't have been easy for him.

He watched a robin hop from the silver birch Molly had planted at the bottom of the garden and smiled as it cautiously eyed him. Robins were funny birds. They somehow sensed his mood. He wondered if this was the same robin that liked to eat out of his hand at the graveyard in Abercrave where Jane, one of his former detectives was buried. Of course it wasn't the same bird, it couldn't be. Birds didn't fly around the country to meet up with old friends. Did they?

The robin hopped to within a metre of him then pecked something from one of the weeds and flew off back into the birch.

He checked his watch. It was time to go. McGuire walked back into the house and dropped his dressing gown on the back of the dining room chair and kissed Molly on the cheek.

"Any idea when you'll finish today?"

McGuire shrugged. "I'll ring you. Love you."

"Love you too, but don't think you're leaving that dressing gown there. You know where it lives."

McGuire sniggered. "OK. Fair cop."

When he arrived at the Incident Room only the night-shift HOLMES officer was there. The HOLMES system was a computer system named after the fictional detective and introduced in 1985. It was developed by a software company to assist in crime investigations. Now, HOLMES 2 was improved but functioned primarily in the same way as its predecessor. As an administrative support system to assist Senior Investigating Officers in their management of complex serious crimes, HOLMES processed the mass of information inputted by officers throughout the country to ensure no vital clues were overlooked. HOLMES could also be used to record reported missing persons and had the facility to store the identities of casualties and survivors of major incidents.

The previous evening had been quiet and not many actions had been generated, which was always disappointing.

Bryn walked in shortly after McGuire and

followed him to the coffee machine.

"Shouldn't be drinking this stuff, my wife says. Still, can't beat a good shot of Columbian to start the day."

Bryn laughed. "Don't know what to say to that, boss, other than I'll take mine black with no sugar."

"I'll introduce you to the team a bit later," McGuire said. "Come to my office, we'll have a quick chat and I'll bring you up to speed with the latest news."

"Sounds good to me, boss."

At six feet four inches tall and with a well-honed body, Bryn was also good-looking. His head was clean shaven, and he had hands like shovels. McGuire knew Bryn could handle himself. Bryn had boxed for the Met during his five-year stint in the smoke and possessed a third-dan black belt in karate. He had even competed at International level for Wales in Kick Boxing. The first time McGuire met Bryn, he thought he had walked into a Johnny Mathis gig. He was a dead ringer - with added brawn but without the hair.

McGuire poured Bryn a coffee. "Cheers, Bryn, sorry it's nothing stronger."

"Never used to drink much, boss. No good for the training." Bryn followed McGuire into the office and closed the door behind him.

"I chose you because of your track record. I know you don't take any crap and I also know you're a team player. That's vital for this team. I know you'll slot in nicely here."

"Looking forward to it, boss. I did a bit of digging into your team when I was appointed, and I know they're my kind of people. I'll slot in no problem. I won't tread on any toes. You'll have no problem from me. I'll just keep a watching brief for the time being."

"So, who do you know on the team?"

"There's Colin, who I've been on a few incidents with years ago, and Julia. I did a few courses with her. As for the rest, only by name and reputation."

"So, you never used to go on the piss with Julia?"

Bryn shrugged and looked awkward. "I still have an occasional jar, and went on a few sessions with her, but that was before she hit it hard," he held up his hands to stop McGuire replying. "I'm not the judging type, boss. We all have our demons. Do you know, the first time I met her she thought I was a Johnny Mathis strip-a-gram. I had hair in those days, he laughed."

"You do look like him, Bryn. Can you sing?"

"Yes, but more like Bryn Terfel than Johnny Mathis."

"Well she's off the sauce," McGuire said. "Been good as gold since she joined the team. I read her the riot act when she joined us, and she knows the score."

"I take every day as it comes, boss. My parents taught me that."

"Well, we've got something for you to work on. A victim by the name of Lenny Stone. He was thirty-nine, from the Rhondda originally, but was living in Pencoed. He was a gay man and a coke user. They found him down by the pier midday Saturday. He'd been manually strangled."

"Is the gay element relevant, boss?"

"Might be, who knows at this stage?"

"Any leads?"

"Nothing pointing us to the culprit yet, Bryn. Plenty of actions allocated to the team to go on with. They've been concentrating enquiries within the gay community in case it's linked."

"Any DNA to go on?"

"Yes, just a matter of getting a match. No hits at the minute. Tracked down a few people who knew him but nothing forthcoming and, as you know, it was Elvis weekend. We had over forty thousand down here. Culprit could be anywhere by now."

"That's true. Well, I'll just shadow for the time being and I'll have the Cardiff Bay officers make a few enquiries amongst the gay community on my old patch, you never know what might turn up."

The team started drifting into the Incident Room and McGuire opened his office door. "Well, this is your moment, Bryn. Let's get it over with."

The room noise had risen several decibels with detectives chattering and swigging copious mugs of coffee. It was going to be another long day for the team.

"Listen up, ladies and gents. Can I have your attention, please?" McGuire shouted above the noise.

"I'd like to introduce you to the new DCI, Bryn Rowlands."

Julia was at the coffee machine, saw Bryn and smiled.

"I understand you know Bryn personally, Julia," McGuire said. "I'll let you introduce him to everyone later."

Julia nodded.

"I'm sure you all know of Bryn's reputation and I'm equally sure he'll fit in well and will do us proud. I've brought him up to speed on the Stone murder, so we are now back to full strength. Bryn, do you want to say a few words?"

The big guy stepped forward and smiled warmly. "Cheers, boss. I have to say that I feel honoured to be part of the team. I'm not here to tread on anyone's toes, I know how the boss works and I will carry on in the same vein. I will always be on hand if any of you want a chat. I'm a big believer in family and I realise the pressures that come with investigating major crime. I realise that you've all got a busy day in front of you, but I'll have a chat to you all individually as time goes on. If there's anything you want to ask, fire away."

Julia raised her hand with a mischievous grin on her face. "I know it's you're first day, boss, but I have to ask... who killed Lenny Stone? Because, at the minute, we haven't a clue."

The whole room, including Bryn and McGuire laughed.

"I've no idea Julia, but I'm sure you lot will bring whoever did it to book."

"OK, that's the niceties over with," McGuire said. "Have there been any developments that will take us further?"

Colin Boulton stood. Colin was an ex-undercover officer. McGuire swore he had never seen Colin clean shaven. At five foot nine, Colin had joined the job after the height restriction had been removed. Although he was still an inch over the old minimum height, he was short amongst his peers. McGuire despaired at some of the changes he had seen come into effect in the service during his tenure, but he was glad the service hadn't missed out on some of the shorter officers he'd worked with. "We're concentrating our enquiries within the drug and gay communities, boss," Colin said. "We're also trying to identify the tattoos. We know that he had them done a few years ago in Bridgend. The one we're trying to identify is 'TH', we've checked all our data bases but have come up dry..."

Tony Heggerty's name popped into McGuire's head. "Tony Heggerty is missing. He's an Elvis impersonator. He was supposed to perform on Sunday but disappeared. I don't want us shooting off on a tangent but let's keep that in mind."

"Do you have someone looking for Heggerty, boss?" Bryn asked.

McGuire shook his head. "Not yet. There's a private detective looking into it and he's keeping me updated. Let's let him do some work for us and we'll act on it if and when necessary."

"It could be insignificant," Colin Bolton added. "But we have to check all avenues. As for the drugs angle, the victim had been buying now and again from a dealer in Pencoed. The dealer's been nicked and says he supplied him with about fifty quid's worth every Friday night."

"Is the dealer in the frame?"

"No, boss. He had a rock-solid alibi. The drug squad were keeping observations on him, even got Stone on camera getting his gear."

"Anything else, Col?"

"Plenty of actions. Just waiting for that little break, boss."

"OK, ladies and gents, chop-chop. Up and at them," McGuire said.

35.

"His time is up," Rudi fumed. "I warned him, but he didn't listen."

Mrs Harland sat at her kitchen table and smoked a menthol cigarette. Between puffs she listened to Rudi and watched as he worked himself up into a red-faced rage. She smiled. Rudi looked hot when he was angry, and she knew he took things like this personally. "So, what are you going to do about it, Rudi, love?"

Rudi stopped pacing and leaned on the table, his face inches from hers. She blew a puff of smoke into his face and smiled. "You turn me on when you're angry, you know that."

"I'll kill the bastard," Rudi seethed.

"No need to go that far. Just get him to pay up, that's all I want from you. Break a few bones, if you have to but get him to pay."

Rudi straightened and nodded. "I'll break more than a few bones. Do you know how much he's disrespecting me?"

"It's my money, remember?"

"Yes, and it's me he's ignored. He knows I don't let debts slide and yet he's still messing me about."

Mrs Harland placed her hand on top of Rudi's. "Now you mentioned 'messing about,'" she grinned.

Rudi smiled too. He took her hand and pulled her from the chair, he pushed her over the table. "Is this what you want?" he shouted. Rudi knew what his boss wanted, and he was always happy to oblige.

***

The Harley Davidson stopped outside the front door of Tony's house. Rudi wasn't bothered about being seen by Tony; he knew the man couldn't escape. He switched off the powerful engine and kicked down the stand. He decided to keep the helmet on but lifted the visor as he walked to the oak front door.

The doorbell was ignored, as was the angry knocks. Rudi lifted his right motorcycle boot and crashed it against the lock. The thick oak split under the enormous force of Rudi's heavy leg and exploded inwards.

"Who the hell?" someone shouted from inside as Rudi marched in like the Terminator in his black leather jacket and trousers.

Rudi stopped in the middle of the hallway as a man he had never seen before rushed out of an adjoining room and slid to a stop at the sight of the big black man before him.

"Wh-wh-what... what the hell?" the man stammered.

"Who the fuck are you?" Rudi growled.

"K-Kenny... I'm staying here..."

"You Tony's boyfriend or something?"

Kenny laughed nervously. "N-No. I'm just an old friend. I'm his manager."

"Where's Tony?"

"I don't know. He's disappeared..."

"Disappeared?"

"Yes. Since last Sunday."

"You are telling me he's been gone for four days?"

"I don't know where he's gone."

The red mist descended, and Rudi felt the rage building inside again. He had planned what he was going to do to Tony if he didn't give him the money he owed. Indeed, he was still going to inflict pain on the bastard for disrespecting him, but now he was nowhere to be found. Rudi looked around the hall. Large paintings on the wall were probably worth something but Rudi knew nothing about art. There had to be things he could take to go some way towards recompense for his trouble. "All the shit in here is mine. Tony owes us. Do you understand?"

Kenny flushed red. "You can't do that. I'll call the police."

Rudi stepped towards Kenny and grabbed him by the throat. Before Kenny could do anything to defend himself, Rudi butted him with his crash helmet. Kenny's nose took the full force of the blow and shattered. Blood exploded across his face and the helmet. Rudi threw Kenny against a wall and kicked him with his heavy boot. He heard Kenny's ribs crack and kicked him again and again.

Kenny lay still, unable to move. He curled in a foetal position and prayed the beating would stop. It didn't, at least not whilst Kenny was conscious.

Rudi had kicked the man into a state where he no longer felt pain and stepped back. He had other work to do.

36.

The village of Cwmtwrch is a decent jog west of the Swansea Valley, halfway between the city of Swansea and the town of Brecon. Raven, like most others in South Wales had heard of the place. It was famous for for being the home of the former Wales rugby captian Clive Rowlands and, like many communities in the area, appeared to have been exempt for any kind of planning permission. Houses had been crammed into plots that were occupied by other homes and at one time the pubs had outnumbered the chapels - of which there were many. One of these pubs had also benefitted from being on the exact intersection of three counties. With different licencing laws in each, drinkers would move from one room in one country at closing time to the next, until all three closing times had passed.

He had to find Eira, the woman last seen with Tony. He didn't think it would be too difficult, everyone knew everyone in these Welsh villages.

A small village post office ahead on his left caught his eye.

The Post Mistress wore a pale blue and

white, nylon housecoat with her name written in marker pen on a badge. 'Mrs Price' was a typical old village woman; she seemed to know everyone and everything about everyone. In her seventies, Raven guessed she had had plenty of time to develop her local knowledge.

"Eira. Lovely girl, she is. Used to come here every day to get some bread and milk," she said. "Always smiling, and bright too. Not been so smiley or bright since you know..."

"Sorry? I'm afraid I have no idea what you're talking about," Raven said.

She leaned over the counter and glanced around the shop as if she was about to reveal a state secret, even though there was no one else in the shop. "You know? The baby?"

"Oh!"

"Yes, upset her parents, she did, what with not being married and all."

"I see."

"Shame really, especially with the problems the little one was born with."

"Problems?"

"She's under the doctor with her eyes. Bad eyes, apparently. Born with them, she was."

Raven tried not to laugh but felt a smile begin to crack his face. He loved the way old women talked in these parts.

"Blind as a bat, apparently, not that I've seen her, mind. Doesn't come in here anymore, not since the little one was born. Can't be easy, mind, having a baby like that. Bless!"

Raven thanked Mrs Price and followed her directions to the Cwmtwrch Boarding Kennels a short drive outside the village.

The crisp, autumn, morning air made the place look idyllic. The early sun was busy evaporating the overnight dew and creating an ankle-deep mist.

He heard a sound, a ghostly, deep, rhythmic melody hanging in the low-lying haze.

A portly, bald man with a Bobby Charlton comb-over was half visible above the hanging mist, filling water bowls for a multitude of dogs that hopped and bounced excitedly within a wooden fenced enclosure as he sang some Welsh ballad Raven had never heard before.

Raven approached the compound, carefully stepping over a rutted stone track and a scattering dog droppings of various dimensions.

"Dewi Pritchard?"

The man looked up from the bowls and ambled to the fence. He was probably in his early seventies, wearing a grey, worn *dai cap* – a cap others in other parts of the world would call a flat cap. The man had a rugged face, red from his time outdoors with a bulbous purple nose that Raven guessed was the result of his time *indoors* drinking hard spirits.

"I'm Dewi Pritchard, lad. What can I do for ewe? After a puppy, are ewe?"

Again Raven suppressed a grin. He loved

the way the locals pronounced certain words like you. "No, Mr Pritchard, I'd like to speak with your daughter, Eira, if possible?"

Pritchard stared into Raven's eyes, searching for some form of recognition. Had he met him before? Had Eira brought him here? "Who are ewe then? What business 'ave ewe got with our Eira?"

Raven sensed a tension building and smiled in the hope of deflating it. "My name's Raven Connor, Mr Pritchard. I'm a private investigator looking into the disappearance of a man by the name of Tony Heggerty," Now it was Raven's turn to stare into Pritchard's eyes, searching for a sign of recognition. "I believe Eira may know him," there was nothing Raven could detect in those eyes.

"Never 'eard of him, Mr Connor. And anyway, Eira's not 'ere. Me and the missus 'aven't seen 'er since last week," he paused as he brushed an amorous spaniel from his boot. "Private detective, ewe say?" Raven nodded. "Look, you'd better come in the 'ouse, I'm due for a bit of breakfast. Been up since the crack of dawn, I 'ave. These beauties are a full-time job ewe know," he smiled as the dogs jumped and scratched at his trousers.

"I can imagine they are, Mr Pritchard."

"Do ewe like dogs, Mr Connor?"

"Love them, sir. Always have."

Pritchard smiled again and nodded his

head.

Raven followed Pritchard into the main house, where the man's wife was about to plate a large slice of bacon alongside a couple of orange-yolk eggs and fried bread.

"Bron, this is Mr Connor, 'e's a detective, 'e is. Wants to speak with Eira. I told 'im she's not 'ere."

The woman dropped the bacon onto the plate and looked at Raven. She wiped her greasy hands in the apron she wore and extended her right hand that had not surrendered all of the cooking fat to the apron. Raven shook her hand and resisted the temptation to wipe his hand on his jeans.

"We 'aven't heard from her since last week," she said, dropping the 'h' like her husband. "She went to the festival in Porthcawl. Nothing unusual, mind. Sometimes she spends a week down there. She'll probably turn up tomorrow," then she smiled. "Look at me, my mother would kill me if she was alive. I 'aven't offered you anything. Would you like some breakfast? It's no trouble?"

"No thanks, Mrs Pritchard, but a cuppa would do the job nicely."

"Sugar and milk?"

"Milk, no sugar, please. I'm cutting down."

Dewi Pritchard pulled a chair from a small wooden table squashed into a corner of the kitchen. Mrs Pritchard carried the plate of food to him and placed it on the table.

"Smashing, love. Now, what's it all about then, Mr Connor?" he said as he cut a mouth-sized portion of bacon.

"Like I said, Mr Pritchard, I'm trying to trace this bloke called Tony. I know that Eira was with him Sunday evening at the Seaview Hotel, but he's disappeared and a mate of his is getting concerned."

The bacon was paused at Pritchard's lips. "Look, Mr Connor, our Eira's been going to Porth-cawl for 'ears, she 'as. That Elvis Festival, you know? Well, she's obsessed with it. Just goes and we don't see 'er for days."

"Does she contact you at all?"

"No, just goes and then comes back as if nothing 'as 'appened. Doesn't even mention any-thing, does she, Bron?"

"No, not a word, God knows what she gets up to, Mr Connor."

"So, you've no idea who this Tony is?"

"No," she said. "Eira's never mentioned 'im to us. Mind you, this could explain things..."

"What do you mean?"

"Come with me, Mr Connor. I want to show you something."

Mrs Pritchard led Raven into the lounge and there he saw a beautiful young baby girl, sleeping soundly in a wicker Moses basket.

"That's our Grace, Mr Connor," she smiled proudly. "That's Eira's likkle 'un. Three months old she is and she's the love of our lives."

"I take it Eira's not married then, Mrs Pritchard?"

"Oh no, never 'ad a boyfriend, as far as we knew," she snorted. "Me and Dewi think Grace was conceived down at the festival last year. The timing was right. Either that or we have a miracle birth on our 'ands. Do you think this Tony may be Grace's dad? Eira would never tell us who the father was. There's nothing on the birth certificate."

"She's a beauty, Mrs. Pritchard."

"Oh yes, she's our two eyes," she said, then the smile slipped from her face.

"And what about, Eira, how is she with Grace?"

"Loves her to bits, Mr Connor. Loves her to bits, she does."

"I find it strange that Eira doesn't contact you at all when she visits the festival. Doesn't she ring you at all?"

"She's got one of those mobiles, but I suppose no news is good news, and she knows Grace is safe with us."

Raven returned to the kitchen and finished off his tea.

"Have you got a picture of Eira?"

"Bron, get Mr Connor a nice up to date 'un," he cut another piece of bacon and dipped it into one of the eggs. "Mr Connor, do ewe think something's happened to Eira? I'm getting a bit worried now."

"Well, she did go off with Tony in his car, so I take it she's still with him because neither have been seen since Sunday evening. Like you say, maybe he's Grace's dad and they're trying to sort it out, who knows?"

"You're right, Mr Connor." He stuffed the food into his mouth. "Do ewe think we should report 'er missing?" he mumbled through the food.

"Give me a day or two. She's an adult, she's not what you'd class a vulnerable person and the police wouldn't do much anyway."

Pritchard nodded.

"Has Eira got a car, Mr Pritchard?"

"Yes, it's a blue Ford Fiesta. Nothing fancy, like."

"And the Registration number?" Raven produced a pen from his coat pocket.

"DNY 850C."

"Bloody hell that's an old number."

"Aye, I 'ad an old Anglia in the 70's, loved it, I did. Just kept the number when we scrapped it, like."

"I've got a mate in the police, I'll see if we can have the number circulated, you never know, we may get lucky," Raven said as he jotted down the number onto the back of his hand.

"This Tony bloke, Mr Raven, who the bloody 'ell is 'e?"

"He's an Elvis tribute singer, Mr Pritchard. From the Rhondda originally, but now he travels all over Europe doing these festivals."

"Eira's never mentioned 'im to us, 'as she Bron?"

"No, never. If 'e is the father, we'd like to meet 'im," then she paused for a brief moment. "I 'ope 'e's not married?"

"No, he's not married, so you can put your mind to rest on that count."

"Is there anything else, Mr Connor. If Eira turns up we'll give you a ring, shall we?"

Raven nodded. "I'll do likewise, here's my card," he produced a business card from the pocket he had taken the pen. "If you hear any-thing in the time being, please let me know, and thank you for your time."

"Not a problem, is it Bron?"

Bron shook her head and smiled.

Raven walked back to his car and decided to pay Kenny another visit in Treorchy. His gut feeling was that things were not right.

37.

He had no idea how long he had been unconscious. The mad man had hurt him, hurt him bad. He ached all over. He knew his ribs were broken – at least four – and God only knew what his face must look like. Perhaps it was God's way of making him pay for all the bad things he had done throughout his life? Perhaps his brother was exacting some kind of sick revenge from beyond the grave? If so, he knew he deserved it. That thought eased the pain for a brief moment until he tried to move. He lifted his head and his eyes began to focus. There was blood everywhere. The tiled floor was covered in his claret.

A sharp pain in his chest stopped him from moving further. He was struggling to breath and began to panic. What if his lungs were punctured? How would that feel? He'd heard of ribs breaking and piercing the lungs. Had that happened to him, was he going to die?

Kenny remembered his phone. He carried it everywhere – everyone seemed to carry phones everywhere these days. He carefully moved his hand down to his back pocket and pulled the phone from his blood covered jeans.

He pressed the button to unlock the phone but the blood on his thumb prevented identification. He'd have to tap in the code number. What was the code number? He had never forgotten it before. Perhaps his brain was damaged too? SHIT!

He lay still for what seemed like ages. He couldn't move and he struggled to remember his pass code for the phone. Was it 0-1-0-4-6-8? That was a number that meant something to him but why?

He tapped the number into the phone and sighed with relief as the phone flashed through to the dial screen.

Kenny tried to type the emergency call number but struggled to focus. Thankfully, he didn't have to dial it. Kenny heard footsteps outside. Then he heard a voice.

"What the hell?"

Kenny saw a pair of white trainers and blue jeans and felt panic once more. Had the attacker come back or sent someone else to finish him? Then everything went black for the second time.

***

When Raven arrived at the house, he found the front door slightly ajar.

Raven called out for Kenny but didn't get any reply and sensed something was not right; a gut feeling, Raven had been involved in enough conflict all over the world to know when things weren't right.

He called out once more and slowly pushed the front door open, it was then that he saw Kenny on the hall floor, there was blood everywhere, it was obvious he had taken a terrible beating.

Kenny was barely conscious, and blood was pouring from his mouth and his front teeth had been broken, but the man was holding his mobile phone.

Raven rushed over to him. "What the hell?" he said as Kenny dropped his phone and blacked out.

Kenny was placed into the recovery position. Raven called for an ambulance and waited by Kenny. After a few minutes, Kenny's eyes flickered open again. "Who did this, Kenny? Who did this to you?"

Hardly able to speak, but Kenny tried to form the words.

"Big... black... after... Tony... and... money"

The man was in a bad way, but the ambulance arrived within five minutes. The paramedics quickly saw to him, made him comfortable after giving a shot of painkiller. Then they rushed him off to the Royal Glamorgan Hospital at Llantrisant.

Now alone, Raven thought it would be a good opportunity to have a good look around the house. The first thing he did was check for any

CCTV, only to find that the system wasn't even functional. He had barely rummaged through the nearest bedroom when a voice shouted from downstairs.

"Hello, is there anyone here? It's the police!"

"I'll be down in a minute" Raven replied.

When he trotted down the stairs to the hallway, Raven was greeted by the severe face of a young detective .

"What's been going on here then? Bit of a mess by the looks of things."

Raven told the detective what he knew, which wasn't much.

"And his name?"

"Kenny Vincent, he's a close friend of the owner."

"And you are what to them?"

"Just a friend of Tony and Kenny."

"Oh aye? You're a friend of Tony, our very own local celebrity Elvis? So, where is he?"

"Well that's it, my problem. He's gone AWOL. That's why Kenny was here."

"Probably on tour somewhere, no doubt."

"You know him, obviously?"

"Oh aye. Done a few charity gigs for the locals. He's a valley boy. Done good for himself."

"Do you know him personally?"

"Mr Connor, I'll ask the questions, if you don't mind?"

Raven grinned. "Oops, sorry officer, didn't mean to tread on your toes."

"Don't get smart, Mr Connor, or I may even nick you for this lot."

He could tell that the detective was not in the mood for banter, so Raven thought better of replying.

"By the way, Mr Connor, why are you here?"

"Like I said, just an acquaintance of Kenny's, he asked me up for a few beers."

The detective nodded sagely - clearly not convinced. "Have you any idea who's responsible for this lot?"

"Not a scooby, officer," Raven shrugged. "Now, is there anything else you need me for? It's just that I've got places to be."

Sharpe looked puzzled. "What line of work are you in then, Mr Connor?"

Raven shrugged his shoulders. "Bit like you, I suppose. I investigate when the police are too busy, or don't give a rat's arse to do what they're paid for."

Sharpe didn't look impressed. "Are you investigating anything at the moment?"

"Strictly confidential, officer, you know the score," Raven pulled a card from his pocket. Here, give me a bell if you want a chat again."

The card was torn in two and Sharpe let the halves flutter to the tiled floor.

"Thought littering was an offence," Raven cracked. "I suppose you'll get the old fingerprint boys out to dust the place, but I wouldn't bother with the CCTV. I've checked the system. It's not even working."

"I could nick you for obstruction, Mr Raven, you realise that?"

"You could, but your time would be better occupied if you paid poor Kenny a visit," Raven turned to leave then stopped and looked back over his shoulder at Sharpe. "I'll leave you to lock up, unless you're going to slip the bracelets on me?"

"On your way, Mr Connor, before I change my mind."

Raven walked back to his car. He thought about giving McGuire a ring. The case was taking a turn for the worse and Raven still had no clue as to where Tony the Elvis could be. He waited until he returned to his office before making the call. "Terry, Raven here. I'm in a bit of a dilemma. I don't know whether I should be ringing you. I know you've got a lot on the go at the minute..."

"What is it, Raven? Must be bothering you if you're ringing me. We're partners now, re-member, so crack on."

"Well, you know this missing person, this Tony Heggerty, the Elvis impersonator? I've got a feeling something's not right."

"In what way?"

"Earlier this afternoon, some big black guy broke into his house in Treorchy and beat up his mate, Kenny Vincent. Kenny's the bloke who hired me. He's in the Royal Glamorgan with his front teeth gone, and a few ribs broken, I reckon."

"Any idea why?"

"Money, I guess, what else? Kept asking where Tony was and that he owed money."

"He's a grown man, Raven. He'll turn up somewhere, I've no doubt."

"I don't know, Terry. It's not right."

"Perhaps he's done a runner until the heat's off, did you think of that?"

"I suppose it could be, but the woman who was with him is missing as well. Her parents haven't seen her for a week, not since she left home to visit the festival."

"Like I said, he's keeping his head down in more ways than one, Raven. Get my drift," McGuire chuckled.

"Smutty, Terry, very smutty. Can you do me a favour then?"

"Go on, what is it?"

"Can you circulate their vehicles?"

McGuire sighed. "Go on, give me the numbers."

Raven read out the numbers and the makes and models of the two cars.

"OK leave it with me, I'll sort it. Who's dealing with the robbery up at Treorchy?"

"Some young DC by the name of Sharpe, arrogant little prick."

"Oh, Sharpie? There's plenty of go in him. He'll be on my team in another six months. A tenner says he'll nick the culprit within forty-eight hours."

"You're on, Terry. Money's already in my bank."

"Raven, watch this space. I'll circulate the vehicles and give you a bell for me to collect the tenner. I'll also give Sharpie a bell and get the official story."

***

The smiling face was peering down at him. Everything seemed white, bright and the light hurt his eyes.

"How are you feeling?"

Kenny tried to answer but the pain in his chest stopped him. He raised his right hand gently off the bed and waved it briefly.

"What am I doing here?"

"You're in hospital. A man called Raven Connor found you and called us and an ambulance. You were in a mess."

"I was b-beaten."

"So I've been told. I'm from Treorchy CID. I'm dealing with the break-in and the assault on you. Can you tell me what happened?"

Kenny tried to speak through broken teeth.

"Take your time," Sharpe said.

"A-a man. A b-big black guy... b-broke-in and-did-this," he said. It was clear that Kenny was in considerable pain. In addition to Kenny's front teeth missing, his nose was a mess. Both eyes were turning black and the whites of his eyes were red.

"Do you know the man?"

Kenny rocked his head on the pillow, a shake was too painful. "No."

"The place was ransacked but nothing obvious seems to have been taken. Do you know what he was after?"

"M-money. He wanted... Tony. Tony... owed him money."

"The operator said that you told her it was your house, but it's actually Tony Heggerty's?"

Kenny nodded, almost imperceptibly.

"Where *is* Tony? Was he there with you at the time?"

Again, Kenny rocked his head in the negative. "Missing... for... days."

"Do you live with him?"

"No. Staying...I'm his... manager."

"How can I get hold of Tony?"

"Don't know. He's... missing, I said. If... I knew... he wouldn't be... bloody missing, would he."

Sharpe sighed. He was beginning to regret letting Raven Connor leave. He had his business card. He checked a pocket before he remembered he'd torn it up and tossed it away.

Shit!

38.

Midday Saturday in the Pontypridd CID office meant corned beef pasties for those on the team not watching their weight. Powell's Bakery on the high street had the best pasties in the country, at least that's what DC Mark Sharpe believed. Unlike many other versions he'd tried over the years, they actually contained corned beef. He had become a connoisseur of the savouries. He had sworn off the local chain-bakery versions produced with barely a scrape of the processed meat. Sharpe had just got off the phone to the Royal Glamorgan Hospital as he bit into the first of two pasties he had bought. Kenny's condition had been considerably more serious than initially thought. He had taken a turn for the worse during the night and the surgeons had operated on his damaged spleen and lung. His wounds would heal but his spleen had to be removed, so he wasn't going anywhere any time soon.

There was no information locally that could point Sharpe in the direction of the assailant – other than his name. There was no doubt that he must have a bit of form to carry out such a brutal attack.

Haydn Naylor, the crime scene investigator, a man as wide as he was tall, came into the office and sniffed the air. "Am I too late?"

"Pasty orders were an hour ago," Sharpe confirmed. "Hope you've got something for me, Haydn, I'm treading water at the moment."

"Good news, Mark. I found loads of prints, but only one set is on the database."

"Please tell me?"

"They're Rudi's Gumms," Naylor said as he dipped his head closer to the pasty sitting on the desk and sniffed the air. "I can tell you he's a handful. Stack of form, been out about twelve months after convictions for GBH, possession, supplying. You name it, he's into it. He's on licence at the moment under the probation order. Are you going to eat that?"

Sharpe sighed, shook his head and pushed the pasty towards Naylor.

Naylor grinned. "That's nice of you. I was wasting away."

"You could live for a month in the desert and still not waste away," Sharpe said.

"No need for that. I'll have you know I'm in training."

Sharpe snatched at the pasty, but Naylor was too quick. "Pasty is no good for you, then," Sharpe said.

"I need my protein," Naylor said before biting into the snack.

"What's his full name and address?"

Haydn Naylor checked a scribbled note on the back of his hand. "Rudi Gumms. Born in Kennington, now resident at The Halfway on Coity Road, Bridgend."

"Any intel regarding use of weapons?"

"No, he's only muscle. I'd advise you to take a few of the boys down and do the business at the address. I'll come and have a rummage, probably got a room there."

"OK, I'll round up the troops and run it by the DI. We'll hit him around six."

"Sounds like a plan, hope he comes quiet."

***

Sharpe and his team of four uniforms and one extra DC arrived at The Halfway dead on six and spoke to the warden who told them that Rudi was in his room because he'd signed in an hour earlier.

The Halfway was a bail hostel and operated strict signing protocols to ensure the 'residents' complied with the order of their bail.

The building was a large semidetached Victorian property that had once been home to some influential family. With eight bedrooms, five up and three in a ground floor extension out back and three reception rooms in the original part of the building on the ground floor, it was fit for purpose.

Rudi's room was on the ground floor in the

extension. Sharpe sent three of the uniforms to cover the back yard in case he decided to try and escape.

Sharpe waited a few minutes, guessing the length of time it would take for the uniforms to get into position before he approached room 3 and knocked the door. "Rudi Gumms, this is the police, open the door, we want a chat?"

Sharpe could hear someone inside, heavy, clumping feet.

"What do you want? I've done nothing. Leave me alone," a voice deep and angry shouted back.

"Open the door or we'll put it in."

"You the big, bad wolf?"

"Open the door or I'll huff and puff and all that bollocks," Sharpe snapped.

Nothing. Then more shuffling of heavy feet.

"Put the door in, boys?"

A burly uniform PC swung a heavy metal ram at the door, which crashed inwards under the splintering blow. Rudi was squeezing himself through the window in an effort to escape, but soon discovered the waiting arms of the boys in blue outside.

Sharpe sniggered and leaned out the window as he saw the officers cuff him. "Rudi Gumms, I'm arresting you for robbery. I must caution you, blaa, blaa, blaa, you know the caution better than me. Take him back to Ponty, boys. Book him in for me, I'll follow you later," he turned to Haydn who had followed in behind. "Haydn, we'll have a look around, see if we can find anything from the house in Treorchy."

A search has to be methodical, but Haydn knew that it was best to first stand and peruse the scene and ask the simple question, 'where would I hide stolen gear?' It was only one room, and a sparse one at that. The best investigators tried to put themselves into the shoes of the criminals. But after about half an hour searching, Haydn and Sharpe drew a blank and both sat on the bed.

"Well, Haydn, we've struck out here, mate."

There had to be something incriminating – if indeed Rudi was the man they wanted. Haydn saw a small screwdriver next to a shaing mirror on a glass shelf. stood and stepped over to the washbasin and picked up the plastic shaving mirror. He shook it and it rattled.

"What have we here, Sharpe?" he said.

The mirror had four small screws holding the glass to the frame. Haydn used the screwdriver that could only have been left there for that reason and grinned at what he found within the frame. He dropped the contents onto the bed.

"What's this?" Sharpe said. He picked up a driving license. "Tony Heggerty's driving licence. A credit card in the name of Andy Horgan. A bracelet engraved 'Eira.' A number of rings and a gold watch engraved 'Hound Dog.' I think old

Rudi's up the creek without a paddle. Got to be good for a ten stretch. Bag it up and let's get cracking," he lightly punched Haydn on the shoulder.

Gerwyn Croft, a twenty-year officer promoted to the role of custody sergeant at Pontypridd station four years ago had already authorised Rudi's detention before Sharpe arrived.

Like an old pro, as soon as Rudi entered the cell, he sorted out his blankets, lay on the bed and shut his eyes.

"I don't think he'll give you the time of day," Sergeant Croft said as he slammed the cell door and walked back to join Sharpe.

"Well, I won't lose sleep. I've got the property from the house. He's on licence, so he can stay mute as far as I'm concerned."

"You going to interview him tonight, Sharpie? He doesn't want a brief."

"No, I'll do him in the morning. Then I'll charge him and have a special court Monday. You OK with that?"

"Sounds good to me," Croft said as he made a note. "What's the latest on the bloke he gave a tuning to?"

"Lost his spleen," said Sharpie. "He'll be in hospital for a few weeks."

"What about an ID parade?"

"Sarge, where am I going to get twelve like Rudy Gumms in Pontypridd? Push comes to shove, we'll do the ID on photos."

39.

He checked the rear-view mirror of his Toyota pickup. A plume of dust looked like the Mini Countryman was on fire as it bounced over the unmade lane to the clearing in which Pete Allen had parked his battered Japanese truck. He checked the clock on the dashboard; Stan was nearly an hour late. The sun was already well into the sky and Pete always resented any loss of available light.

The dive had been planned for over a week and there was no excuse for Stan's late arrival. Pete had unzipped his wetsuit and rolled it down to his waist.

The Mini pulled up alongside the Toyota at the edge of the quarry and Stan's stupid grin was hard to resist. "What time do you call this?" Pete shouted through his open window.

"I call it plenty of time," Stan shrugged. "It's a quarry dive not the bloody Maldives," he said.

Pete sighed. Stan was never good at keeping to schedules but this was taking the piss. "Got your kit?"

"Do bears shit in the woods?"

Pete stepped out of his Toyota and walked

to the load area. A single tank fitted with a regulator was strapped down to the floor. He released the latch on the strap and lifted the tank onto his shoulder. He turned to find Stan ready, tank on his wetsuit back, facemask on his head and swim fins in his hand. "Come on," Stan laughed. "I'm always waiting for you."

Pete shook his head. "How do you do that?"

Stan shrugged. "Come on. It's getting on. No time to lose."

"You're unbelievable," Pete mumbled.

The water was as expected; frigid. Pete immersed himself and dunked his head under the water. The sharp cold penetrated his skull, but he knew the pain would ease as the water inside his suit warmed with his body heat. The exertion of the trek down the winding man-made ramp cut into the earth had left him sweating prior to dropping into the azure blue water of the old limestone quarry.

The old workings were still partially intact at the bottom of the deep lake. Pete had dived the quarry twice before with Stan and knew only too well the risks the industrial debris posed to unwary divers. Several had died since the quarry flooded many years before, but the allure of the place was hard to resist on a crisp and clear Saturday morning.

Stan waded out to Pete and both men checked their equipment, pulled on their fins and dropped below the surface of the cold water.

Visibility was no more than five metres but that was exceptionally good for quarry diving. Many quarry pools were full of silt that permanently obscured the view making them even more hazardous to divers.

Stan kicked slowly ahead and down at a shallow angle, the beam from his powerful flashlight illuminated the particles suspended in the water. Both men knew where they were going, they had been there before.

The remains of the limestone quarry buildings soon came into view, at first like ghostly apparitions that became clearer with each gentle kick of their fins. The block structures were still in good condition, the wooden doors had not yet succumbed to decay and inside the small office building the accoutrements of a thriving business could still be seen, left like the Marie Celeste. Coffee mugs, pencils, ballpoint pens, desks and chairs, all left untouched when the company pulled out and the quarry flooded from a natural watercourse that had been continually pumped away during the years of business. Visibility had been better the last time they had explored the place. Something had stirred up the silt and it was getting harder to see the further they descended.

Pete saw Stan turn and point to a small concrete block house that was devoid of windows. No more than eight feet square at the foundations, the walls rose another eight feet or so to a sloping corrugated roof that dipped at a shallow angle to the back. Pete made the 'OK' signal with his thumb and finger and kicked after Stan.

The single steel door on the small building had begun to rust on the hinges and around the padlocks that secured the door at the top, bottom and in the middle of the door. A sign warned 'Caution Explosives.' Two of the locks had been forced from the bolts in the door. Only one remained. Stan had used a jemmy to remove the locks last time they were there. It wouldn't take long to remove the last. He carefully removed the jemmy from his belt and began to force it into the lock.

Pete kept a lookout, not that they expected to see anyone else down there, but it paid to be cautious when the theft of volatile explosives was concerned. The two men knew the value of any kind of explosives on the underground market. If the rumours were true that several kilos of plastic explosives had been simply abandoned in the store, then there was a good pay day ahead. Stan had the connections to fence the stuff through a contact on the island of Jersey. Where the explosives ended up was of no concern to either of the divers.

Pete's dive light swept across the bottom of the quarry. Large boulders, probably weighing in at more than a ton each, littered the bottom. Then the light reflected off something bright and shiny. He swam slowly towards the object which was obscured by three of the large limestone rocks. As he approached, he could see what looked like the wing mirror of a car. He kept swimming until he was on top of a silver BMW that was partially buried in the thick silt. Pete shone the torch into the cabin then froze. He knew he couldn't afford to panic. Panic under water could easily result in a horrible death. He willed his breathing to slow, but his natural reaction and impulse was to swim away from the gruesome sight of the two bodies inside the car.

40.

Images of blue-arsed flies flittered around the inside of Jake Marler's head, he wondered which of the little blighters represented him. All attempts to gather pertinent information on the Lenny Stone murder had been ruthlessly swatted thus far. He was leaving no stone unturned but still getting nowhere fast.

He'd spoken to all his narks and exhausted every avenue of enquiry and had come up blank.

It was a little before eight when a call came through to the CID office. Marler was reading through his notes, looking for anything he might have missed when Gary Bastion, a DC of ten years' service picked up the call. "What can I do for you?"

"Got a good one here for you, Gary," the female Operations Room voice said. "The local boys are up at the Cornelly Quarry. Some local divers have found a vehicle submerged with two bodies in it."

Bastion switched the phone to loudspeaker and covered the mouthpiece out of habit rather than necessity. "Sarge, vehicle in the Cornelly Quarry, better have a listen to this… make and registration?" he asked of the woman on the other end of the line.

"Silver BMW, Registration number ELF111S."

"And the registered owner is...?"

"Tony Heggerty of The Firs in Treorchy."

"Is it still under water or has it been pulled out?"

"Still submerged. There's a diamond T recovery vehicle there as I speak, about to retrieve it. The locals want you up there a bit sharpish."

"And definitely a couple of bodies in it?"

"Yes, without a shadow of a doubt."

"Tell the boys I'm on my way with DS Marler. We'll assess when we get there, but you can call the Force Medical Officer and CSI's as a matter of course."

"Will do."

"Don't like the sound of this, Sarge," Bastion said.

"Me neither, Gary boy. This Heggerty bloke is the Elvis tribute act that never turned up last Sunday night at the Pavilion. Let's hope it's just an accident or some bloody sick suicide pact, we can certainly do without a double murder on top of the Stone enquiry."

"You're a callous bastard, Sarge," Bastion grinned.

**

Within fifteen minutes, Marler and Bastion

arrived at the scene and checked in with the local uniform Inspector, Norman Slater. Slater stood at the rear of a large mobile recovery vehicle equipped with a high-power winch. The inspector smiled at the detectives as they parked the pool car clear of the recovery scene. He watched Marler and Bastion stroll towards him. Slater had also been a detective. He had spent most of his career as a detective but had been promoted back into uniform three years ago and decided he was enjoying the change.

"Morning lads, thanks for being so prompt. We'll have her up in no time, doesn't look good. One male, one female, no idea how long they've been in the water. Looks like another busy day for you, Jake."

"You can say that again, Inspector," Marler frowned. "If it's Heggerty, the Elvis impersonator, I'd say the timeline would be from last Sunday evening until now. He didn't turn up to perform in the Elvis Festival. There were ructions there, apparently, when he failed to appear. He was a big noise in the event... literally," he continued. "Who found the vehicle?"

"Couple of local divers, here most weekends." Slater read a pair of names he had scribbled on the palm of his hand. "Peter Allen and Stan Fraser. They saw the bodies, got the registration number off the plates and called it in."

Marler nodded sagely. "How are they?"

"How are they?" Slater snorted. "Have a

look over the edge, they're down there now, hooking her up to the winch. Must be crackers to dive in the first place, if you ask me."

The winching operation had begun, and the vehicle was pulled at a slow, methodical pace from the deep murky waters on to a narrow ledge of limestone just above the water level.

Marler followed Slater along a narrow path as it switched back several times down to the ledge nearly a hundred feet below. Slater stayed away from the vehicle and let Marler check it out. The divers had already removed their diving gear and had begun the arduous trek back up the narrow path lugging their gear behind them.

The driver's door was unlocked and Marler opened it and stepped back as a gush of brown cloudy water rushed from the interior. Both air bags had been activated, the male driver was strapped in, as was the female passenger. The hand brake was not applied, and the gears were set in neutral and the keys were in the ignition. Marler sighed. This wasn't what he wanted to see. Unless the driver managed to slip the gear into neutral as the car went off the edge, it was quite obvious the vehicle hadn't been deliberately driven off the cliff. "I think we'll leave this one to the FMO and CSI's, Inspector," he said. "I don't want to contaminate anything more than I already have."

The 'cavalry,' in the shape of CJ, Glyn and Marigold, arrived less than thirty minutes later.

Marler watched the three men scramble down the path towards him, laden with boxes and aluminium flight cases essential for their tasks. Marler chuckled as he watched CJ. The Force Medical Officer must have a screw loose, he thought. CJ wore a knee-length, black leather coat, with a multi-coloured scarf that made him look like Doctor Who. His knee-high black leather boots had treads like an off-road motorcycle's and clearly helped him descend far quicker than Glyn and Marigold.

CJ nodded at Marler and waited for Glyn Walcott to catch up with them. Marigold was unsure of his footing and taking far longer to reach the bottom.

Glyn Walcott was approaching retirement and had spent most of his career on the Scenes of Crime unit. What Glyn didn't know wasn't worth knowing. Typical of the breed who gravitated to the unit, Glyn had an 'odd' sense of humour. Nothing was out of bounds for Glyn and political correctness was something that applied to others and not him. Anyone who worked with him would quickly understand that sick jokes were Glyn's way of dealing with the horrors the majority of people would never have to witness, let alone deal with. "Strange place to park a bloody car," he sniggered.

Marler shook his head and grinned. "I opened the door but that's all," Marler assured Glyn.

Glyn nodded. "Always a pleasure to attend a scene where contamination is kept to a minimum. Now let's have a look to see how these poor souls met their maker," he looked at CJ. "Over to you."

CJ looked inside the vehicle and did a cursory examination of the two bodies. "I can tell you they're both dead," he said.

"No shit?" Marler teased.

"Well, that's a cracking start, don't you think?" CJ smiled. "I'm worth every penny of my meagre salary. I'd say they've been in the water about five or six days but will get a better idea when they're on the slab."

"Can you see any injuries for cause of death?"

"Well, apart from the fact that drowning is a cause I can't rule out at present... the bloke's had a bang on the nose, but that could be from the air-bag," he kept inspecting the gruesome finds. "Nothing facially on the woman, however, both have distinct blunt force trauma to the head, and marks on their necks, two little puncture marks. Mmm... if I had to stick my neck out, I'd say some kind of prodding instrument has been used... again, the PM will give us a better idea. I'd get the Home Office Pathologist out if I were you and give old McGuire a bell."

Glyn and Marigold spent over half an hour photographing the bodies in situ then both bodies were carefully removed from the vehicle and laid out on to some sterile body bags where CJ got busy on a more thorough examination.

"Can't see any other injuries, gentlemen," he said. "The quicker we get them to the morgue the quicker we can get to the bottom of it all."

"I'll arrange for the vehicle to be taken to the nick in Porthcawl" Glyn said. "Marigold, you go with it and make sure that it's dried out properly, you know the score. I'll accompany the bodies to the mortuary with CJ. Jake, you give the boss a ring, bring him up to speed, tell him it *may* or *may not* be a double murder."

"No problem, Glyn, I'll get right on it," Jake said.

***

"Boss, Jake Marler here, I'm in the Incident Room, it looks like we may have a possible double murder up at the Cornelly Quarry. Male and female found in a submerged vehicle, the vehicle is registered to a Tony Heggerty, the Elvis impersonator."

"Heggerty? Jake, are you sure?"

"Well, the vehicle's registered to him, boss."

"And the woman, any ID for her?"

"No, not at the minute. The vehicle is being taken into Porthcawl nick and Marigold's going to sort it."

"What about Glyn?"

"He's on his way to the mortuary with CJ."

"Any significant injuries to the bodies?"

"The bloke's got a bang to the nose, may have been caused by the air-bag activating, and they've both got blunt force trauma to the head, and marks to the neck, probably caused by a prodding instrument."

"I'll check that the Home Office Pathologist is on his way out and meet everyone at the mortuary. You crack on in the room there, start the ball rolling."

McGuire ended the call and sat back in his high-back office chair. He stared at a picture on his wall. It was a class photo of thirty or so young new recruits on their passing-out parade nearly thirty years ago. McGuire could see the monochrome image of himself at one end of the assembled group. All the young faces looked serious, smartly dressed and excited as they embarked on their new career. Only six of those thirty had made it through to today. Four had failed to finish their probationary period, several had left of their own accord when they quickly discovered the realities of the job and at least another six had sadly passed away. A thirty-year officer was a rare beast and something to be celebrated. McGuire was rapidly closing on his thirty and knew he had to seriously think about his future. At least now, thanks to his old pal Ed, he had the option of going into business with Raven. He tapped Raven's number into his phone.

***

Raven flipped open his laptop and clicked on the email server to find a message from Terry McGuire.

Tony the Elvis is dead. Found with a woman in his car at the bottom of a local quarry. Give me a ring at your earliest.

Terry.

Shit! Now things had exploded in his face. From a routine missing person enquiry to a brace of deaths. It could be a simple case of Tony or Eira driving off the edge or perhaps something like an argument that went wrong. Whatever it was, it was now the end of Raven's involvement and he had hoped the case would have kept him employed a little longer. He needed the fee.

Raven also needed a drink. A single can of best bitter sat on a shelf in what was an empty fridge apart from a half bottle of milk, a small piece of cheese and two chilled ready meals. He decided to leave the beer.

He poured a coffee and carried it back into the bedroom. Sue hadn't looked up from her soap opera.

The coffee was good, and he sipped half before his phone began to ring. It was McGuire.

"I was just about to call you," Raven said.

"Had to speak to you. Did you get my email?"

"Yes."

"We have two bodies in a car registered to Tony Heggarty but don't have identification on either yet. I'd put money on it that it's Tony though. Both victims have been beaten by a heavy object and both were dead before they hit the water. The PM is clear that they were dead before they entered the water."

"Shit!"

"You can say that again. We think we have a suspect, but I can't say anymore at present. I'll update you as soon as I can."

"I'd appreciate that."

"Sorry to put an end to your job."

"Have you found Eira's car?"

"No, we haven't," McGuire paused a beat. "Raven, you've got to give me everything on this and I mean *everything*, every last detail. What's your take on it?"

"The only connection is that Rudi bloke. The big black guy who put Kenny, Tony's mate, in the hospital."

"Oh aye, the one young Sharpe dealt with?"

"Aye, that's the one. Apart from that, just a dead end. I thought Tony and Eira had just gone off for a bit of rumpy-pumpy."

"I need them identified. Who'd be best for that?"

"Eira's parents have got a puppy farm in Cwmtwrch and, as for Tony, try Dafydd the bloke from the Pavilion."

"OK, so it looks like Rudi is top of the list of suspects. I'll ring Sharpie before I go to the mortuary and I want you at the briefing tonight at eight. You can give the team everything you've told me and anything else you think of."

Raven took another gulp of coffee. "It's alright. I've got something I promised myself I'd clear up. Seems now is as good a time as any. See you at eight."

41.

"You know why you've been arrested. I've got to tell you that your dabs are all over the house you broke into, so what's the story? This wasn't random. Who put you up to it?"

Gumms sat back, linked his hands behind his head and glared at Sharpe - a clear 'fuck you' expression on his face.

"So, what's it going to be, Rudi, the sound of silence and perhaps the odd no comment or are you going to tell me what's going on?"

Rudi Gumms leaned his big frame forward; the table affixed to the concrete floor shuddered as his meaty arms thumped down. "I've been in the house before, so those prints don't mean jack shit," he glowered at Sharpe.

Sharpe snorted. "Never?" he said with a disbelieving tone. "And when was this, Rudi?"

"Couple of weeks or so. Tony had a party there. I went with my boss."

"And who is your boss, prey tell?"

"Why should I tell you? Seem like you've got a lot to prove that I have anything to do with this."

"Well, if your boss can vouch for you that

you had access to the house that would make things a lot easier for you. Give us his name and I'll go and check and who knows you may be off and running."

Rudi hooted. "Fuck you, you prove it, all you've got is a few prints by the sounds of it."

Sharpe frowned. He knew Rudi was right but also knew Rudi was lying. "When you visited the house, you must have been upstairs, downstairs, and in the lady's chamber. Your dabs are everywhere, even on the oven, can you explain that?"

He smiled. "No comment."

"Oh, here we go, touched a nerve, have I? What if I say I believe you, and your employer does substantiate your explanation, how do you explain the property we found in your room when we arrested you?"

He shook his head. "No comment"

"Don't you want to know what property we found, Rudi?"

"No comment."

"Do you want me to show you, Rudi?"

"No comment"

Sharpe retrieved the property bag from an envelope on the floor next to his chair and tipped it onto the table.

"There it is, Rudi, in all its glory. How do you explain that?"

"You've planted that to make your case. You're all fucking bent," he snarled.

"Now why would we fit you up, Rudi? I've never even heard of you until this. And, of course, there's the small matter of the bloke you nearly killed, he's fighting for his life after complications. Have a think on that."

"No comment."

"It seems Tony Heggerty owed money and you were on a mission to get it back. But I don't think it was you he owed. I think it was your boss because, let's be fair, you aren't the sharpest tool in the box, are you?"

Rudi snarled. "Fuck you. No comment."

"Just to let you know, the bloke's not going to snuff it, he was just in the wrong place at the wrong time."

"Do I give a fuck? I don't think so."

"So, this is how it's going to go, Rudi. I'll be charging you later with the full dram... Robbery, GBH, the whole shooting match. You're on licence, so bye bye, I reckon, for a long time."

"Fuck you."

"Whatever, Rudi. Just get your head down. I'll charge you later and you can have a special court all to yourself on Monday morning. If, in the meantime, you want a chat, just ask for me."

***

McGuire gave the Pontypridd CID office a call.

"Get young Sharpe to the phone, please."

It was less than three minutes before

Sharpe picked up. "DC Sharpe, what can I do for you, boss?"

McGuire asked Sharpe for an update.

"All sorted boss, I've charged a guy buy the name of Rudy Gumms with robbery and assault," Sharpe said. "He's banged up for special court."

"Any property recovered?"

"Yes, some cash, rings, and a woman's bracelet engraved with the name 'Eira.' I reckon they're from the house. Just waiting for Heggerty to turn up and positively ID them"

"I think you'll have a long wait, Sharpey. Tony and Eira have just been fished out of a local quarry. We haven't a positive ID yet, but it looks like it's them."

Sharpe whistled. "Do you think Rudi's responsible, boss?"

"Well, he's all we've got at the minute. Keep this under your hat, don't speak with him again. I'll send a couple from my team up later as soon as we have a positive ID on the victims. That should be later on this afternoon."

"I understand, boss. Mum's the word."

It was midday when McGuire arrived at the morgue. He'd already made the arrangement for formal ID and picked up Bryn, his second in command.

The band was all there, including Selina Hamilton the pathologist who had already made a start on Tony. Her assistant was in the process of prepping Eira.

Selina lifted her visor.

"Ah, Detective Superintendent McGuire, right on cue."

McGuire introduced DCI Bryn Rowlands. "He'll be the Senior Investigating Officer on this one," he explained.

Selina smiled, flicked her visor back down and carried on with the post-mortem."

McGuire spotted CJ across the other side of the mortuary and walked past the lifeless remains of Tony without looking at Selina's handiwork.

"What you think, CJ? Have you got a rough idea as to cause of death?"

"Probably drowning, Terry."

Selina looked up, flicked her visor up from her face. "One down, one to go. I suppose you want some answers?"

"Yes please."

"Cause of death is drowning, but with a rider. I believe the marks on the neck are probably from something with a double prong. I've seen them before from a stun gun. Tony here has also got an injury to his nose, nothing serious though and I would say he sustained that before entering the water. He's also got a large contusion on the side of his head, under his hair. That's from a heavy blow. It didn't fracture the skull but would have hurt. So, in my opinion, he was alive when he entered the water. But I think he was probably unconscious. He then drowned."

"What about the woman, any sign of assault on her?"

"I've had a cursory examination. The same marks on her neck, and blunt force trauma. Give me an hour and I'll have all the answers for you. Are you going to stay?"

"No, I'll leave you in the capable hands of Glyn and CJ. Bryn and I will make our way back to the Incident Room. Conference at eight. We'll be able to formerly ID them a bit later on and then we can put out an urgent press release."

42.

The theme music for Eastenders was the regular cue for Raven to head to his bedroom.

Sue sat quietly, transfixed to the television, ready for her dose of the popular soap that Raven despised. As much as Raven loved to see his sister happy, that didn't mean Raven had to sit through it.

He was bothered by the file he had found in his new office. The McGuire mentioned within it was Terry's father and now he didn't know whether to tell his new boss or not. Perhaps he'd leave it a while and make some enquiries beforehand. The last thing he wanted to do was upset the man bankrolling his business.

The Harland woman had bothered Raven too. It was clear he'd been duped into giving Collins – the Grand Hotel manager – a good hiding for reasons over and above the despicable treatment of his staff and the illegal recording of hotel guests in the act of sex. Why would Collins record the guests anyway? Was it just because he was a sick pervert or was there another motive? And, if so, what could that be, and how did Mrs Harland get involved with the girls at the hotel.

It didn't make sense. He wanted to drive down to the Gower and force her to tell him.

He remembered the disc he had taken from the recorder in his room at the hotel.

The disc was in his overnight bag. The bag was in his wardrobe. He dropped the bag on his bed and tipped the contents onto the duvet. He needed to wash the clothes he had used at the hotel anyway. The disc was amongst his dirty socks and underwear.

He slipped the disc into the computer DVD slot and waited for it to load. It flashed onto the screen at the start of the recording.

Raven checked the date – 31st of Dec' 2019. The first recording was nine months ago. That meant he couldn't have recorded many guests on the disc. Perhaps he had a method to the madness? It was clear that Collins was using the same disc to record the 'events' until it was full, but this disc still had forty percent capacity left.

He pressed play and watched as the first thirty minutes of the first recording showed an empty room. Then, just after the thirty-minute marker, a young couple entered the room. Both in their mid-twenties, Raven fast-forwarded the video through the action Collins had obviously wanted to record.

The second clip started the same way. Raven guessed Collins had started the recording each time when the guests were booking in at reception. This time, two men entered the room and Raven recognised them. It was the same face he had seen on the posters at the Elvis Festival. It was Tony the Hound Dog Heggerty and a man Raven had met just a few days ago.

***

Sue had gone to bed by the time Terry McGuire knocked on Raven's door.

Raven had rung his new friend to tell him about the contents of the disc and McGuire told him he'd call down straight away.

"Can't offer you a drink, I'm afraid," Raven said as he let McGuire in.

"No problem. Let's see the disc."

Raven had paused the disc at the point where he had seen the two men engaged in an act that proved Tony was clearly fond of men as well as women.

"Bloody hell," McGuire said. "Any idea who the other guy is?"

"It's the manager of the Seaview Hotel in Porthcawl, the place where Tony stays each time the festival is on."

"OK. Let me have the disc and I'll show it to my team. We need to get this manager in tout suite."

Raven nodded. Pressed eject, and handed the disc to McGuire. "Is this a spurned lover case?"

McGuire shrugged. "Who knows. Could be. All I know is we need to get this fella in for questioning… quickly… and I need you to come in and brief my team. We need to know everything you know."

Raven checked his watch. "I'll be there at eight."

43.

They were now dealing with a triple murder enquiry, Lenny Stone, Tony Heggerty and Eira Pritchard and McGuire had called the team of detectives together for a briefing.

The Incident Room was a large space on the first floor of the station. Cream colour vertical blinds diffused light from windows on one wall. A large glass, portable scribble board stood on castors at the front of the room. The board was a new addition to the room with a built in LED system that cast light up through the screen to illuminate the coloured marker pens. Photos of the victim and suspect – Rudi Gumms – were affixed to the glass and were linked by coloured pen lines.

"OK team, things have taken a turn for the worse. This morning the bodies of Tony Heggerty and Eira Pritchard were recovered from the waters of the Cornelly Quarry. They were murdered. This, coupled with the murder of Lenny Stone, casts a different light on the enquiry. Is there a connection? I think the best way forward is to re-evaluate everything we have, anything and everything we know, and I hope this will help us to better understand what we don't know," he paused and glanced at Raven who was sitting in McGuire's office. Several detectives had seen Raven when he arrived, clearly wondering what he was doing there. "So, I've taken the un-precedented step of asking Raven Connor, who some of you know, to divulge what *he knows* about Tony and Eira. I'll ask Raven to speak at the end, he won't be present for the main body of the briefing."

McGuire nodded at Marler in the front row. "OK, we'll start with Jake. What have you got Jake?"

Marler stood and turned to face the others. "Well, as far as the Stone murder goes, boss, we're no further on than when he was found. Certainly looks like a robbery. We know he was homosex-ual and a drug user and pretty much a loner. Whether or not his demise is connected with today's events is anyone's guess.

"As for Tony, I've checked all ANPR records and can put Tony's vehicle travelling towards Cornelly past the Porthcawl cemetery at seven p.m. last Sunday night. As you can imagine, there'd be hundreds of cars using the road at that time. There are no other sightings. I'm pretty sure now that the car was being driven to the quarry." Marler sat and watched CJ stand.

"CJ, what have you got for us?" McGuire asked.

"Cause of death for both Tony and Eira was

definitely drowning and there's no doubt they were alive when they hit the water. Both had marks to the neck. The pathologist believes they were caused by a stun gun. Tony and Eira had injuries to the head and nose, both were ante mortem, suggesting they had been in some sort of altercation prior to death."

"Any sign of sexual assault or drug use, CJ"

CJ shrugged his shoulders. "We're waiting for tox at the minute. There's no doubt that Eira had been sexually active before her demise, however, if push comes to shove, I'd say at this time that it was probably consensual."

"With Tony?"

"Highly likely. No bruising or anything that suggests otherwise, and her underclothing was intact."

McGuire nodded and look at Glyn. "Please tell me you've got something?"

Glyn remained seated. "Not a lot at the moment, boss. The scene has been examined thoroughly, I've got the car drying out, the inside is totally saturated. All samples have been taken to the lab for fast-tracking, so hopefully we'll have something more positive tomorrow. There are a couple of anomalies though. There was no property on the bodies, which I find very strange. Suggests to me it could be a robbery. I can't think of any other motive, considering the facts."

"I agree, Glyn, but I think they knew their killer."

"What makes you think that, boss?" Marler enquired.

"Too much of a coincidence for a killer to just happen to be at the quarry when Tony and Eira arrived. The killer must have followed them or known they would be there?"

Marler didn't look convinced.

"OK, now I know Raven's been trying to trace Tony and Eira for a week, he's probably done a fair bit of leg work for us. At the moment, our number one suspect is actually in custody up at Pontypridd. He's a face called Rudi Gumms, he's been charged with robbery. He was in possession of property from Tony's house. One of the items is a bracelet engraved *Eira*. Julia, you and Kirsty get up to Ponty and nick him on suspicion and bed him down at the Bridewell for the night. Duggan, you go with them. You can keep the twat company in the back of the car and you can have a crack at him in the morning. He's a tough cookie, so make sure he's trussed up like a turkey. After Raven's given his input, I'll call a press conference and hopefully we'll get some information tomorrow. As you all know, Tony was a popular bloke in the town and a press conference might well throw up some additional leads."

McGuire stepped out into the corridor and shouted. "Raven, your audience awaits."

Raven appeared and strolled into the Incident Room.

"Ladies and gents, for those of you who don't know him, this is the infamous private eye, Raven Connor," McGuire grinned. "Like I said earlier, he's been trying to trace Tony and Eira and I've no doubt he'll be able to fill in a few blanks."

Raven stood awkwardly at the front of the assembled detectives. "I realise I'm not one of you, but I hope you'll understand that I have a job to do? Mr McGuire knows I've been employed to find Tony and Eira, but I was also involved in another case a few days ago where I was employed on a matrimonial job, the usual stuff, following a suspected cheating husband."

"Sounds interesting," Marler smiled.

Raven returned the smile. "In more ways than you can imagine." He described the events at the Grand Hotel, including the illicit video recordings and watched the wide-mouthed expressions of the detectives as he did so.

"In one of the recordings, Tony, one of the victims of the quarry find, was caught in a... shall we say... compromising position with a man who is the manager of the Seaview Hotel in Porthcawl." The detectives began murmuring amongst themselves. "So, it looks like Tony was fond of women and men."

"This puts a different slant on things," Jake Marler said.

Raven nodded. "I think so."

"It means that someone might well have

been blackmailing Tony, and possibly the manager. If this is the case, then perhaps this bloke called Rudi is not our man?" Marler added.

"That's true," McGuire said, "but we have to check out Rudi Gunn before we rule him out and start looking elsewhere," he turned to Raven. "Who do you think is behind the videos at the hotel?"

"I thought it might be the manager of the Grand but I'm not so sure anymore..."

"Why?"

"Because I suspect someone else is the brains behind it."

"Any ideas?"

Raven sucked air through his teeth as he thought. "I think the woman, Mrs Harland, who hired me in the first instance to check out her husband might be hiding something. Things are not as straight forward as I first thought they might be."

44.

Thirty-minute breaks were a luxury for Raymond Stroud, even though he was entitled to the time from his duties, his duties rarely permitted him to take his full allocation of 'downtime.' At fifty-three he was getting too old for caring for others. The job was hard enough as it was, but his own recent health scare hadn't helped. The minor stroke had come without warning. He had never smoked and had always kept himself fit but six months ago he had been struck down by something he had always dreaded. Strokes were in his genes, he had always known that. Stroud's father had died from a stroke and his mother had spent the last five years of her life struggling with the aftereffects of her own. Life was just unfair. Stroud had dedicated his life to others but that didn't make any difference to the genetic time bomb that had triggered as he took his early morning jog. At least he had recovered well, almost a hundred percent and he was back in work, so perhaps the lifestyle had been worth the effort in retrospect.

The staffroom was quiet, as it usually was. He couldn't remember the last time he had been able to take his break with any of the other staff but at least the kettle was all his for the duration of his break and so was the microwave. Six minutes for a beef stew.

The high note of the microwave 'ping' demanded his attention from the early evening television news, but Stroud's eyes were fixed to the screen. It was rare to see news of events in Wales but the recent murder at the Elvis Festival in some South Wales coastal resort had probably captured the imagination of the syndicating editors. Now Stroud too was captured by the police appeal playing out before him.

***

"Got a call from someone in a rehabilitation centre in Oxfordshire, boss," Marler announced as Bryn Rowlands carried his fourth mug of coffee past the line of desks manned to answer calls from the public. The Incident Room had been set up to take the calls after the public appeal for information had been broadcast thirty minutes earlier.

"Rowlands stopped and placed his mug on the desk. He lifted the incident log and read the notes. He nodded. "Get someone to call him back and make arrangements for two of our team to pay a visit as soon as possible."

"Yes, sir."

***

Jake Marler had volunteered for the three-hour trip to Oxfordshire. Marler drove whilst Bryn spent the first thirty minutes of the journey reading through everything they had on the case, which was more speculation than fact and nothing near evidence. Bryn had initially thought about getting someone from the Thames Valley Police to pop over to take a statement but that was always asking for trouble. It was vital that whoever took the statement knew everything about the case. Anything missed at this stage could jeopardise the case further down the line.

The village of Swerton was off the beaten track, even the sat nav had trouble pinpointing the place.

Marler turned off the main road and onto a country lane that was no bigger than the width of a small truck. Uneven and rutted in parts, the lane made a sharp right, but Bryn spotted a sign affixed by nails to a tree and pointed down an even narrower and rougher lane. The pool car bumped along the track, down past a small lake and then rose to the left towards a large house set in trees.

"Certainly secluded," Bryn said.

"Never know it was here," Marler agreed as he pulled the car to a stop between the house and a small stable block.

A grey-haired man smiled as he stepped out of the main entrance to the house. Marler noticed he had a slight limp and his left arm seemed to be out of synch with the rest of his move-ments.

"I'm Ray Stroud. I called you," the man said. There was nothing wrong with his speech but Marler guessed he'd had a stroke at some time in the past. Marler had seen it before. It was in his own genes.

"I'm DS Jake Marler and this is DCI Bryn Rowlands."

They followed Stroud inside the grand house and along a corridor to a room with a sign for 'Staff Only.'

"Tea, gents? You must be parched."

"White, no sugar," Bryn smiled.

"Same for me," said Marler.

The detectives sat as Stroud popped two Tetley bags into mugs and soaked them with hot water from a small table-top boiler.

"Nice place, but not exactly easy to find."

Stroud grinned. "Not meant to be. It's all about seclusion, taking our clients away from the bustle of life and giving them time to find themselves."

"Are you the manager or owner?"

Stroud laughed. "God no. I wish. I'm just a therapist. I spend most of my time just listen-ing."

"And you have a lot of... clients?" Bryn said.

"Twenty-three at the minute. Fourteen outpatients and nine residents."

Marler sipped his tea and then spoke. "So how do you know Kenny?"

"Kenny was here as a resident a couple of years ago."

"And you remember him?" Bryn asked.

"I do," Stroud said as he sat opposite them on a low armless chair. "I was a client mentor at the time, someone who had gone through what some of the patients had experienced and had time to listen. I was a volunteer then but was offered a full-time job here just before Kenny left us."

Bryn placed his mug on a low table between the two rows of low chairs. "And what was your impression of Kenny?"

Stroud shifted on his chair. "This is awkward for me, but I've had clearance off my line manager to tell you what I know. We operate a confidential service here, but I'm not bound by that because at the time I was just a volunteer and what Kenny told me was thought to be... well... let's say... bluster."

"Bluster?" Bryn said.

"Yes. You know, we often get people with deep seated troubles, often caused by experiences that have scarred them and Kenny was one of those. But it was his way of describing things that I just thought was bluster... bravado, you know? Talk of revenge?"

Marler set his mug down and leaned forward. "Revenge?"

"Kenny was pretty messed up. He was reluctant to say anything at first but, after talking to him over several days he finally opened up and began to say things that I thought was just bullshit."

"So you keep saying, but we need to know what he said," Marler said.

Stroud nodded. "I'm sorry. Kenny told me that things had become awkward between him and his wife. They started to row and things became nasty."

"Violent?"

Stroud shrugged. "Not sure but he said it started after she confessed that before she met up with Kenny she had been having an affair with one of his close friends from Wales."

Bryn sat forward in his chair. "Who?"

Taking a small notebook from the table, Stroud opened it to a page he had dog-eared and read the name. "A bloke called Tony Heggarty."

45.

Most ordinary, law-abiding people think that criminals are the low life of society. They saw the results of the crimes committed but rarely understood the minds behind those crimes. After twenty-odd years, Julia understood them and had already brought herself up to speed with everything that was known about the murders. Experience had taught her that when interviewing hardened criminals for any serious crime she had to be on top of her game. The majority of villains were sharp as ticks, and they could smell bullshit.

"What do you make of this Rudi Gumms then, Kirsty? What did he say when you arrested him for the murders?"

"Not a lot, boss, just stayed crashed out on the cell bed, didn't really give a monkey's, it seemed. Hardly spoke a word at all on the way back to the Bridewell. I think we're going to have a job with him."

"What did he say when you told him the victim was Tony?"

She shrugged. "Didn't faze him at all. He's an arrogant bastard, boss."

"Does he have a brief?"

"No, seems dead cocky, boss. Knows he's going down for the robbery but seems to be accepting it."

"OK, get him into the interview room and we'll have a crack at him."

***

"I won't beat about the bush," Julia said. "You've been arrested on suspicion of the murders of Tony Heggerty and Eira Pritchard, what have you got say about it? Remember, for the tape, you're still under caution."

Rudi Gumms made a sucking sound through his teeth as his eyes wandered slowly around the small interview room. No windows, just a recessed strip light behind a wire grill. The light was bright and reflected off the gloss white paint covering the four walls. "Look man," he finally said. "I haven't killed any fucker, especially not that ponce, Heggerty. What would I want to kill him for?"

"You tell me, Rudi," Julia said as she folded her arms across her chest and stared at the big man.

"If I had anything to worry about, I'd want a brief. I'm going to pull a fair bit of bird for the robbery, but murder? Do me a fucking favour. Tony Heggarty owed us big time, did you know that?"

"Us?"

Rudi shrugged his big shoulders and turned his head away.

"Who do you mean by 'us?'"

Rudi smiled but kept his head turned away.

"OK. First things first. Can you tell us where you were...say...between midday on Friday and midday on Saturday?"

The big man turned his head back to face Julia. "Is that when they were topped?"

"Just answer the question, Rudi. It could help you in the long run."

Rudi leaned back in his chair and cupped his hands behind his head. He laughed loudly, an exaggerated, mirthless laugh.

"Not a problem, man. I was with a woman, a white woman to be precise. She'll vouch for me. I've been with her all week. Her old man's away," he grinned. "Do I have to paint a picture?"

"Not that old chestnut, Rudi? Just give us her name and address, if it's not too much trouble?" Julia matched Rudi's grin.

"Harland. Geraldine Harland, She's got a big house down on the Gower. Everybody knows the Harlands."

"And she'll alibi you?"

"Without a shadow of a doubt."

Julia stifled a frustrated sigh. If the Harland woman confirmed Rudi was with her then they were back to square one.

"Let's get back to Tony Heggerty. What can you tell us about him?"

Rudi snorted. "A fucking ponce, no, not just a fucking ponce, a fucking ponce with a few nasty and expensive habits."

"Tell us more, Rudi?"

"Well, he puts on this show of having it all, but he owes a fair old wedge, but you must know that, eh?"

"He owes you, then?"

"Not me. It's my boss. Tony owes him about thirty 'K'. He gambles and, with his coke habit, I'm not surprised some fucker topped him."

"And who's your boss?"

"Well that's a bit tricky because I'm giving his Mrs one. He's away on business at the minute."

"So, I take it Mr Harland calls the shots, but not in the marital bed?"

Rudi sniggered.

"So, what's he into?"

"All sorts."

"Like what?"

"He's a bookie, got his fingers in loads of pies."

"This business up at Tony's house, what was that all about?"

"Just wanted some cash off him, but he wasn't there. So, I gave that other bloke a few slaps. He was a cheeky twat and wound me up."

"A few slaps? The poor bloke is still in hospital. He'll be there for a while by the look of things."

"Do I give a toss? Shouldn't have got in the way. Should have just let me get on with my business."

Julia unscrewed the top off a plastic water bottle and took a swig. "Did you ever meet Eira Pritchard?"

"Who?"

"Eira Pritchard. The other victim found with Tony."

"No, never met her in my life. Why would I want to kill some piece I'd never even met?"

"Well, amongst the property you stole from Tony's house was a bracelet with her name engraved on it."

"So? Means nothing to me. I'd have just flogged it. Anyway, what's he doing with a bird?"

"What do you mean?"

"He was gay."

"Enlighten us, Rudi."

"He never flaunted it, never tell from looking at him, but he was gay. Kept it in the closet, but I knew everything about him, knew who his dealer was, the whole nine yards."

"His dealer?"

Rudi grinned. "You seriously expect me to grass?"

"Worth a try," Julia grinned back. "When did you speak to Tony last?"

"In the week, just put the squeeze on him. My boss wanted his money, pronto like. Tony didn't come through, thought he'd done a runner. That's why I paid him a visit. Thought he was lying low, the little scrote."

"Oh, he was lying low, Rudi. At the bottom of the Cornelly Quarry."

"No chance of getting the cash then," he smiled. "My boss better start talking to the receivers. What do you reckon?"

"You're full of heart, Rudi. I just hope your alibi comes through."

"She will, no sweat."

"It would appear you know a great deal about Tony, so if you didn't do the business, who did?"

"Could be anyone. Like I said, he was into drugs and the gay scene. Take your pick."

"I notice you haven't asked how Tony and Eira were killed Rudi?"

"Means fuck all to me how they died. All I know is that I didn't kill them."

"This dealer you mentioned, if you tell me who it is it'll help your case."

"You're having a fucking laugh, aren't you? Go fuck yourself."

"As I said, it would help your cause if you were forthcoming."

"I don't think so. Look, I've said enough as it is. I'm screwed, end of, man. So just take me back to the cells."

"Just a few more questions. The bloke you beat up at Tony's, had you ever seen him before?"

"No. Thought he was one of Tony's bits of

stuff, you know what I mean?" he winked.

"Did he know where Tony was?"

"Don't think so."

"Well, Rudi, we'll check with Mrs Harland and if she confirms you spent the week with her, looks like you'll be in the clear. Do you want me to be discreet, bearing in mind her husband is your boss, or shall I confide in him?"

"Do your worst, I don't give a toss."

46.

He had drawn the short straw. Chris Duggan's task for the day was to break the bad news to Kenny that his closest friend was dead.

The High Dependency Unit at the hospital had confirmed that Kenny was fit to be spoken to. He'd sustained a hell of a beating at the hands of Gumms, and at one time his injuries were life-threatening. He was lucky to be alive.

The on-duty staff nurse greeted Duggan and warned him that Kenny was still seriously ill and that he would only be allowed a few minutes with him.

Ushered into a side room where Kenny was wired up like something from the Matrix. Duggan pulled up a chair and sat beside Kenny. Kenny managed to nod acknowledgement.

"He did a job on you, didn't he?"

"I hope you've got him?"

"He's been charged and is in custody. He'll be off the streets for a few years, have no worries about that. His name is Gumms, Rudi Gumms. Do you know him?"

"No. The man's an animal. I thought he was going to kill me. He was after Tony. Thank God he wasn't there. Is there any news? Has Raven found him and Eira?"

"Well, that's why I'm here, Kenny. I've some bad news."

"What's happened?"

"I'm afraid both Tony and Eira are dead. We believe they've been murdered."

"Murdered? Did this Gumms do it?"

"That's what we're trying to find out."

"How did it happen?"

"His car was found submerged in the quarry at Cornelly. It appears that Tony and Eira drowned. But we're treating it as murder."

"If they drowned, why is it murder? Perhaps it was an accident?"

"No, Kenny, we've ruled that out. They were murdered."

Kenny's bottom lip began to tremble, and a single tear trickled down his left cheek. "Find the bastard, please. Tony was like a brother to me."

"When did you see Tony last?"

Kenny groaned as he lifted a bruised hand to wipe away the solitary tear. "Sunday evening... in the hotel. He went off with Eira in his car."

"Where were they going?"

"I've no idea."

"How did they seem at the time?"

"Well, I know things weren't right. I'd never met Eira before. She was in a bit of a rip with Tony. She wasn't happy."

"What did you do after they left?

"I went to the Hi Tide for the finale, where Tony was supposed perform later. But Tony never turned up."

"What did you think of that?"

"I knew it wasn't right and the fans were disappointed."

"Is that why you got Raven Connor involved?"

"Yes. Davey and I reported it to you lot on the night. The copper on the phone said he was a grown man and that was it. Nothing the police could do. I knew there was something wrong. I just knew it."

"Tell me about Tony. What sort of bloke was he?"

"Like a brother, he was. I hadn't seen him for years until last week, but it was like we'd never been apart."

"So how did you drift apart, Kenny? I understand you grew up together."

"We were in care together, but we went our separate ways. Tony became famous, and I became a drunk and drop-out. I went off to the smoke, did a bit of singing in the clubs and worked on building sites."

"So, you came together last week? Frst time for years?"

"Yes. I've lost my wife. So I came down looking for Tony. I haven't got a pot to piss in."

"Sorry. But in the few days you were with

him, did you hear anyone threaten him or anything?"

"Only that German, Fritz Mueller. Him and Tony had a bust up at a press conference. But that was all smoothed over."

"Anyone else?"

"Well, not threatening, as such, more of a nuisance, I think. I think his name was Larry, a proper Elvis lookalike in a blue suit."

"Did Tony spend any time with this Larry?"

"No, but he said he'd meet him down on the pier. I didn't take a lot of notice. Don't know whether he did or not. It wasn't my business."

"When was this, Kenny?"

"Friday, at the press conference."

Duggan circled his notes. This new information might well solve the death of Larry. It was a lead, and that was more than they had before.

"What about Gumms, had you seen Tony in his company at all?"

"No, never. He just broke into the house. He's a fucking animal. I wouldn't be at all surprised if he killed Tony and the girl."

"But why? If he'd killed them, why would he come looking for Tony?"

"Who knows why? Look, I'm tired, officer. Can we speak again tomorrow?"

Duggan smiled and nodded. Kenny was looking exhausted. He'd had a real outing at the end of Gumm's fists and boots. "Not a problem,

Kenny. Any idea how long you'll be in hospital? I'll come to see you at home if you'd prefer?"

"Who knows how long I'll be here. They've done a load of tests and I think there's something they're not telling me. Before you go, can you do me a favour? Can you get that private detective to pop in? I'd like to thank him for what he's done."

"Not a problem, Kenny. I'll pop by tomorrow and take a full statement off you about the robbery and some more background on Tony. You OK with that?"

"Yes."

***

Colin Boulton was staring at the timeline on the board in the Incident Room when Duggan entered.

"How did it go, Chris?"

"He's in a right mess, boss. Gumms did a job on him. He'll be in for a while, I reckon."

"Write it up then, Chris, and action out anything you think relevant."

"Yes, boss."

***

Sue was watching Eastenders again, but this time on catch-up. Raven had taken her to the local hospital to have pre-op checks. Now all they had to do was wait for the date of the long-awaited procedure. Both had been surprisingly upbeat, apart from the fact the tests ran on longer than anticipated and Sue missed her regular dose of the soap opera. "Thank God for catch-up" she had said upon return to the flat. "Yes, thank God for that," Raven said with less enthusiasm.

The small items of furniture had already been boxed up in preparation for the move to Ed's house. Only the big items were left for comfort and, of course, the television would be the last thing to go.

The call to Raven's phone was a welcome relief for him. The number displayed was unknown, but he answered anyway.

"It's Chris Duggan from the CID. I've been in to see Kenny today and he's asked to speak with you. I think he wants to thank you for what you've done."

"Oh? That's not a problem. I'll pop in tomorrow. Has the enquiry moved on any further?"

"Not really, Raven. It's a bag of worms."

"Can't argue with that. There's more to this than meets the eye. Thanks for letting me know."

47.

The battered Vauxhall engine sounded as if a cylinder had given up the ghost and the oil light kept flashing intermittently as Caroline and Bryn headed down to the Gower. McGuire had told them to corroborate Gumm's alibi – or otherwise – but Bryn wasn't sure the car would get them there. He nursed the car through the gears and made an unspoken promise to the car that he'd book it in to the workshop immediately upon return – as long as it got them there and back. It was a deal.

"What do you make of it all, boss, do you think it's him?"

"Well, for a bloke who's looking at a fair stretch for the robbery, he doesn't seem all that worried. He's taking it on the chin, no brief, nothing at all. As for the murder? If he's right about this Harland woman giving him an alibi, I can't see it being him, to be honest."

"I agree. Why go looking for Tony if he'd already topped him? And why kill Eira? What's that all about?"

"Things don't add up, and then there's Lenny Stone. Is it the same killer? If so, what's the connection between all three victims?"

"Raven's done some work for this Harland woman," Kirsty said. "What's her role in all this?"

"We'll soon find out..." the car missed a beat and Bryn swore under his breath before continuing. "...who knows? Harland and her old man are worth a few shillings, by all accounts. Fingers in lots of pies."

Bryn sighed with relief as the car finally reached the destination. He whistled when he saw the size of the property. "We're in the wrong bloody job."

They were greeted at the front door by Geraldine Harland.

Bryn and Caroline produced their warrant cards and showed them to the woman.

"I'm Detective Chief Inspector Bryn Rowlands and this is my colleague DC Caroline Williams, we need to have a word with you and your husband."

"What's this all about?"

"May we come in? I'll explain everything."

"Of course, but my husband isn't here at the moment. He's away on business and won't be back until mid-week."

They followed her into the lounge and this time Caroline whistled. "Nice place. Love your taste," she said.

"Thank you. Sit down. Can I get you anything, tea, coffee, perhaps something stronger?"

"No thanks, shall we just get on with it?"

Bryn said.

"By all means. Fire away."

"Mrs Harland, we are at present investigating the double murder of a man by the name of Tony Heggarty and a woman named Eira Rowlands. Do you know either of them?"

Harland sat on the arm of a white leather settee that looked like a quality piece of furniture. "I heard about this. What's it to do with my husband and I?"

"Did you know either of the victims?"

"Yes. We did business with Tony, but I've never heard of the woman."

"What sort of business are you and Mr Harland in, exactly?"

"We've many businesses. Bookmaking, IT, a casino, we're very diverse."

"So, what's the connection with Tony?"

"You probably know this already. Tony was a big gambler. He owed us a lot of money."

"How much all told?"

"I reckon... over thirty-grand."

"That's a lot of debt to run up. Seems you've lost that money now."

"Chief Inspector, that's the name of the game. Tony was regular as clockwork with his debt, up until a couple of months ago. Then he started ducking and diving. My husband and I spoke to him on a few occasions about payment, but he just kept bullshitting."

Caroline said, "What, did you do about it?"

"Nothing, really. We knew we'd get the money eventually, one way or another."

"One way or another?"

"Just a turn of phrase."

"Do you know a Rudi Gumms?" Bryn asked.

"Yes, he works for us."

"In what capacity?"

"Have you met Rudi? He's built like a brick shithouse. Can you guess why we employ him? We deal with some right toe rags, he's our collector of debts, but it's his size we employ him for. We insist that no one is ever hurt."

"At present, he's in custody. He's been arrested on suspicion of killing Tony and Eira. When did you see him last?"

Geraldine took a sharp intake of breath. "No that can't be. I know he's a bit handy, but murder? I don't think so."

"So, when did you see him last?"

"Last Thursday morning, he was around here."

"Of course, he's denying the murders, and he's put you forward as his alibi."

"Alibi? How can I give him an alibi?"

"Did you have any idea that he was in custody?"

"No, I didn't."

"Have you been having a relationship with Rudi?"

Geraldine face flushed red and took another sharp breath.

"What has he said?"

"Just that you've been having a sexual relationship whilst your husband's away. If it's true, just tell us, and if you can alibi him, we can move on with the enquiry."

"Look, it's not how it seems."

"Mrs Harland, we're not here to judge you. We're trying to find out who killed Tony and Eira, period. If you've been having a bit of nooky while the old man's away, so be it. We're not at all interested. Now can you help us?"

She sighed. "Rudi's been staying here with me for over a week whilst Tom's been away in Jersey with business. We're opening a casino over there."

"When was Rudi with you, Mrs Harland?"

"Tom flew a week last Saturday morning, so he was with me until the Thursday morning. I can certainly vouch for that."

"Are you sure, Mrs Harland?"

"Am I sure? Of course I'm sure. Best sex I've had for many years," she smiled.

"I take it you haven't heard from him since?"

"No, but that's not unusual. He's a free spirit. He does what he wants. If he's required, we give him a bell."

"Have you ever met Tony in person?"

"Many times. Usually at the Elvis Festival."

"When did you see him last?"

"About a year ago, he was on stage."

"Mrs Harland, last Thursday, Rudi broke into Tony's house up the Rhondda. It seems he was looking for Tony to reclaim the money that was owed. But Tony wasn't there, and he seriously assaulted a man by the name of Kenny Vincent who was in the wrong place at the wrong time. Were you responsible for sending him there?"

"No. Rudi said he'd get the money, but as for breaking in the house, no that's nothing to do with me. Where was Tony?

"No idea. He'd gone missing the Sunday before."

"Well there we are then. Why would Rudi go looking for him if he was already missing? Rudi didn't kill them."

Caroline said, "Mrs Harland, I understand you hired a private detective by the name of Raven Connor, is that correct?"

"You obviously know the answer. Yes I did."

"For what purpose?"

She waved her hand around the living room. "Look at this house. Look at me. I've all the trappings of success. I've been a faithful wife, stood by my husband through hard times, why do you think I hired Connor?"

"Sounds to me like there's a divorce in the offing?"

"You got it in one, girl. I'm going to take him to the cleaners, the cheating bastard. He must think I'm green."

"Raven told us about the Grand Hotel. What's the score there?" said Bryn.

"Raven's probably told you that's where my husband entertains his women. I hired him to get evidence for the divorce."

"Raven is in possession of a disc with pictures of individuals in somewhat compromising positions, do you know anything about this?"

Geraldine turned away and said nothing for a moment. "Look, I paid some of the young girls at the hotel to plant some cameras in a few rooms so I could catch my husband at it, it worked. But I hired Raven as a sort of back up insurance. I was only concerned about my husband's antics. I've already put it in the hands of my solicitor. I paid the girls because Collins, the hotel owner, is a touchy, feely, scumbag who treats women with contempt. I wouldn't be at all surprised if he's on the disc."

"Is there anything else, Mrs Harland?"

"No, I don't think so. I've told you everything. What will happen with Rudi?"

"Reckon he'll pull at least a ten stretch for the robbery."

"Is there anything I can do for him?"

"You may want to get him a brief for his court appearance. I can't see him getting bail mind you. He seems resigned to it all."

"For what it's worth, I don't think he's killed anyone."

Bryn said, "Thank you for your time, Mrs

Harland. Here's my card. When your husband gets home, can you ask him to give me a ring? Caroline will take a quick statement off you and that'll be that."

"I take it you'll be discreet, and you won't let the cat out of the bag?"

Bryn tapped the tip of his nose twice.

"Not a problem, Mrs Harland. Need to know basis."

Bryn and Caroline headed back to the Incident Room as fast as the clapped-out car would permit.

"Boss, she's a sharp cookie," Caroline said as Bryn concentrated on the driving the sickly Vauxhall. Actions that would be subconscious had become very conscious as he carefully teased the power from the dying engine. "I was watching her all the time you were questioning her," Caroline continued. "I wouldn't like to get on her bad side."

"She came over quite genuine, but we'll keep an open mind. It looks like she's put Rudi in the clear. Anyway, we'll let the boss to sort that one out."

"The car began to rattle as they neared the station then coughed and died on the street outside. Bryn patted the steering wheel. "Time to keep my end of the bargain," he said.

"What's that, boss?"

Bryn grinned. "Nothing."

48.

A crime scene investigator has to have patience, and on occasions think outside of the box. Glyn and Marigold had plenty of those qualities between them. They could still remember the old days, when they were known as Scenes of Crime officers. Although the title of the role had changed, their main aim was still to identify, record and recover forensic evidence from all types of crime scenes, ranging from murder to criminal damage.

It was a painstaking job, that called for total dedication and a sense of humour. One day they could be examining a stolen vehicle for fingerprints and the next they could be down the morgue fingerprinting a body that had been floating in the sea for God knows how long.

This week, both Glyn and Marigold were working full tilt, involved in the investigation of three murders.

Glyn was vastly experienced and would go through a crime scene with a meticulous precision. On many occasions he came up trumps on major incidents where SIO's had felt that the trail had gone cold and there would be no result. In Marigold he had the perfect foil. They worked well together, almost telepathically, not *telepathic*, as a DC once said in a briefing.

Tony's vehicle had been completely dried out, both inside and out, and Glyn and Marigold began to do the business on it. They were looking for anything that might give the team an idea who was responsible.

Marigold began dusting both the interior and exterior for fingerprints. They both knew that the vehicle had been submerged in the freezing cold water of the quarry for the best part of a week, and that certain evidence would have degraded, however they both were determined to get something the team could use.

Once they'd dusted the vehicle, they got to work on the interior, taping all the seats, door panels and any other surfaces that hadn't been printed.

"Do you think it was a robbery gone wrong or was it premeditated?" Marigold said to Glyn.

"Who knows? The gear was in neutral and the ignition was on, so I would rule out a suicide pact, that's for sure. As for the marks on the neck, that looks pretty shocking."

Marigold opened the glove box compartment and started rummaging through it. He pulled out a mobile phone charger, then a tin of travel mints and lastly a small sealed plastic folder with what appeared to contain coloured pictures. He fumbled with the folder seal and finally slipped a rubber glove inside to remove the pictures.

"Bugger me, Glyn, have a look at these. Make your eyes water, they will."

There were ten pictures in total. They'd obviously been taken with an instamatic camera - square format with a heavy, white border at the bottom. Marigold laid them out on the car bonnet.

Glyn whistled. "Isn't that Tony and Lenny Stone in that one, and there again in those four? Must be a third person taking these who must be involved too."

"You mean like a 'menagie-twat'?"

"Aye, but I think it's ménage à trois, but whatever, Marigold. The boss will be interested in these, of that there's no doubt. We'll check for prints, the killer's dabs might be on them."

It took another two hours before Glyn and Marigold returned to the Incident Room and conferred with McGuire.

"Boss, we've done the car," Glyn said. "Plenty of marks, fibres and what looks like pubic hairs on the back seat. But even more interesting are the pictures that Marigold found in the glove box." He handed them to McGuire and grinned as he watched his expression change from mild interest to shock to highly interested.

"Well, there's no doubt what's going on here, Glyn. Tony, Lenny Stone and some third person engaged in a nice little threesome. Stick them on the board. Perhaps one of the team may recognise who it is."

"By the way, boss, we've had the tox results from the lab. Both Tony and Stone tested positive for cocaine. Eira was clean as a whistle, poor girl."

Glyn grabbed a handful of magnetic fasteners from a plastic pot and began sticking the pictures on to the new board.

McGuire watched him then took a sharp intake of breath. It was staring him right in the face. The tattoo on Stone's arm. TH-LS, obviously Tony Heggarty and Lenny Stone, he couldn't believe how he hadn't put two and two together. It was now quite clear that the murders were linked, but he still had no idea who had committed them. At least the list of suspects was diminishing at a rate of knots.

McGuire put out a call for the troops to gather and had sunk two cups of coffee before they were all present.

"Ladies and gents, we're nearly four days into the enquiry and we're running out of suspects. It looks like Gumms is in the clear. However, our friend Gumms isn't going anywhere. He's on toast at the minute in Cardiff Prison. The German Elvis and his manager have been eliminated, they were at the Elvis final all Sunday night, so they've been ruled out. But now we've got a fresh lead," McGuire turned and pointed at the cork board. "Glyn and Marigold found those ten pictures in Tony's car, does anyone know who the third man is?"

Jake Marler stood. "That's Andy Horgan, the manager of the Seaview, boss. I'm sure it is. I recognise his face..." he paused and grinned. "But not his arse."

The others laughed.

"Nice one, Jake. Now get your own arse up the Seaview and drag him down here if necessary. Take Duggan with you. If he starts any nonsense arrest him on suspicion."

"Bryn, Colin, let's have a chat in my office."

The team dispersed amongst a cacophony of scraping chairs and mumbled conversations. Bryn and Colin refilled their own mugs from the percolator and followed McGuire into his office. Bryn closed the door behind him and took a seat alongside Colin.

"Boys, I've got a feeling these murders are getting away from us," McGuire declared grimly. "I'm more than happy that it's the same killer, but what's the motive and why would he or she kill Eira?"

"Look, boss, it's obvious that the killer's robbed them," Bryn said. "No mobiles, wallets, nothing. So, is it a rogue killer from outside of our area, down for the festival? If it is, I totally agree with you, the longer the enquiry goes on, the less chance of an arrest."

"What's your take on it, Col?"

"Tony's the key," he said emphatically. "I believe his lifestyle has got him caught up in the mess, the drugs, gambling, his promiscuity, it's got all the signs that he knew the killer for him or her to get near enough to stun him. The use of the stun gun might be key too. The killer couldn't have been confident of overpowering him and took the stun gun. That could mean it's a woman. I'm convinced we're not far off the mark. Is it possible Tony killed Stone? There was definitely friction between them."

"We'll see what the Horgan says when he's interviewed," McGuire nodded. "How are the team doing?"

"Working their bollocks off, boss," Bryn grinned. "I've never seen such enthusiasm, they're a good bunch."

"Good, keep them like that, Bryn. I'll do another press release in a couple of days, maybe we'll get lucky."

49.

This would be interesting, Jake Marler thought, as he and Duggan drove a marked panda to the Seaview Hotel in Porthcawl, not knowing how Andy Horgan would react when they eventually showed him the compromising photographs. The panda car was a borrowed Kia from the uniform coppers. One of the CID pool cars was off the road, having died when Bryn took it to the Gower, and two other cars were out on other jobs. The transport problems were beginning to mount since the government cutbacks had bitten deeply into daily operations. It was something that had adversely impacted upon all areas of policing and Marler wondered what would go next. Things couldn't carry on like this for much longer before the service ground to a halt.

There were too many distractions, he thought, as he tried to focus on the task in hand. Duggan's question was a relief from the thoughts that he knew he had no control over.

"Have you had any dealings with him Jake?" Duggan asked.

"Met him a few times over the years. He's

well respected in the area and, in fairness, he runs a tight ship at the hotel. Never any trouble there."

"Do you think he could be involved in the murders?"

Marler shook his head. "I don't think so. He was more than co-operative when the team interviewed him with the hotel staff last week."

The hotel was quiet when they arrived, the handful of staff were clearing away after a large business luncheon, but guests were few and far between.

Horgan was in conversation with one of the receptionists behind the desk as they approached.

"Can we have a quiet word please? It's very important," Duggan said.

Horgan sighed. There was no need for identification, he had seen Jake Marler before. "Come into my office, we won't be disturbed there."

"Mr Horgan, there have been some developments in the Tony and Eira Morgan murders," Marler said as soon as the door closed behind them.

"How can I help? I've already made a statement about Tony and everything else."

"Perhaps there's something you're not telling us? Have a think," Duggan prompted.

Horgan's head dropped, and he took a deep breath. "Is it about the CCTV disc I gave to the private detective, the one where Tony and the girl got into his car?"

"No, that's all been sorted. Look, we have a lot to talk about and I think it's best if we go down the nick."

"Are you arresting me? Do I need a solicitor?"

"No, it won't come to that."

Horgan shrugged acceptance but didn't look happy.

***

The interview room was fully equipped with the standard recording gear used throughout the UK. Horgan sat on a chair opposite the two officers as they checked through notes.

"Mr Horgan, you're not under arrest, have you any objection to this interview being taped?" Duggan asked.

"No, I've nothing to hide."

"Can you just give us some background on yourself, please, like where you were born, that sort of thing," he said.

He nodded. "Well, I was born in Neath. Left school at sixteen with no qualifications. I was a disappointment to my parents in more ways than one. They had high hopes for me. They wanted me to follow them into teaching. They were also fanatically religious... and being gay didn't help."

"I suppose it was a difficult time for you?"

"Yes, it was. Very. I couldn't stand living

with them and I left home at seventeen, the first chance I got, and began working in hotels down the West Country, waiting tables, washing dishes, anything and everything to earn money."

"Well you've done well for yourself," said Marler.

"Yes, I suppose I have. I self-funded all my business courses and gradually worked my way up to management. It's been hard, but well worth it."

"How long have you been at the Seaview?"

"Five years this summer, but I'm sure you know that. I've built the business up, we've got five stars, probably now one of the best hotels in Wales."

"OK, now let's get down to the nitty gritty, shall we? We're in possession of a number of photographs. You're in a few of them. Have you any idea what we're talking about?"

"I can only guess. Are you going to show them to me?"

"Well, they're a bit graphic and sexually explicit."

"Just show them."

Marler laid the pictures out on the table and said, "Can you identify the individuals?"

Horgan wasn't fazed. He pointed, "Well that's me and Tony in those two. That's me and Tommy Harland in those. I don't know the name of the other bloke, only met him that night."

"Where were these pictures taken?" Duggan asked.

"In Tony's house, up the Rhondda, a few years ago."

"What if I told you that the bloke you don't know is in fact Lenny Stone, our third murder victim? Surely you've seen his picture on the news?"

"If I did, nothing triggered recall, I'm sorry."

Marler leaned forward and pointed to a man in one of the pictures. "OK, tell us about Tommy Harland, who is he?"

"He's a millionaire businessman who lives down the Gower. Tony introduced me to him when we were together."

"Where did you meet him?"

"Up at the hotel. It was a businessman's lunch."

"When did you see him last?"

"Over a year ago, I would say. Not seen him since."

"Let's go back to the photographs," Marler said. "Was this a regular thing?"

"Once or twice, back at Tony's, but usually me and Tony would find a quiet hotel. He liked to keep a low profile. The less that knew he swung both ways the better for his career, so he said."

"Did you ever see Tony do cocaine?"

Horgan snorted. "Ever see him? Yes, he was a regular user. Couldn't get enough of the shit. Never did anything for me. I had too much to lose, we both did, but addiction is a bastard and Tony was an addict. We were complete opposites. That's why we called it a day on our relationship. There were no hard feelings. Truth be told, I really miss him. He had a good heart. He meant well."

"What about this girl, Eira, did you know her?"

"No, but I knew *of* her. Tony told me he was seeing a young woman, but I knew that was Tony trying to deny the truth of his sexuality. Tony was a dreamer and I don't think the truth would ever have been allowed into his reality."

"Have you ever met a man by the name of Rudi Gumms, he's a big black feller?"

Horgan nodded. "Tommy's minder. An evil bastard. He's homophobic too. I think if he had his way, he'd have given me a good kicking. Tommy had to reel him in a few times," he paused before continuing. "Do you think he killed them?"

Marler shook his head. "No, he's got an alibi, but he's locked up. So you won't be seeing him any time soon."

Horgan sighed. "Look, officers, I wasn't involved in these killings. I would never hurt Tony and I didn't know Eira. I think I loved Tony once upon a time, but not enough to lose everything I've worked for."

"We'll take a full statement off you covering what we've spoken about," Marler said. "Then we'll take you back to the hotel. When we do, we'll have a quick look through your room and your car, OK?"

"Do as you must, officers, anything, if it helps find the killer."

Marler left Duggan to take the statement and spoke to McGuire in the Incident Room.

"Boss, we've just finished with Horgan. I think he's in the clear and he's been fully co-operative with the photographs. He's identified the fourth bloke as a Tommy Harland who is Geraldine Harland's husband. The plot thickens. The pictures were taken at Tony's house a while ago."

"Good work. Bryn said Harland's away at the minute so action him out as a person of interest. I want him interviewed as soon as he returns. Have a chat with Bryn, he'll fill you in on Harland. Do a complete background on him. Who knows, he could be in the frame. According to his wife, he was in Jersey at the time of Tony's disappearance."

"I'll crack on, boss."

50.

Raven sat in the new office of Raven Investigations. He smiled at the email detailing the purchase of the boat he had fancied in Swansea marina. The take-over by McGuire had freed up Raven's personal account. There would be no need to dip into it and he had paid a deposit for the vessel and the rest would be on finance. Sue would love it, after he had spent some time changing the interior and sorting the exterior paintwork. It had been a few years since he had been on a boat and he knew he'd have to brush up on the recent maritime law changes, but he had already had a good grounding in it during his time in the SBS.

He clicked off the email and began reading the 'McGuire' file that Ed had been compiling at some time before his death. The earliest entry in Ed's handwriting was dated fifteen years ago. The man had clearly been dipping into the file every so often, but the final page showed no satisfactory conclusion. The killer or killers were still at large.

The file concerned the unsolved murder of Detective Sergeant Patrick McGuire, who'd been stabbed to death in Dock Street, Porthcawl, over twenty-five years ago.

At about an inch thick, and made up of numerous newspaper cuttings, copies of witness statements and photographs of the murder scene, many of which were quite graphic, the file was dog-eared and well-worn. Ed had made a comprehensive summary of the murder and it was obvious he'd been doing a lot of digging himself prior to his own sudden and tragic demise.

There was no direct evidence in the file pointing Ed to the culprit or culprits, however there were many named suspects who'd been interviewed and eliminated.

Raven closed the file and stared at the ceiling. He watched a fly crawl across the fluorescent strip light. He wondered if fly's had names in the fly community and grinned at the stupid idea.

Terry McGuire's father had been murdered. Raven had no idea that his new partner in the business had carried the violent loss of his dad all this time. He had decided he wasn't going to mention anything to the man, unless McGuire brought the matter up first. He wondered at the connection between Ed and the case and whether he had told McGuire of his investigation. Raven doubted it. He was grateful for McGuire's timely intervention into his failing investigation business and, as he saw it, it was the least he could do to carry on with Ed's work – surreptitiously, for the time being.

He closed the file and locked it away in the top draw of his desk and then rang the hospital. He needed to visit Kenny. There was no need for the man to thank him. Raven had no intention of staying there long. He hated hospitals.

He dialled the number and spoke to a ward nurse. "I'm sorry, Mr Connor," the male nurse said, "but Kenny's been transferred to our oncology ward for tests and observations."

That was a shock. "How is he?"

"Are you a relative?"

"No, he's a client of mine and has asked to speak with me. Do you think I'll be able to visit?"

"You could either ring or pop in on the off-chance, but I can't divulge anything over the phone."

Why had Kenny been moved to the oncology ward? Oncology mean cancer, in lay-men's terms, and he didn't like the sound of that, but then nobody liked the sound of that. The poor bloke had taken a fair old beating from Gumms, so the quacks must have found something serious during the medical investigations. He'd find out soon enough.

Raven took the VW and listened to some John Miles on a CD he had bought some time ago and had never listened to. He arrived at the hospital reception less than an hour later and was directed into a side room just off the main ward.

Kenny was sitting up in bed, propped up by a couple of large pillows, head enveloped in the soft, white folds. He'd lost weight since the last time Raven had seen him and his skin was tinged a sickly yellow. He didn't look good. There was something seriously wrong and it had nothing to do with the beating that Kenny had sustained at the fists and boots of Gumms.

"Kenny you look like Homer Simpson, what's happening?"

"Things aren't too clever," Kenny smiled, but the expression lacked humour. "Fact is, I don't think I'll be leaving here. Had a bit of bad news this morning."

"Well I guessed something wasn't right. What's the score?"

He shuffled himself further up the pillow. The effort looked far from easy. "When they operated on my spleen and lung, they did a few biopsies whilst they were poking around inside. I've had ultrasounds and just about every other test."

"What's the prognosis?"

"One or two, perhaps?"

"Well, at least you know you've got some time to fight the thing. Two years isn't a lot of time but…"

"Fucking weeks," Kenny interrupted. "I've got about two weeks, tops. They said I can have treatment but I'm refusing, it's for the best. What's the point if it's gone that far?" He sighed. Raven could see him fighting back the tears and his bottom lip trembled. "At least I can put it all to bed now, that's the reason I want to see you."

"What are you talking about?"

"I've pancreatic cancer and tumours all over the bloody place."

"Then take the treatment. The doctors know what they're doing. They can do amazing things these days, could give you a few more years."

"No, I've had my day, Raven. Now I've got to clear things up. I've got no-one now. I lost my wife and now Tony's gone. It can be the three of us now, me, Tony and my little brother, Andy, all back together, like when we were young and we didn't have a care in the world."

Raven said nothing. Who was he to tell anyone, who had just received the worst possible news, what to do? He sat silently, waiting for Kenny to take the lead again.

"Any news on who killed Tony and Eira?"

"No, nothing at the moment," Raven said. "But looks like there's a connection with the murder of Lenny Stone, the bloke they found dead down on the pier."

"What? They think the same person is responsible for all three?"

"Looks like it. I'm sure McGuire and his team will get to the bottom of it."

Kenny laughed and started to cough. Raven poured him a glass of water.

"It's bloody ironic, isn't it?"

"What's ironic?"

"It's not the same killer."

"How can you be sure?"

He grinned. "Because I killed Lenny Stone."

Raven spilled the jug as he returned it to the bedside cabinet. "Stop fucking about, Kenny, this isn't a joke."

"I'm serious, he deserved it, the little weasel. Imagine, if I wasn't going to bloody die, I'd have got away with it too. I sound like a villain off Scooby Do. *If it wasn't for those meddling kids*," he said in a poor American accent and laughed. "Lenny was going to mess with Tony's career, I had to do him. Tony had given me a job, a chance to find my feet again and that little twat comes along to ruin everything."

"Listen, Kenny, don't say any more," Raven warned him. "I'll give McGuire a ring. Bloody hell, this will set the cat amongst the pigeons. Don't say another word, just hang fire."

"What will McGuire do?"

"How the hell do I know? You've just admitted to killing a bloke. I just hope you're on the level, because it'll have to be more than just your word. Have a rest whilst I make the call."

The confession had taken Raven by surprise, he'd been in many ropey situations whilst in the SBS and had seen things no man or woman should ever see, some of it the inevitable outcome of human frailty, fear and anger, but this was something unexpected.

He gave McGuire a ring.

McGuire sounded tired as he told him that the investigation was progressing but not yet concluded.

"Is it the same bloke?" Raven fished.

"Looks that way. Why are you asking?"

"Well, I'm up on the oncology ward visiting Kenny."

"How's he doing?"

"Not too clever, Terry, he's terminal. Got pancreatic cancer. He's in a terrible state here with just a few weeks to live, but this is the reason I'm calling you..."

"Go on," McGuire sounded intrigued.

"Kenny's just admitted to killing Lenny Stone.

"What?" McGuire shouted. "You're winding me up?"

"You'd better get someone up here, double quick, his health is on a downward spiral. The only way he's leaving here is in a box."

"Are you serious?"

"Serious, Terry. He's just coughed it. I haven't asked him anything more. Just get the boys up here."

***

McGuire carried his phone out into the CID office. Colin and Julia were paper shuffling and looked up as he entered. "OK. Colin and Julia will be there in twenty minutes," he said loud enough for the two detectives to hear. They looked at each other and both shrugged.

Covering his phone with his hand, McGuire nodded to the door. "Get your arses up to the hospital, tout suite. Raven's with Kenny and Kenny just made a death-bed confession to killing Lenny Stone".

"Jesus!" Julia said. "Is it on the up?"

McGuire shrugged. "Who knows?"

***

Raven ended the call and returned to speak with Kenny.

"I've spoken to McGuire, he's sending someone up. I've filled him in on the situation. Just lay back and rest.

"Thanks."

"Don't thank me. You probably won't thank me when they grill you over the murder."

"It's the truth. I did it and I'm going to die. What more can they do to me?"

***

Colin and Julia arrived on the ward and before interviewing Kenny they spoke with the on-call doctor and explained the situation. The doctor confirmed that he felt that Kenny was still fit enough to be spoken to, however, if at any point he became distressed the interview would have to be terminated, he warned.

Raven stood to one side as Colin made the introductions, then Colin said, "I'm arresting you for the murder of Lenny Stone." Colin cautioned

Kenny, who just nodded his head.

Julia produced a small Dictaphone and switched it on.

"This interview will be taped, Kenny, and you have a right to legal advice. Do you understand that?"

"Yes. I don't need a brief, but Raven stays. Otherwise I will deny everything."

"Not a problem," Colin said. "So, what have you got to say?"

"Like I told Raven. I killed Stone. I didn't intend to, but things just escalated."

"Raven's filled us in on your background, Kenny, we know about your condition, but we still need to get to the bottom of this. We need you to tell us everything."

He nodded. "Well, there's not a lot to say, really. I'd got back together with Tony after many years apart," he smiled. "It was going to be a new chapter in our lives, I was going to be Tony's road manager. We made plans."

"So, what went wrong, Kenny?"

He shook his head. "I couldn't believe it. We went to the press conference during the Elvis Festival and that German bloke and Tony had a big bust up, it all kicked off. Then, the following day, there was the big apology, all made up crap. It was all for show. That's when that twat Lenny Stone turned up. I could see that he'd upset Tony over something, then Tony said he'd meet him on the pier later in the evening."

"You're not covering for Tony are you, Kenny, what with him gone and you wanting to keep his name clean?"

Again, he shook his head. "I can prove it, but I'm losing my thread here. Shut up and just let me finish."

"Carry on then, Kenny, the floor is yours."

"We got back to the hotel and I could see Tony was wound up over Stone. I calmed him down and told him not to worry about the bloke. I convinced Tony to let me go and meet Stone. I was his manager, after all, and I told him that if he seriously wanted me to do the job then he had to trust me to sort it. We had a bit of grub later and Tony went to bed. I strolled down to the pier, I didn't have to wait long."

"Yes, carry on."

"Well, Stone approached me and asked me where Tony was. I told him that he wasn't coming, and he told me he wanted five grand off Tony or he'd go to the press and say Tony was gay and a coke addict."

"What did you do then?"

"I lost my rag. I grabbed him by the lapels of that stupid blue Elvis suit and pulled them tight to his throat, called him a piece of shit and threw him to the floor. I thought that was it, but as I turned my back the bastard got up and grabbed me by my trouser belt and yanked me back. That really did it. I threw him around, gave him a couple of digs to the face and left him."

"You left him on the ground? Was he knocked out?"

"More stunned, I would say."

"Did you go back to the hotel?"

"I was going to, then I turned back. I knew things would have to end. People like Stone don't give up. I went back, grabbed him around the throat again and squeezed the life out of him. Then I pushed him off the pier. I had to protect Tony," he shrugged.

"Now, when Stone was found, he had nothing in his pockets. Did you take anything from him?"

"Yes. His phone, wallet, keys and a block of cannabis."

"Where is that stuff now?"

"If you go up to Tony's and have a look in my car, a Ford Focus, you'll find them in the spare wheel housing wrapped in a white handkerchief. I never expected that bloke Gumms to turn up and give me a hiding."

"I must say, you're a change from the others I've dealt with over the years," Colin said. "Is there anything else?"

"No, only that you have to catch the killer of Tony and Eira before I snuff it. I want us to get buried together. Raven, you'll see to that, won't you. Promise me?"

Raven looked surprised but nodded. Kenny was his client and if that was the last thing he could do for him, so be it.

"Is that it?" Kenny said. "I don't see any point in charging me. You got the confession and the property. Case closed, surely?"

Colin and Julia looked at each other, and Julia switched off the Dictaphone.

"You'd better put that back on," Kenny said to Julia. Julia did as he said and made the introductions once more for the recording. "What else do you want to say," she said.

"I killed my wife too."

Raven glanced at Julia. Her wide-eyed expression was all he needed to see to know this was totally unexpected.

"I wasn't going to say anything about it but, what the hell? In for a penny in for a pound," he grinned.

"Go on," Colin said.

"I found out she was shagging Tony, my old mate, Tony. I couldn't blame Tony. Tony was Tony. He'd always been the same. But my wife had been in the home with us for a while and then moved away when she was adopted. Went to London.

"I met up with her again and we started dating and things went on from there. I had no idea that about the same time, my dear wife was slipping away for Tony to slip her one."

"Jesus!" Raven sighed.

"What did you do?" Colin said.

"She had cancer too, ironic, eh? Anyway, she didn't have long to go. I'd accepted everything, her with Tony, the cancer. She was in pain, so she asked me to give her pills and to use a pillow."

"And?" Julia said.

"So, I did. It was heart-breaking, but I knew it was the right thing to do. She took the pills, a big handful, and then, when she became drowsy, I used the pillow. She didn't fight. Just slipped away."

"When was this?" Julia asked. "Date?"

"Twenty-first of November twenty-seven-teen. The PM focussed on the overdose. If they picked up on the smothering bit they never mentioned it."

"Anything else? You're not going to tell me you killed JFK as well are you?" Raven joked.

Kenny laughed. "Now you mention it, I was on the grassy knoll," he joked.

"Kenny, I've got a uniform outside. They'll keep an eye on you from here on in. It's procedure, you understand?" Colin said.

Kenny nodded then closed his eyes.

They all took that as the cue to leave.

Colin and Julia waited in the corridor for Raven.

"Cheers, Raven. I'll bring Terry up to speed. Good job, mate. I've no doubt he'll be in touch. Pop into the nick at your leisure to make a statement. Kenny's not going anywhere."

"Will he be charged?"

Colin shrugged. "Like he said, it's not going

anywhere. He might get charged, but even if he goes to court, he won't see a day inside a cell, not with his prognosis."

51.

The Rialto Casino was Thomas Harland's jewel in the crown of his business empire. It was the main casino on Jersey and was a homage to Las Vegas casinos, a conglomeration of deco styles that somehow worked.

Lavishly decorated and operated twenty-four hours a day, three hundred and sixty-five days of the year, the Rialto was making more money for the Harland empire than all his other businesses combined.

Being the tallest building on the island, at thirty stories tall, and housing a hundred top end apartments, all tastefully decorated, Harland believed it was his greatest achievement. It was no wonder his wife Geraldine wanted to take him to the cleaners to get a piece of the Rialto action.

Harland liked to mingle with guests, shaking hands with the punters and smiling politely. He believed in a personal service and was sure it was why his clients were always returning.

His mobile rang. He checked the caller ID, it was Geraldine - the snake.

"How are you my darling, what are you up to?" he asked through gritted teeth.

"Not a lot. Guess who I've had knocking the door?"

"Pray tell, my darling."

"The murder squad, asking questions about three murders, one of them being Tony."

The high spirits he had felt just seconds ago quickly evaporated. "What did you tell them?"

"As they say on telly, I helped them with their enquiries. They want to speak with you now. I haven't told them anything controversial, they know that Tony owed us and wanted to know about your relationship."

"I hope you told them it was strictly business?"

"Of course. Did you know Rudi's locked up?"

"What's he done this time?"

"He's only broken into Tony's house and battered some mate of his. He's been charged. He's in custody and the copper said he'll probably get a ten-year stretch."

"Did he ring anyone?"

"No, he's taking it on the chin."

Harland sighed. "I'll sort something when I get home, probably in a few days. Are you sure you haven't said anything else to the police?"

"No, I told them you flew to Jersey on Saturday, so nothing that would drop you in the shit."

"That's good. We'll have a good chat when I get home. It's time you and I saw a bit of sun. Do you fancy a few weeks in Barbados?"

"Sounds nice. So it's all going well there?"

"You know what it's like, sweetheart. A lot of socialising and greasing of palms."

"You'll drop yourself in the shit one day, you can be sure of that. I hope you're not dabbling with the hostesses?"

"You know me, darling. Always true to one. Look, I've got to go, got an appointment with a few councillors, planning permission for the extension."

"Before you land, give DCI Rowlands a bell," she read out a number. "He's based at Porthcawl. Perhaps you can call in and see him on the way home? Get it all over with."

"No problem. I'll sort. Bye for now, darling, love you."

Harland took one of the four glass lifts to the penthouse suite where Pauline Phillips was taking a bath. The bathroom was the size of most people's living rooms. Tiled completely in a copper stone, the carved stone bath stood on four copper plated legs.

"You look a bit flustered," she said as he poked his head around the door.

"Just got off the phone with Geraldine," he stepped inside and walked over to the bath. He kissed Pauline on one of her breasts. "The police have been around asking questions about a bloke I know, Tony, the one they fished out of the quarry with some bird."

"Oh yeah, it's been all over the news. Porthcawl is now the murder capital of the world," she joked.

"It's no fucking joke. They want to interview me. They've already had a crack at Geraldine, but she's been around the block. Probably didn't give them the time of day. If they start digging, I could get drawn into it all and, if push comes to shove, I'll need an alibi. Can I rely on you?"

"Of course."

"When we get back to Wales, I'll get the pilot to drop you off and I'll get down to Porthcawl and sort it. It may not come to it, but if they ask questions, I've been with you all the time, do you understand?"

"Of course. All the time. I understand."

Harland rang Bryn Rowlands from the bedroom of the apartment.

"I take it Mrs Harland has filled you in on the nature of the enquiry?" Bryn said.

"Yes, the murders. Very sad news. I knew Tony well. We were very close friends. So, how can I help you?"

"It's just some background, really. We understand Tony owed you a large amount of cash?"

"Yes, that's correct. But in my business, you win a few, you lose a few."

"When can you come to meet me?"

"Can't we do it now, on the phone?"

"Sorry, it has to be face-to-face. We'll need a statement."

"Do I need a brief?"

"I wouldn't have thought so, Mr Harland. Do you think you'll need one?"

Harland said nothing.

"You still there?"

"Yes. I land at six, tomorrow evening. I've hired a helicopter to pick me up and take me to the landing pad at the Grand Hotel. I'll see you around eight, would that be OK?"

"Not a problem, Mr Harland. I'll be looking forward to it."

Harland ended the call and tapped in the number for his brief, Royston Morris.

"Were you involved, Tommy?" Morris asked. Morris had worked for Tommy Harland since Harland had first set up his gambling business.

"Look, Roy, just be there. Do you understand?"

"I'll be there, Tommy, not a problem. Just stay calm. If you're not involved, there'll be no problem. But I need to have the heads-up. Is there anything I should be aware of?"

"No, nothing."

"From what I've read, the victim went missing on a Sunday night and his body was found a week later, they'll probably want an alibi. You OK with that?"

"No problem, but I don't think Geraldine

will be amused when she finds out who my alibi is."

"I've been warning you for years, Tommy. Your dick has ruled your head. I'll see you tomorrow."

Harland paced the thick pile carpet. It was true, he had always sailed close to the wind, but Geraldine had always been happy to turn a blind eye as long as nothing upset her lifestyle. Now that upset was as good as guaranteed and Harland knew Geraldine was not a woman to upset.

52.

Jake Marler had been a busy man, collating information on Thomas Harland. The main purpose was to eliminate Harland from the murder enquiry, by whatever means were available. He knew that Harland was going to be interviewed by Bryn, so it was only natural that he'd be involved, after all, he held all the information on Harland. Marler had already shared all that information with the team, and it had lifted their spirits.

This, together with Kenny's admission to the killing of Lenny Stone, and the murder of his own wife, had created a buzz of excitement. They were on a fast-downward roll to the finish line and all they needed now was the physical evidence they'd use in court.

It would be all down to the interview of Harland, and how he would respond to questions that were put to him.

Marler knew that Harland was a smooth operator, he was a multi-millionaire and was well into the gambling business. Born with a silver spoon in his mouth. His father, Tommy Senior, was himself a bookmaker and owned a chain of shops in and around the Gower – an area where there had once been a lot of disposable income to lose on horses, dogs and just about anything else worth betting on.

Tommy senior sold the shops for millions to a national chain and then went into land development.

It was only natural that Tommy junior would take over the business at some time. However that came a bit earlier than had been planned after his father suffered a fatal heart attack.

There was no doubt Harland was as bent as a butcher's hook, and most certainly had many councillors on his pay roll too, both in Wales and in Jersey. He was a rich, corrupt bastard who needed his wings clipped, and in Marler's mind, today would be the day, if things went to plan.

If he wasn't involved in the murders, there was no doubt that his sexual preferences would make headlines, once leaked to the press. It was a tactic that was far from ethical, but it was also a means to an end if it ended his dodgy dealings.

Marler and Bryn met in the canteen and had a quick chat over a cuppa to discuss the structure of the interview. They had to get it right. Everything might well depend on the outcome of the interview.

"You can lead on the interview," Bryn said. "You've done all the leg work, so it's only right that you have a crack at Harland. We'll go in softly-softly, then you can hit him with every-thing. We'll see how he reacts. I reckon, if you hit a few nerves he'll turn turtle and spill a whole lot more."

"Cheers, boss, it's much appreciated." Throughout his service as a detective, Marler had been involved in many serious criminal enquir-ies. He'd sat in on murder suspect interviews, but he'd never been the lead interviewer. This was a first for him and it set his nerves on edge.

It was just turning eight when both Har-land and his brief, an ageing man in a grey pin-striped suit, turned up at the nick.

Bryn had already made his way to the interview room.

Marler did the introductions and shook their hands like a prize fighter before battle.

Roy Morris, Harland's brief, took a large notepad from his brown leather briefcase and thumped a gold pen on to the top. "I hope this won't take too long, sergeant, my client is a busy man. I take it he's not being treated as a suspect?"

"No, Mr Morris, not at this stage," Marler lied. "Let's pop upstairs to the interview room. My DCI is already there."

"Lead the way," Morris smiled, but Harland looked nervous. Understandable, under the cir-cumstances, Marler thought.

When they entered the interview room, Morris seemed somewhat startled. It was obvi-ous he knew the DCI.

They shook hands.

"I thought you were down the bay, Bryn?"

"Good God, Roy. Long time no see. Thought you'd packed in all this nonsense years ago?"

"Just keeping my hand in, Bryn. Keep the wolves from my door."

Bryn nodded. He knew Roy Morris had once been a sharp defence solicitor. He'd faced him many times over interview tables and the dock in court. The last time they had faced-off had been over the case of a serial paedophile. Morris had won the case, he'd got the man off the charges, but Morris had changed, rather than smugly celebrate his victory, Morris had apologised to Bryn outside the court. Bryn had blamed himself, rather than Morris. He had been the DI in charge of the case and had failed to cover all the bases. The paedophile had walked out of the court a free man because Bryn had failed, and he had sworn he would never let that happen again. Several weeks later, Bryn had heard that Morris had resigned his position with the law firm and retired. It was a shock to see him back in the station, defending Harland, but Bryn knew he had to be on his top game with Morris on the case.

"Let's get down to business," Bryn said, and stared at Harland. "Mr Harland, thank you for co-operating. You're not a suspect at this time. This is purely an interview to eliminate you from enquiries relating to the murders of Tony Heggerty and Eira Pritchard. I assume you know all about the murders?"

"Of course, it's common knowledge," Harland said.

"DS Marler has a few questions he'd like to put to you."

Marler leaned forward to engage Harland. "OK, I've looked into your background and it's clear to me that you're a very successful businessman..."

Harland puffed his chest and nodded. "I work hard."

Marler smiled. "Can you tell us what your connection with Terry Heggerty was?"

Harland looked to Morris, who nodded in the affirmative.

"I've known Tony, or I should say *knew* Tony for a few years. He was a client of mine, met him a few years ago in the Seaview Hotel."

"What do you mean by a client?"

"Like you say, you know my background. I run an on-line betting company and Tony was a client."

"Was he a big gambler?"

Harland nodded, "I would say so."

"Did he always settle up with you, did he owe you any money?"

"No and yes. No, he didn't always settle up and yes, he owed me a few bob."

"How much, exactly?"

"Thirty grand or thereabouts."

Marler whistled. "Wow. That's a lot of

money."

Harland shrugged. "To some, it may seem to be, but it was the nature of my job. I'd usually get it back some time, sooner or later."

"Did you ever socialise with Tony?"

"Yes, but not often. I'd see him in the odd function."

"What about other than that, had he visited your home or vice-versa?"

"No, never. I live down the Gower. I don't get involved with clients. I believe he lives up the Rhondda, and no, I've never been to his house. Why are you asking?"

"Just for elimination," Marler said. "As you probably know, Tony's home is now a crime scene, even though he was found in a quarry. We'll need to take elimination fingerprints as part of the elimination procedure."

Harland looked briefly at Morris who was jotting notes into the big jotter with his gold pen. "Fire away," he said.

"Do you know Andy Horgan?"

"Yes. I know Andy. He manages the Sea-view, and I've been to many functions there."

"As a friend?"

Harland now looked confused. "What do you mean?"

"I mean, were you friends? Did you social-ise outside of those functions?"

Harland shook his head.

"Could you please confirm for the recording? You shook your head."

"Sorry. No. We didn't."

"What about Larry Stone?"

"Larry Stone?" he said as he looked up to the ceiling as if trying to find an answer there. "No, I've no idea about him. Never met anyone by that name that I can remember."

"Have a good think, Mr Harland. Larry Stone is an associate of Tony and Andy. Stone was, in fact, murdered and his body dumped off the pier in Porthcawl."

"I heard about that as well, but it means nothing to me."

"Can you tell us about your movements from, say, midday a week last Sunday, and midday on the following Monday?" Marler grinned but there was no humour present. "Again, it's just to eliminate you from the enquiry, you understand?"

Harland raised his eyebrows and looked to Morris. Morris raised his too but said nothing. "Well, I flew to Jersey on the Sunday morning, landed at around ten a.m."

"Were you with anybody on the flight?"

"No, I was alone. I've been in Jersey until today. My missus rang me to say that you wanted a chat, so here I am."

Morris then raised his pen. "Is that it, officers?"

"Not quite," Marler said. "Let's rewind, Mr Harland. I asked you earlier if you knew Lenny

Stone. If I show you a picture it may very well jog your memory?"

The photograph of Stone was the most recent they had, supplied by his brother, and Marler laid it on the table in front of Harland. "I need to be sure of this. Are you still saying you don't know who this man is, Mr Harland?"

"Never seen him before in my life, that's the God's honest truth."

Marler nodded and slipped the photograph under his notebook. "Going back to Tony, are you sure you've never visited his home in the Rhondda? Think carefully."

"Look, I've never been there, and I don't know Stone."

Marler leaned down below the table and retrieved a brown envelope from a folder he had left on the floor for this moment. He laid out the compromising photographs, taking his time to let the tension build.

"Do you recognise anyone, Mr Harland?"

Harland stared at the photographs, his mouth fell open and began to mouth silent words.

"I do believe that's you with both Tony and Stone," Marler said. "Also in the photographs is Andy Horgan, he's confirmed these photographs were taken at Tony's home."

Morris held up his hand. "Can I have a minute with my client, officers?"

"Not a problem," Bryn said and stopped the

recording. Both he and Marler left the room.

Bryn grinned and patted Marler on his back. "Good job, Jake." He then tapped out a number on his mobile phone to bring McGuire up to speed.

"Boss, it's going well here. Harland is lying. Jake just hit him with the photographs and his brief has stopped the interview. I reckon he's about to clam up. When Jake mentions the airport and his bit of stuff on the side, he'll probably make no comment."

"Not a problem," McGuire said. "Pauline's been picked up and she's on the way to the Bridewell. She doesn't know her arse from her elbow. Caroline and Kirsty will sort her."

"If Harland goes no comment, I'll arrest him, boss."

"If you're happy, Bryn?"

The door to the interview room was knocked from the inside and Marler opened it to find Morris standing in the doorway.

"Officers, you can carry on with the interview. I've advised my client," he said.

Marler switched on the tape and video recorder as he and Bryn sat once more in the same seat as before.

"Well, Mr Harland, you've had time to think. Can you tell us why you've lied about knowing Stone? It's quite obvious you'd been having some kind of sexual relationship."

Harland flushed red. "No comment."

"You realise that you're not under caution?"

"No comment."

"I've a few more questions, and how you answer these may determine your future, Mr Harland."

"No comment."

"I've checked with the airline you said you used to fly to Jersey. You didn't fly on the Sunday morning, you flew on the Monday morning. You were also accompanied by Pauline Phillips who hails from Cowbridge. She's a lady you're having an affair with, and before you answer I must warn you that this can all be proved."

"No comment."

"Mr Harland, you're obviously lying through your teeth regarding these murders. Now this is where it gets serious. Thomas Harland, I'm arresting you on suspicion of the murders of Tony Heggerty and Eira Pritchard and I must caution you."

Marler reeled off the caution as Harland stared at the floor, mumbling.

"No Comment."

Harland looked about to cry, his eyes welled, and his lip trembled, then Jake hit him with the last piece of the jigsaw. "Pauline Phillips, at this moment in time, is being interviewed at Bridgend Bridewell. I'm sure, once she realises that she may be caught up in a double murder enquiry, and that you're using her as an alibi, she'll soon give us chapter and verse. So, have you anything to say?"

Harland shook his head again. "No comment."

"What next, Bryn?" Morris said as he finished jotting notes and checked his watch.

"Your client will be taken to the Bridewell and detained pending further enquiries."

"From what I see, you haven't got enough to charge him."

"We'll see how it goes, Roy. We'll see how it goes," Bryn frowned.

"Could I have five minutes with him, just to update him on what's going to happen?"

Bryn shrugged. "He's your client. Let us know when you're finished. It'll take us a while to sort the paperwork for his transfer."

The solicitor nodded. "Thanks. Won't take me long."

53.

Harland was the killer. McGuire was now convinced. He had already spoken to Andrea Edwards from the CPS about charging the man and although she warned that there was strong circumstantial evidence, she wanted more to authorise a charge of murder.

The reams of paperwork that documented the evidence was faxed to Andrea at the Crown Prosecution Service and then he called a briefing to bring the team up to speed. They'd been working for a fortnight on the case and now they were nearing the end of the road.

"Ladies and gents, this is what we've got at the minute. You're all aware that the Lenny Stone murder has been resolved, although there's not a hope in hell that Kenny Vincent will ever stand trial. That's not a problem," he said as he held up his hands to quell a growing murmur of discontent. "Stone's property has been recovered in Kenny's car up at Tony's home. I know what you're all thinking, how was it missed? Just forget about it. I'll sort that bollocks out, once the dust has settled.

"Now, getting on to our double murder.

Thomas Harland has been interviewed and arrested for both murders. He's been conveyed to the Bridewell as we speak, where he'll be detained to appear in court for remand. His vehicle has been impounded. Glyn and Marigold are examining the tyres for comparison to ones found at the quarry scene.

"Harland has no alibi for the relevant timeline, Kirsty and Caroline are interviewing his girlfriend, Pauline Phillips, as we speak. Hopefully, if they can put pressure on her, she may blow the case wide open. The girls will give us a bell shortly with some good news, I'm sure. Now, I suggest you all have a blow. Go for a pint, or whatever. Be back here at ten in the morning, that's all."

McGuire returned to his office and sat waiting for news from Glyn and the girls. He didn't have to wait long. First to call was Glyn on the mobile.

"Boss, compared the tyres on Harland's vehicle to all the casts taken at the quarry, got two matches, so that's another nail in the bastard's coffin."

"Do the business, Glyn. Then you and Marigold go home to the family. Thanks for everything. I've called a briefing in the morning, hopefully we can put it all to bed then."

McGuire nodded his head, he knew Harland's world was starting to crumble, but what was the motive for the killings? The only thing that McGuire could think of was jealousy. There was no doubt that Tony and Harland were on intimate terms, perhaps Stone was the fly in the ointment, a lover scorned? If so, the killings must have been premeditated. There was also the matter of thirty grand owed to him, but killing Tony would mean he'd never see a penny of it. That was the real fly in the ointment.

He stared at the photo of himself with Molly and the kids taken years ago in some seaside resort in Devon. The frame was dusty, and the photo had faded in the sunlight from the window behind him. He checked his watch and called home. "Hi, Molly, I won't be too late. You go to bed."

"No, love, I'll wait up for you. The new series of Line of Duty is on tonight. I've got a bottle of Merlot and a big bag of share crisps ready."

"Sounds great."

"Since you've been promoted, I'm seeing less of you now than ever."

"Sorry, Molly. I've been thinking about that. Now we've got the money from Ed I'm thinking of retiring. I can let Raven do all the work at the detective agency and act as an adviser. We could go and visit the kids."

"And before you ask, the kids are both in fine form. I've just spent three hours on Skype with them."

"You can read my mind, Mols."

"I've had enough practice over the years."

"We've nearly topped and tailed the cases. We'll put it all to bed in a couple of days. I've got a week's leave then, so I'll sort the business out with Raven. Then you and me can have a bit of quality time. Go to Hong Kong, pay for the kids to meet us. What do you say?"

"Sounds lovely, but I'm not going to hold my breath."

McGuire grinned. She was right to not bank on his promise, but this time he meant it. They both deserved a break. "I love you, Mols. Where would I be without you?"

"Probably in a rehab' centre."

McGuire laughed but knew it was probably true.

***

This was too much to handle. Pauline began to panic. Thomas may well have his interests sorted but that was no guarantee that she'd be safe too. There was only one thing she could, strike first and cover herself before the police came knocking her door.

She drove to Porthcawl police station where two women detectives met her and took her into an interview room.

***

"Pauline, I don't think you realise the position that Tom Harland has put you in," Kirsty said. "You said when you came in earlier that you were with him on the Sunday in question, flying to Jersey. That couldn't have been correct because you flew on the Monday morning. We've got you both on CCTV, and *you* booked the tickets"

"I must have been mistaken. It was the Monday."

"OK, so what about the Sunday? Now think carefully because depending on what you say will affect our decision on whether we arrest you or not. Tom Harland has been arrested for the murders, so please don't lie for him."

Pauline looked horrified. Suddenly, something that seemed at first to be a simple bending of the truth to protect her lover from the wrath of his wife had become far more serious. "I don't know what's going on, and I certainly don't know anything about murders. All Tom told me was that if you ever asked about where he was I was to say he was with me all the time."

"So, was he with you all day Sunday, as you first said?"

"No, I never saw him at all on the Sunday."

"What about Monday?"

"I met him at the airport, and we flew to Jersey."

"Did you know that Tom was having sexual relations with different men, including Tony Heggerty?"

She scoffed. "I don't believe that for a minute. No that can't be."

"We've got the evidence, Pauline, I'm sorry

to say."

She shook her head and thumped her fist onto the table. "The bastard. Are you telling me that he's gay and he's been having it off with me and his wife at the same time?"

"We're afraid so. Puts a different light on it now, doesn't it?"

"The bastard. Look, I'm not involved in anything. I didn't realise he was involved in anything like that, you've got to believe me. I know he's a dodgy dealer, but murder? I can't believe that."

"We believe you, Pauline, but we'll take a full statement and then get you home."

Pauline began to tremble as the anger began to subside. "Can I see him."

"Not at the moment, Pauline. Why would you want to? He's let you down and has been using you for some time. He even wanted you to lie for him, he's capable of anything."

She nodded. "You're right. Perhaps the less I see of him the better. But what about all his things? You lot can have all the stuff in my safe."

"What stuff would that be, Pauline?" Kirsty said as she glanced quickly at Caroline. Caroline's eyes were wide in surprise.

"Files, computer discs, a briefcase, and piles of cash. He said it was safer with me because nobody really knew me or our connection."

"Look, when we get you home, we'll take care of that. I'll take a full statement off you now."

Caroline left the interview and rang McGuire. "Boss, just finished with Pauline. Kirsty's taking a statement off her. She's seen sense and doesn't alibi Harland for the timeline. He's knackered. There's also property at Pauline's: cash, discs and briefcase. We'll collect it when we drop her off."

"Cracking, Car, once you've done that, get yourselves home. We'll see you both in the morning."

Caroline and Kirsty arrived at Pauline's home two hours later. It was a beautifully maintained detached cottage on the outskirts of Cowbridge.

"Nice place," Caroline said.

"Thank you. And before you both say anything, this cottage is nothing to do with Tom. It's mine. Bought and paid for by me. I lost my husband a few years ago and he left me very well off. Tom's nothing to do with it."

Pauline led them into the house and up a narrow dog-legged staircase to the main bedroom where she opened a wardrobe and the safe that was housed in a wall behind a rack of expensive clothes.

"There you go, help yourselves. That all belongs to Tom."

Caroline pulled out a brown Barbour leather briefcase and placed it on the bed. "That's a nice bit of kit, worth a bob or two, have a look at that, Kirsty?"

Caroline could also see bundles of notes, together with computer discs in the back of the safe.

"Have you any idea what's on the discs, Pauline?"

"I've no idea, this is all down to Tom."

"I wouldn't worry too much about that lot, Caroline. Take a look what we've got here," Kirsty said.

In all its glory, a Vipertex stun gun, two mobile phones, two bunches of keys, a purse and a wallet were inside the briefcase.

"We've hit the jackpot here, Caroline. We'll bag and tag it. The boss will be over the moon with this, I'll give him a bell."

***

McGuire was sipping a glass of red and watching the end of Line of Duty when Kirsty called.

Molly shook her head as he answered and walked out into the kitchen to talk. "What can I do for you, Kirsty? Thought you'd be tucked into bed by now."

"Sorry to bother you so late, boss, but it's important. We've just recovered a stun gun and what we believe to be mobiles and property belonging to Tony and Eira. It's all bagged and tagged. We'll get it to Glyn and Tec' support in the morning."

"Excellent news. Looks like it's all coming together. Do the business first thing and I'll see you in the briefing at ten. Now get home, both of you, and very well done," he grinned.

The wine tasted somehow nicer with good news. He finished off his glass, poured himself another and carried the bottle in to Molly.

"Good news?"

He poured another for his wife and kissed her on the forehead. "Very," he said. Then the smile on his face slipped as his phone began to vibrate again.

"Shit," he said as he mouthed an apology and stepped out onto the patio. The chill made him shiver and the urgency of the voice on the other end of the line made his blood run cold too.

"Sorry, boss, got some bad news."

"What's happened?"

"It's Harland, sir..."

"Go on..."

"He had a heart attack, in the Bridewell."

"Is he alright?"

"Oh aye, boss, the bastard's alright. We called for an ambulance. They got him in the back to stabilise him. He seemed OK. The solicitor asked if he could travel behind the ambulance in his car. We got to outside A&E and he seemed to be recovering. All seemed good. Made a remarkable recovery. Then the bastard pulled a knife on one of the ambulance crew in the back of the Ambulance and held it to his throat."

"What?" McGuire couldn't believe what he was hearing.

"Seems he got a knife from somewhere, God only knows how. Ambulance staff say it wasn't one of theirs."

"Don't tell me he wasn't searched?"

"The officers transporting him said they searched him properly and he was searched again at the Bridewell. His brief wanted to talk to him in private at the Bridewell before the heart attack."

"That's not possible. The knife has got to have come from the brief."

"That's what I think too, boss, but it happened so fast we just had to deal with it as it happened, none of us had time to think about that at the time. He must have had it in his car. One of the lad's escorting the ambulance said the brief threw his case in his boot before they took off for casualty. He must have given it to him.

"What about the firearms team, are they available.

"All out on a job, boss. I'm sorry. He drove off in the brief's car, with the brief still inside.

"Tell me we've got the number, and are traffic on the case?"

"Yes boss, all sorted."

"It's got to be the brief. Get the bastard in. Bleed him dry. His career will be over after this. I'll see to that."

"That's the other problem, boss…"

"You mean there's more?"

"One of our traffic lads was in the area and picked it up quickly. He got behind it and followed the car. Harland was driving and they got to the junction with the M4 and the passenger door opened, and the brief was pushed out. Throat cut."

"Is the bastard alive?"

"Dead, boss."

"Jesus. Where's Harland now?"

"We lost him. The traffic officer following stopped to check on the brief."

"I can't believe it," McGuire raged. "Get someone on the CCTV's, track the car. I want the bastard stopped now."

54.

Lynette had brought Sue a boxset of early Eastenders episodes. Raven smiled as his sister hugged her and thanked her. It was as if Lynette had given her news of a lottery win. Could there be an addiction for a television series? He wondered. He hadn't told Sue that the appointment for surgery had come. He guessed she would be OK about it but couldn't be sure. They had both come to accept that perhaps it would never happen. Now there was hope again and Raven was excited by the prospect ,but also worried. The surgery was a major event, something he had been warned could end Sue's life. He knew doctors always warned for the worst. They had to cover themselves.

He joined the hug and kissed the two women in turn. "Thanks for that. Another Eastenders box set for us to watch, yippee," he joked.

"You know you like it really," Sue said expectantly.

He nodded. "OK, it's alright."

Sue laughed.

Lynette broke free of the hug and kissed Sue. "Got to go. Full timetable of visits today. I'll try and look in on you later. We'll watch a few episodes and force Raven to watch them with us."

"That'll be lovely," Raven said, faking a frown. His phone rang.

"Who is this," he said as Lynette turned to leave. He waved to her as she opened the door and blew a kiss at Sue.

"It's Mrs Harland. Thought you'd like to know that my murdering bastard of a husband is heading for The Grand Hotel. He's on the run from police."

"What?"

"He was interviewed today and got Roy Morris to slip him a Mickey Finn, and a knife. He faked a heart attack, and when they got to the hospital, he threatened a para medic, and drove off in his Roy's car. He rang me on his Roy's phone to tell me he was leaving for France, and he told me that he's killed Roy. He's that desperate, he's lost the plot."

"How do you know he's going to The Grand? That's inland. He'll never get away from there?"

"He came back by helicopter to speak to the police. Must have gone bad for him. He's always got a backup plan. He's cunning. I'm guessing the chopper is still there."

"What car is he in?"

"If it's Roy's, it's a black Merc. He's got a private plate; RM1, you can't miss it, but you better be quick."

Raven ended the call and ran out into the hallway. He called to Lynette as she was getting into her car.

"Got an emergency. Could you check back on Sue as soon as you're free?"

Lynette thought about it for a moment. "I'll call in and tell them. They can get someone else to cover the jobs. I'll stay with Sue until you get home."

Raven raised his thumb then blew an enthusiastic kiss. He checked back on Sue. Put the DVD in the player and told her he wouldn't be long.

He rushed down to the RS parked in the garage of the new house. He had never had a garage attached to a house before. The automatic door rose as he ducked under and opened his pride and joy. The old Ford was the best vehicle for a fast jaunt through country lanes. The car fired up with a roar as he pressed a pre-dial on his phone and waited for McGuire to answer. The call went to answerphone.

Raven left a message. Everything he could get out quickly before the call recording ended.

The RS got him to the M4 from the exclusive estate in Bridgend in less than five minutes. He got the car up to full speed, a little under a hundred and twenty and kept his foot pressed to the floor as he flashed his headlights to warn vehicles ahead to clear the road. Only at sites of speed cameras did he slow down to avoid setting the cameras off. He guessed Terry might well be able to work some deal with the ticket office on his behalf, but he didn't want to take the chance. He needed his driving licence. Harland had a head start on him, but Raven knew the roads to Llandovery probably as well as Harland. There was a chance Raven could get there in time to stop him.

He checked his watch as he neared the Pont Abraham junction that signified the official end of the M4. He took the third exit, sliding the rear of the RS around the corner to flashing lights and blaring horns of other vehicles. He knew there was at least another half hour before he could reach Llandovery and that, depending upon Harland's route, the man might be in the air by that time and well on his way to sunny climes.

***

Harland realised the M4 would be too easy for the cops to track him. He turned off at Port Talbot just before the speed restriction and headed towards the steelworks, a massive three-mile steel producing facility on the coast. He dumped the car outside the perimeter fence, clambered over it and began checking the site vehicles used to convey workers around the huge complex. A Ford Fiesta sat open, the keys in the ignition. He didn't think they had problems with car thefts on the secure site. He donned a high-vis jacket and a safety helmet and goggles from the back seat, started the Fiesta and headed for the security exit.

He thought about using the M4, but it was too much of a risk. He knew another route, up the Swansea Valley and over the Black Mountains. It was a longer route, but no one knew where he was going. He had to make sure he didn't draw attention to himself.

Making good time, the turn for the village of Cwmtwrch appeared ahead and he made the turn at a leisurely pace. Within twenty minutes, he was on the top of the Black Mountains. He saw an ice cream van parked in a layby at the top overlooking a stunning vista of patchwork fields and thought about stopping for a cone but thought better of it. The view of the sprawling valley from the mountain top was stunning and made him smile. He could see for at least fifty miles in all directions. He wondered what view he would be gazing on tonight. The helicopter would take him to France and then he'd hire a car and head south. His money was secure in bank accounts in the Cayman Islands. He was set for life. He had plenty of time.

***

The town of Llandovery was a market town, a town that had historically been a stop-off point for the old sheep and cattle drovers travelling between their farms and the market. The local rugby team had kept the nickname of The Drovers and the local private school had a reputation for good education whilst providing many up and coming stars for the Welsh rugby development system.

Raven drove the RS at a steady pace through the town and on to the road that led towards Brecon. He knew the lane for the hotel was just ahead. He changed down to third for a sweeping left-hand bend then the road opened up and he saw the sign for the hotel. He noticed a Fiesta catching up quickly behind.

He braked and pulled onto the rough track just as the dusty Ford Fiesta pulled in behind him. He checked his mirror and did a double take. It was Harland. He knew Harland had not seen his face, other than perhaps in passing the last time he was at the hotel, but he had been too busy with his girlfriend to notice him.

Keeping the RS at a steady speed, the Fiesta caught up with him on the track as he reached the brow and began the descent to the hotel. The Fiesta kept pace. Raven checked his mirror and could see Harland looking off to his right. Raven looked the same way and saw the helicopter, the blades were turning slowly, probably beginning their build up to take off speed.

His phone rang. He pressed the green button. It was McGuire.

"Harland. I gather you lost him?"

"Aye, bloody cock up," McGuire said.

"Well, I know where he's heading. There's a helicopter at the Grand Hotel near Llandovery. I'm there now and Harland is in a green Ford Fiesta behind me."

"A green Fiesta? He stole his brief's Merc. How the fuck's he in a Fiesta?

"He's in a Fiesta. I assure you."

"No wonder we lost him. He must have stolen it. Leave it to us. I'll get officers on the way."

"You'll be too late. I'm here and he's right behind me. He doesn't know me. I'll update you." He ended the call before McGuire could argue. He pulled into the gravel courtyard out front of the hotel and kept the engine running – just in case.

His phone rang again, and he pressed the green icon once more. The hands-free set he had fitted to the RS amplified McGuire's voice. "I've got Dyfed Powys police on the way to the hotel. The nearest unit was in Ammanford. Can you believe that? That's a thirteen-minute drive but you know what the roads are like out there."

"I'll sort it."

55.

The Fiesta had served him well. Harland grinned and gathered the mobile phone from the passenger seat. He was pleased to see the pilot had started the engine as he had told him to do when he called him from Llandovery. The blades were ripping through the air and looked like the craft was ready for flight.

He parked the Fiesta and left the keys in the ignition. He stepped from the car and checked the car park. Only three cars were there; a Jaguar XF, a Mercedes and an old black RS Escort that looked like it had just come out of a new car sales room. Then he realised he'd seen the car before. Some time ago when he had been at the hotel. He looked again and saw the driver. He was sitting in the car with the engine ticking over. Harland could see the exhaust fumes and the driver's eyes in the mirror, looking directly at him. He stepped a pace from the Fiesta when the door to the RS opened.

Harland looked to the helicopter. It was standing on a concrete circle with a yellow painted H in the centre. He could make out the yellow letter, but the chopper was at least two-hundred yards away. The helipad was well away from the main building for safety reasons he understood but now he cursed the health and safety brigade. Should he run? He heard the footsteps of the RS man as he walked towards him.

Pulling open the door, Harland jumped back into the Fiesta and turned the key. The diesel engine rattled then fired. He looked at the man. He reminded Harland of someone he had seen on tv. Some movie star. He had stopped. He was too far away to get to him before he drove off.

The man ran back to the RS. Now Harland was in no doubt he was there for him. Harland threw the car into reverse and dropped the clutch. The front wheels spun and sprayed small stones in all directions as he swung it around and headed in the direction of the chopper. There was only a footpath that led past a pillared concrete canopy that was probably used for wedding photos, a pagoda of sorts. The Fiesta headed for it just as the rear wheels of the RS were spinning in the gravel car park and snaking after it.

***

Fiesta's were no match for the RS 2000, especially not off-road and the Fiesta was bouncing over the car park verge onto the immaculate lawn and heading towards the pagoda and the helicopter beyond.

Raven floored the accelerator and the RS took off over the verge and quickly gained on the

Fiesta, which suddenly braked hard and Raven jammed his foot on the brake and then the clutch and steered to the left. He missed the rear of the Fiesta by inches and breathed a sigh of relief. The Fiesta had already driven off again, wheels spinning and tearing up the turf as the tyres tried to grip.

The helicopter pilot must have seen the cars heading towards him and was now lifting the craft off the ground. It rose twenty feet into the air, well clear of the cars spinning and circling on the lawn around the pagoda and hovered there. The pilot was clearly conflicted. Should he wait for his client, or leave?

Raven began following the Fiesta as it drove around the pagoda. He began to enjoy letting the rear end slide out, keeping the power from his foot smooth and adjusting to ensure he didn't apply too much and send the car into a spin. Then the Fiesta front end slid away, the front wheel drive losing all grip.

Harlandyanked the handbrake and spun the car to face the RS.

Cursing, Raven patted the steering wheel of his old car. "Sorry, dad," he said as the Fiesta accelerated straight at him and crashed into the droop snoot of the classic RS.

Upset, furious, and out for blood, Raven floored his throttle and pushed back at the Fiesta. It was no contest. The Fiesta wheels spun but failed to find grip. The RS gained pace and rammed the Fiesta into one of the pillars of the pagoda. The crash dislodged the concrete cap that spanned two uprights – like the big stones of Stonehenge – and toppled off its pedestal and onto the roof of the Fiesta. The cabin collapsed under its weight. Raven saw Harland's head rammed down into his shoulders and then below the steering wheel into the footwell.

The RS idled as Raven got out to check the damage. The chopper rose higher then banked with nose down to gain speed as it disappeared over a line of trees.

The damage to the front end of the RS was bad but not as bad as that caused to the Fiesta. Raven touched the cracked nose cone of his old car and wondered what his dad would have said. Then he thought he'd better check on Harland but there was nothing he could do for him. He was trapped in the footwell.

The sound of police cars could be heard in the distance as Raven called McGuire.

This time, McGuire answered on the first ring.

"The bastard smashed up my RS," Raven said.

"Did you get him?"

"There's at least a grand's worth of damage. These cars are not cheap to get parts for any-more."

"What about Harland?"

"Aye, he's lucky... he should be dead. He'll

have a hell of a headache if he survives the night."

***

Harland did survive the night but the injury to his head proved even more serious than Raven had imagined. It would take months if not years of medical intervention before the man could ever be considered fit for trial, if at all. That bothered McGuire as much as it bothered Raven.

They sat together in the bar of a pub less than a hundred metres from their new office. They had sipped a brace of bitters and talked about their business and their families, getting to know each other better.

They avoid talk of Harland, both knew the subject would only anger them both. They had to accept the medical prognosis and there was no point in moaning about his escape from justice, if serious brain damage was any kind of escape.

"I need a few weeks before I commit to the new job," Raven said.

"I thought you already had committed to it?"

He nodded, "I have, but I want to do something for my sister, take her somewhere while I still have the chance."

McGuire finished his pint and placed the empty glass on the table. "Family is important. You do what you need to do. Never put the job first. I made that mistake and it's something that I regret and something I'd change if I had my time again."

56.

Tomorrow would be the day that would signal the start of a new life for Raven in more ways than one. Tomorrow, he would officially sign the legal documents McGuire's solicitor had drafted for his share in the new detective agency that had once been Ed's. It would still be Raven Investigations, but he now had the financial backing and professional support from a man who had spent nearly thirty years doing the job Raven had fallen into in civvie street.

His time with the Special Boat Service had developed a love for the sea and, if the new venture proved to be a success, he could look forward to taking the boat and Sue to France or Spain or even further afield like the Canary Isles. He had driven home from the meeting with McGuire in the pub and booked two tickets on the Eurostar for Disneyland Paris. He couldn't wait to tell Sue in the morning. He didn't think she'd be disappointed they weren't taking that boat trip just yet. Disneyland would make up for that.

He had had to endure another hour of Eastenders – split into two half hour episodes. Why would anyone want to watch an hour of a soap that left him feeling suicidal every time he watched it? No accounting for taste, he thought.

Sue had gone to bed after the second episode. She had taken a shower, ready for her admission to hospital in the morning. It was going to be a busy day. He had to get her to admissions by nine and then, after ensuring she was OK, he'd head off to Bridgend to sign the contract. He hated the thought of not being at the hospital with Sue, but he'd only be gone for a couple of hours and be back with her by the time she came around from the operation. It would be OK.

He poured himself a beer from a can and thought about McGuire and what he had done for him. He didn't have to. He was taking a bloody big risk investing in the business and letting him and Sue move into the house Ed had left McGuire. The house was large, a detached property in a new development just outside of Bridgend.

Sue loved her new bedroom and had already planned on the colours and new curtains she asked Raven to get for her. Raven had called into IKEA and picked up the items after detour to McGuire to get the update on the Elvis murder. At least that was now done and dusted, and he had played a part in the successful outcome of the case.

Whilst Sue was in hospital – the doctors said she'd be in for a few days, post-op – Raven would put up the new curtains for her and paint the room just as she wanted.

He sipped his beer and flicked through Netflix for something to watch.

It was just after midnight and Raven couldn't sleep. A zombie movie set in London had raised a few laughs but he just couldn't concentrate. Part of the reason was worry for Sue and also excitement for the new life they were about to begin. It kept him wired. He clicked on play for a new series of SAS – Are You Tough Enough, a series where former special services soldiers put civilians through their paces to see if they would be good enough to pass the elite selection process and he grinned as he saw his former colleague, Andy Sommerville, grinning back at him. He had worked closely with Andy on many operations during their time together on the SBS. It was strange to see him openly talking about his time with the service on a world-wide tv network. At least Andy seemed to be doing well for himself, but it was something Raven would never do. Andy hadn't changed a bit. He still looked fit and his thick black beard hadn't lost any of its colour. He was a good-looking bastard – ideal for the telly.

Raven took another sip of his beer and decided to look in on Sue, it was something he always did, every night before he went to bed, not that he had any intention of retiring just yet.

The nightlight was on and he noticed a piece of paper on the bedside table, in the glow from the lamp. He crept in and picked it up. Sue was lying on her back, with the duvet pulled up beneath her chin, something she rarely did. She looked peaceful.

The note had been scrawled in Sue's child-like hand.

Don't worry. I'll be fine. I can't wait for the boat trip to France. I love you.

Sue XXXXXXX.

Seven kisses. He smiled then placed the note back on the table and leaned closer to kiss her forehead, but her forehead was cold.

"Sue, it's me, Raven," he said quietly, his voice breaking as he began to realise that Sue wasn't going to reply ever again. He would never see that cheeky smile or hear her nag him to watch Eastenders with her ever again.

"Sue, I love you. What will I do without you?"

Sue didn't respond and he checked the pulse on her neck but knew it was a pointless task. Sue was dead. She had simply slipped away peacefully in her sleep.

Raven sat on the bed next to her then swung his legs up alongside her. He lifted her head and slipped his arm beneath it and lay with her for a while, like they had done so many times in the past.

TERRY MCGUIRE SERIES OF CRIME THRILLERS

Based in South Wales, UK, McGuire has risen through the ranks as a hard-nosed detective. Admired by friends and colleagues, hated and feared by the criminals, McGuire will do what it takes to keep the streets clean and he's not afraid to crush toes to do it.

Unethical Conduct

Corrupt police officers, a murder, a rape, and a flasher. Can DI Terry McGuire's day get any worse?

Terry became a copper to uphold the law and protect the innocent. When he investigates a former friend and colleague, and a body buried on a beach, he has his work cut out for him. Especially as the carelessly buried corpse appears to have been frozen for five years.

The life of a police officer isn't like the TV or films: there isn't the luxury of working one case at a time. McGuire has to juggle the complexities of a number of offences, and get to the truth.

Can Mcguire stand up for what he believes and bring the perpetrators to justice, whoever they might be?

Authors Cole and Williams have nearly 50 years of real-world policing experience between them. And it shows in the gritty, pacy writing and glimpses of what really happens on a police investigation. The cases for Terry McGuire might be fiction, but they draw heavily on real life police-work.

Edge Of Integrity

Promoted to Detective Chief Inspector, Terry McGuire is given control of the drug squad that had once been under the influence of the corrupt senior officers McGuire brought to justice. An international drug bust, a flasher and a deadly vendetta against McGuire test his own integrity. "Gritty 'real' feel to this fast-paced thriller. Number two in the Terry McGuire series of thrillers."

Death And Depravity

Sex and Drugs and Corpses

A young man is found dead from an overdose in a secluded wood.

A young woman with a false name is found dead from an overdose in an office toilet. Enquiries suggest she is part of a human trafficking network.

DCI Terry McGuire believes a particularly nasty batch of heroin is on the streets and the race is on to catch the supplier before more people die. But Terry is still haunted by the flasher case that has run cold.

Angel Of Death

An arsonist is on a rampage - an abandoned nightclub is torched and the forensic evidence suggests it's the same arsonist that struck a school years before.

Someone is killing the residents of local nursing homes.

The flasher has finally made a mistake.

A normal week in the life of Terry McGuire and his team as they work on several fronts to solve the crimes. But Terry will uncover something during the investigations that will shock him to his core.

Nest Of Vipers

One man's terrorist is another man's hero.

As Terry McGuire continues his mission to un-ravel the mysteries of an Irish diary, the action moves to the lawless badlands of Northern Ire-land and the murky world of Irish Republican terrorism.

What is the connection between a small-time Belfast criminal-turned-terrorist and a recently deceased catholic nun who retired to the South Wales' Gower Peninsula?

When Terry discovers that his investigation is endangering the life of his family, the case be-comes personal. And you don't want to get on Terry's wrong side when that happens.

Nest of Vipers is another in the fast-paced series of books following police officer, Terry McGuire, in his South Wales patch.

Night Hawker

When the daughter of a friend and work col-league is raped, Terry McGuire is determined to bring the culprit to justice. But, when the suspect is brutally attacked, Terry has to dig deeper to find the truth.

The cases come thick and fast for Terry and his team. Their resources are stretched as they investigate missing children, the rape, a dumped corpse and a brutally murdered young man.

As Terry closes in on his prey, he faces his greatest danger. Will he pay the ultimate price in his attempt
 to protect the innocent?

Redemption

DCI Terry McGuire is believed to have died in a terrible fall into a flooded ravine.

A terrorist attack on a London bus and an MP shot dead in the streets appears to be the work of a fundamentalist group hell-bent on bringing the capital city to its knees. But a top secret security briefing document suggests a more sinister plot is being played out. When two South Wales police officers discover the document, one is killed and the other becomes a target.

Gavin Millner returns from Basra suffering from Post Traumatic Stress Disorder, having lost his friends on a routine patrol. Unable to cope with life at home, Gavin finds himself living rough on the streets until he's persuaded to seek help at The Haven rehabilitation centre in Rest Bay, South Wales. When a homeless man disappears, leaving his beloved dog behind, and the body of a homeless woman is found brutally murdered on the beach, the patients at the home become suspects in what appears to be the evil work of a serial killer.

But there is an even darker secret deep in bowels of the The Haven. Could Terry have survived the fall? Is there a connection between the terror attacks and someone from Terry's past? Is the murder of the woman linked to the missing man and, if so, what are they hiding at The Haven?

Betrayal

How can a series of brutal killings in New York possibly be linked with a 200-year-old murder in Wales? Is it conceivable that the President of the United States is involved in a cover-up?

Private detective and former Special Boat Services Marine, Raven Conner, is hired to investigate and becomes a key figure in one of DCI Terry McGuire's most frustrating cases.

Meanwhile, angry at his failure to catch the murderer of the Bag Lady, McGuire must reluctantly accept that he has let the killer slip through his fingers.

Dead bodies are discovered, apparently the racially motivated slaughter of a respected shopkeeper and his wife. The team interview a number of suspects. Just when McGuire thinks things can't get worse as he tackles multiple crimes, a former prostitute is attacked and left for dead.

With resources stretched to the limits McGuire and his team must connect the dots and solve the cases.

Printed in Great Britain
by Amazon